Critical acclaim for

WHAT HAPPENED TO *Anna K.*

"Literate and fun . . . an uncommonly ambitious book."

—PEOPLE (PEOPLE PICK, 4 OUT OF 4 STARS)

"Reyn manages to capture the moving-train moodiness of the classic while creating a fresh, addictive story that has a tragic appeal all its own."

—THE WASHINGTON POST

"Irina Reyn is a marvelous writer, with the ability to capture a character or set a scene in just a few sentences." —SAN FRANCISCO CHRONICLE

"Delicately nuanced . . . [Reyn] makes Anna's downward spiral not only credible but horrifically beautiful." —NEW YORK NEWSDAY

"Witty and compelling . . . recalls, contemporizes, and illuminates the classic story from which this fearless first novel takes its inspiration and its shape."

—O, THE OPRAH MAGAZINE

Praise for
What Happened to Anna K.

"A smart, witty, at times downright funny read."

—*Christian Science Monitor*

"Tolstoy's Anna Karenina survives a transition to twenty-first-century New York City and still captivates."

—*Houston Chronicle*

"Fascinating, compelling fiction."

—*Pittsburgh Post-Gazette*

"With humor laced into this story, Reyn explores aging, love and marriage, ethnic identity, the power of tradition, and the pull of family and community."

—*The Jewish Week*

"[Reyn's] characters inhabit the interstitial place between immigration and assimilation, tradition and innovation, poised to create a postmodern culture of their own design."

—*Booklist* (starred review)

"Tolstoy himself would surely have given a nod to Reyn's re-creation of his Karenina."

—*Library Journal*

"Deft . . . offers wit and insight, and a pungent portrait of New York."

—*Kirkus Reviews*

"Irina Reyn's sly wit and perfect-pitch dialogue make this modern-day retelling of *Anna Karenina* a delight to read. . . . Readers should love this novel, whether or not they know the original Anna."

—Lynne Sharon Schwartz, author of *Ruined by Reading* and
Leaving Brooklyn

"Irina Reyn's debut offers a feisty reimagining of the original tale, with contemporary Russian-Jewish characters in Queens, Manhattan, and Brooklyn brought to vividly detailed life—and with the conundrums and consolations of immigration itself rendered compassionately and smartly."

—Martha Cooley, author of *The Archivist* and *Thirty-Three Swoons*

WHAT

HAPPENED

TO

Anna K.

A NOVEL

———

IRINA REYN

A TOUCHSTONE BOOK
Published By Simon & Schuster
New York London Toronto Sydney

FOR ADAM

 Touchstone
A Division of Simon & Schuster, Inc.
1230 Avenue of the Americas
New York, NY 10020

FIRST TOUCHSTONE TRADE PAPERBACK EDITION MAY 2009

TOUCHSTONE and colophon are registered trademarks of Simon & Schuster, Inc.

For information about special discounts for bulk purchases, please contact Simon & Schuster Special Sales at 1-800-456-6798 or business@simonandschuster.com.

Designed by Mary Austin Speaker
Photograph by Kramer O'Neill

Manufactured in the United States of America

10   9   8   7   6   5   4   3   2   1

Library of Congress Cataloging-in-Publication Data
    Reyn, Irina.
    What happened to Anna K. : a novel / Irina Reyn.
    p. cm.
    "A Touchstone book."
    I. Title.
    PS3618.E95 W47 2008
    813'.6—dc22

                                                                    2007039332

ISBN-13: 978-1-4165-5893-4
ISBN-10:   1-4165-5893-4
ISBN-13: 978-1-4165-5894-1 (pbk)
ISBN-10:   1-4165-5894-2 (pbk)

Only by taking infinitesimally small units for observation (the differential of history, that is, the individual tendencies of men) and attaining to the art of integrating them (that is, finding the sum of these infinitesimals) can we hope to arrive at the laws of history.

~ Lev Tolstoy
War and Peace

The truth is that once we have left our childhood places and started out to make up our lives, armed only with what we have and are, we understand that the real secret of the ruby slippers is not that "there's no place like home," but rather that there is no longer any such place *as* home: except, of course, for the home we make, or the homes that are made for us, in Oz: which is anywhere, and everywhere, except the place from which we began.

~ Salman Rushdie
The Wizard of Oz

1

SAUSAGE IMMIGRANTS

Anna K. was not the only pale woman in a black shearling to glide along 108th Street in Rego Park, but she was the most striking. A Tajik shopkeeper, about to weigh a bag of unripe persimmons, paused in order to follow the course of Anna's backside as it made its way down the block.

What set her apart from the others, at least in her own mind? Her curls, for one—black, lustrous, caressing the bottom of her neck. Her green eyes, the color of leaves in midsummer. Her walk, perhaps, delicate, thought-through, her toes jutting slightly outward. The more observant man might notice the litheness of her torso, her proactive breasts, substantial hips, regal posture, a sharp, even precarious, gleam in her eye.

She walked by the Russian groceries, where women abused store proprietors over the price of sausages. Anna passed stores she had not entered in years. There was European Fashions for Less, and across the street, International Couture and Parisian Chic, with their mirrored walls, their fur-swaddled mannequins, their sequined gowns with padded shoulders. Their saleswomen, who swore that only the most fashionable women of Moscow, Paris, London were stepping out in this leopard-print pantsuit, that fur-collared ballerina dress. Whose skin was overmaquillaged, traces of foundation streaking their cheeks, their plump middles betraying an overindulgence in Stalin sausages. One of them, sporting a severe blond bun and a black apron, chain-smoked outside the front door, watching Anna as she walked past.

By the time Anna left Queens, she grew to detest those stores. But her dear mother would never renounce them no matter how many Longchamp bags Anna bought her. Her mother thought paying retail was for the very rich or the very foolish. Give her a good, crowded Daffy's, squinting women ransacking blemished Italian cashmere, or a T.J. Maxx, with its hope of a decent Ralph Lauren handbag lying unmolested among the tangle of braided straps. According to *New York* magazine and the new wealthy daughters of oligarchs, Anna and her mother were considered "sausage immigrants."

There they were, her parents, just nine blocks away from 108th Street on Sixty-third Road (though in Queens, one must also take into consideration Sixty-third Avenue and Sixty-third Street and Sixty-third Drive, as if the effort of naming were quickly abandoned here), on the fourth floor of an eighteen-story building. Attached to their building was a desolate playground where Anna had played as a child, hoping a sympathetic soul would materialize to form the other half of a seesaw configuration. Later, in her teens, Anna could be found reading on the swings until her mother yelled out the window that it was time for dinner.

In the elevator, just press the number five, walk one flight down (the elevator stopped only on odd-numbered floors), turn left, knock on the lemon-colored door, and voilà, you've reached the Roitmans'!

Her mother had already started planning the wedding; as Anna walked in, she was sprawled in her house robe on the living room rug, the names of family and friends scattered around her on little pieces of paper. "Table twelve," she muttered, dooming several slips of paper to this particular fate.

Anna K. required no pleasantries at the door, no kisses, no inter-ruption of routine. She had her own set of slippers in the hall closet; they were pink chenille, worn down at the heel. She slipped off the shearling, releasing the scent of lavender, the fresh smell of outdoors mingled with Penn Station sweat. She had just seen off her fiancé, Alex K., on a business trip to Philadelphia.

"Hello, Mamochka," she said, giving her mother, then her father, a kiss. Papochka sat in his boxers on the living room couch, buried inside a *Novoye Russkoye Slovo*. His fingers were black with newsprint; he thumbed through the paper in his white, stretched-out tank top, his rolled-up socks.

"Can you believe what's going on in the world?" he said without looking up. "Did you know that we have another Stalin and he has practically the same name?" When not spearheading the demise of yet another unprofitable business venture, Papochka's most sustained interactions were between himself and the paper, lovingly folded and chronologically filed away, only to be thrown out by Mrs. Roitman when he wasn't looking.

"*Nu i shto,* Papa, we know, we know."

The wedding would be at Fabergé, the classiest Russian restaurant in Brighton Beach. The restaurant boasted that its dancers were all former Bolshoi Ballet corps ballerinas, although Anna believed they were shipped directly from Uzbek strip clubs. Only the best vodka for Anyechka's wedding, it was already decided, none of that Smirnoff crap, only the best wine, one that costs more than $20 a bottle. For God's sake, you can't go Loehmann's on everything.

It was her turn now, Natasha Roitman's, and how long she had waited for it to be her turn. Her daughter. How many questions had she been forced to answer about her daughter's single status, her American, non-Jewish boyfriends? Her beautiful Anna unhappy despite all her physical advantages, eyelashes that needed no curling, skin the color of coconut flesh, breasts that called attention to themselves, really they were lovely breasts, nothing at all like her own had been, lumpy and conical. Sure, they had had to work on those thick, snarling eyebrows and leg hair early in Anna's life; they had to buy her a first bra when she was only nine, but what teenage girl didn't have a few adjustments to make when transitioning into womanhood?

And yes, Natasha could admit that Anna tended to stoop when she sat in backless chairs, like a drooping reed, her nose almost in her soup, and she did look thoroughly washed-out in browns and taupes and she could use a little teeth-whitening. And if she followed Natasha's prescription of running a tea-infused ice cube over her eyes in the morning, all that puffiness around her eyelids would be reduced, but considering Rosa's daughter had been dyeing her gray hair for eight years now, Anna was in pretty good shape for thirty-seven.

On the carpet, the future Anna K.'s mother divided people, carefully arranging them into different strata of tables. The Manhattan Russians in the front, closer to the stage—the best seats in the house—followed by the Outer Boroughs Russians, the California Russians, the New Jersey Russians, and so forth. The Midwestern Russians would be squirreled away at the back tables. She didn't blame them, of course, but what could the poor dears do, with nowhere to go in the evenings, among all that snow and industrial soot? How could they know you don't wear turtlenecks to classy Brighton establishments? Or even worse, taking that single "good" dress out of mothballs, forgetting one has worn it to countless birthdays and anniversaries and weddings, the same too-small "special occasion" dress, with its lacy arms, its mermaid shape, its matching fringe-heavy shawl? No, the Midwesterners would sit right there, Anna's mother decided.

In the past, when Anna came to visit, her parents would put on the kettle for tea and ask her questions about the men she was seeing; they would compliment a new blouse, a handbag. They would gossip about their circle of friends. How comfortable to come home, to have a permanent place at the table! Now Anna couldn't sit still; she ran a paper towel under tap water and wiped dust off the bookshelves, caressing her old Austens and Hugos and Alcotts. She rearranged the framed black-and-white pictures on the top shelf: the three of them in Moscow, the studio portrait of eight-year-old Anna, proud in her Soviet school uniform—two years later she would no longer be Soviet. She dialed Alex's cell phone. "Please leave message," the voice mail demanded.

"This is Anna K.," Anna said for the first time, trying it out. She pictured Alex on the train with his colleagues. They might be unwrapping sandwiches from home, salami and cheese, maybe, pressed between slices of cucumber on pumpernickel bread. She was jealous. Ever since she was a little girl, Anna had loved trains.

She still remembered the overnight trains from Moscow to Ukraine taken when she was a little girl, when she and her parents were going to visit her paternal grandparents. The excitement of the long voyage, the strong, bitter tea served in the dining car, the unfurling of a tin of black caviar, the fragrant smell of garlic. All she knew was that by the time she took the train back to Moscow, she would be changed by all the mysteries that greeted her on the other side. Listening to the villagers' exotic Ukrainian accents and words, the simplicity of the local children's games—hide-and-seek, mostly—laced with the fear that the resident Baba Yaga would scoop you into her burlap sack. Gathering mushrooms in the forest (whoever found one would call out, triumphant, before dropping it into the wicker basket)—their scent of minerals and earth when fried with onions. Rising so early to play with the other kids that night still clung to the damp morning air. Drying black currants under the hot sun, the berries spread out in rows on cots, the holes standing for each berry stolen, popped in the mouth. And then the train back to Moscow, couchettes beckoning like cocoons, and then, home with all the sweet pleasures of familiar routine.

"Once you find the right wedding dress," her mother said from the rug, "write down the make and number. Masha will order it for you for half price from her store on Kings Highway."

Anna watched her mother for a while, who murmured to herself as yet another table was completed. If there was a moment to say what was on her mind, to sit her mother down and say, *Mamochka, you see, I've been having some serious doubts . . . ,* to squeeze her mother's hand and wait for her to make it all right again, to make the unpleasantness disappear the way she managed when Anna was young, with a single wave of the hand, a hot bowl of *mamaliga,* and, poof, it was gone. If there was a single moment, a window to change her destiny, this might have been the time, still so early in the whole process, when her mother's heart was not entirely invested in her tables, her linens, her vodka, her Masha, and that awful shop on Kings Highway, with its cheap, imitation Prada bags. Anna knew this was the time to speak, here with Mamochka and Papochka, the paper, the unbrewed tea in the kitchen. But from her vantage point in the chair watching the two of them, the gray invading their hair, all the extra girth and wrinkles they were carrying around (Papochka especially in that tank top, the sagging folds of skin on his forearms, and what about Mamochka—the unnatural coral of her hair, her girdles?), Anna found herself lacking the strength to make them wait for something that did not appear to be coming for her. That train had already passed.

2

THE PROPOSAL, THE
CHOCOLATE RING, THE END

Wasn't it Mama who first uttered Alexander's name to Anna? Yes, Anna was sure of it. Her mother had just attended an anniversary party at Ryba on Avenue O in Brooklyn where her daughter's hopeless thirty-five-year-old state was discussed, her life splayed out side by side with the eggplant caviar, the cheese blintzes with sour cream. After the party, she had called her daughter.

"Anyusha, we finally found you a promising man. I have one word for you: Alexander."

"That's two words, Ma, and why do you always have to talk about my love life with your friends?"

No, Anna, her mother had said, at this point we have a right to discuss you. We are truly worried now. Hadn't Anna frittered her twenties away, dating schmucks who were always leaving the country, men who could barely pay for themselves, who wore frayed T-shirts to fancy restaurants? I mean, it wasn't serious! Why was Anna wasting her time when rich Russian (some even Jewish) oil magnates were infiltrating New York, snapping up wives for their sons along with billion-dollar apartments in the Time Warner Center?

"So what's your point, Ma?" But to be honest, Anna herself was starting to get worried. This was not the way it was supposed to turn out, even if she was ambivalent about marriage, with all its real or simulated boredom, and still glared at babies, propped up in their stroller thrones, blocking her way on sidewalks. All she knew was that the hazy fantasy she had nursed, practically since immigration, had not materialized. How would she know it had? If she were accompanying her husband to the National Book Awards, getting ready in her Upper West Side walk-in closet and flying to pick up furniture at the Art Basel/Miami design show? If he surprised her with Joyce tickets, then popped her into a Hou Hsiao-hsien movie, praising "Hou's mastery of mise-en-scène"? And at the end of the day, in her reveries, her mythical husband would make enthusiastic love to her body, would lavish upon it worshipful caresses, kisses of bottomless awe, and then, still red from exertion, from the pleasure he was able to evoke, would look through her as though performing a biopsy on her soul. They would rise from bed only to part the curtains, to gaze down on the metallic sharpness of the New York City skyline. They would open a bottle of Châteauneuf-du-Pape, blah, blah, blah.

Was this really science fiction? No, she was sure it was possible, otherwise why would Woody Allen's old films always be on television when she was at her most optimistic? Those tastefully decorated loft apartments, those stimulating dinner parties dropping names like e. e. cummings, Kierkegaard, Dostoyevsky, Bergman? How many young women have those movies ruined? For God's sake, even her parents no longer read Dostoyevsky—haven't they suffered enough, they would say; after thirty years of communism, didn't they *deserve* Danielle Steel?

"Well, Viola's grandmother has a sister whose son is single," her mother said.

"Sounds old."

"He probably never found the right woman, the smart woman, to grab him. And I hate to remind you, my dear, you are no young chicken yourself."

"It's spring, Mom."

"What?"

Another Russian date, and what was one more? Hadn't she been on millions of dates with exactly the same guy? "Businessman"-cum-gym-connoisseur-cum-superficial-art-lover. The educated Russian emphasis on culture forcing him to spend a few minutes before a Monet or Renoir. The one book, gathering dust on his bedside table, the *Seven Effective Ways to* or the *Donald Trump's Guide to*. Always a hazy business deal in the works, just one more year and his investment would finally pay off. The loving attention paid to a sports car eternally sitting in some Russian-owned parking lot near the BQE. The Gucci label mysteriously affixed to the outside of his clothing, where it gleamed a chalky silver. A man whose mother, who were we kidding, was still doing his laundry, still fixing him dinner every night. They were always looking for Russian girls who would understand them, the feminine, sophisticated ladies so sorely absent in American culture, they said, but the truth was that American girls didn't automatically do laundry for their husbands; they were not as enslaved by their own beauty, to its future demise, to have to do it.

Okay, Anna said. Bring on another one. But this time, she was not so dismissive. This time, her beloved dream, the one that felt so real that she could practically see the guy, was undulating and starting to disintegrate before her. It occurred to her that all those years of feeling unique, of thinking she was the only Russian immigrant to moon over Heathcliff from *Wuthering Heights,* might have been slightly delusional. (Heathcliff bidding on Deco? No, it was time to permanently put away Ms. Brontë.)

Alex K. had brought her to a restaurant off Central Park West. He was even older than she had expected, well into his fifties, but well dressed, polite.

At the end of the meal, he picked out their cheeses from the cheese cart—he had known which goat would enhance the remainder of their wine. After he had paid the bill, he held her coat open for her, stood behind her as she fumbled with the sleeve, his breath steady on the back of her neck. She thought she would find valet parking pretentious, but she found she liked the convenience, appreciated the way he gave the keys to the waiter, and before she knew it, she had slipped into the car, the two of them cruising down Broadway.

The fresh smell of leather seats, a faint aroma of vanilla. The city unfolded before Anna: the breathless blue of the MetLife Building, slipping beneath it into the tunnel and being expelled onto the wide berth of Park Avenue. Speeding past streaks of light, shadows of bodies in restaurant windows. If she were with a girlfriend, they would have been hailing a cab or, more realistically, trudging down into the subway. Who knew that a Lexus could glide so smoothly? One more date wouldn't hurt, the future Anna K. had thought in the car. Just . . . one . . . more . . . date.

The ease, the ease of it. No worries about money, every pore satisfied. So what if he was Heathcliff's, Darcy's, opposite? He had a reliable travel agent, a Russian woman who understood that her clients needed a few days of pampering at an all-inclusive luxury resort. He had a chauffeur who drove him to the airport; his favorite store was Brooks Brothers, where he always paid retail. He always meant what he said, and nothing subversive, it seemed to Anna, roiled beneath. The print on price tags or bills held no more interest for him, and neither did opera or fiction. He didn't analyze what he saw around him, what he put into his mouth. His world was closed. Flattery oozed out of his lips and it always hit the right notes.

"You are beautiful, *Ty krasavitsa,*" he would say, caressing her cheek, before undressing her. His kisses left a beaded trail of saliva on her belly; she would dab a sheet discreetly, wiping it away. In the morning, she would always find a treat on the other pillow—a chocolate-covered strawberry on an oval silver tray, a peony. He rarely forgot a bouquet of flowers, fresh and abundant, when he picked her up for a date.

One more date, one more date. This would be the last, she told herself; she would break it to him after the muscat or the port, after the trip to Vermont, the gift of the silver Tiffany's starfish dangling on the thinnest of threads. She was not meant for this lack of conflict, she thought, this absence of an opposing force.

But her Chelsea apartment was so constricting, its wood cupboards scraped and uneven, no amount of vacuuming would redeem her carpet and the generations of detritus that lurked beneath. Her cement balcony could only be taken seriously if isolated in quotation marks. She worked by securing rights for foreign books and she was thirty-six. Those were the unimaginable facts of Anna's life, a woman who was whisked to America as a young girl, whose future (searing political essays, powerful lovers, and a work of art shaped by the most idiosyncratic émigré mind since Nabokov) had yet to materialize. And she had waited patiently for the call of the relevant lovers through her twenties and early thirties; she had cocked her ear toward the siren song of divine inspiration. But each day slurred together with the last, with no sharp ideas arriving for Anna; she was leaving no tangible imprint on the world.

But who could have imagined that the future Anna K., of all people, would be proposed to in this fashion? In a French restaurant in SoHo—an open kitchen, Languedoc wines, wood-burning oven, the whole cozy shebang—staring at a diamond ring in the middle of her spoon slathered in chocolate. She had dipped this spoon into her chocolate soufflé (how she loved soufflé, its temperature and texture, the hot and the less hot, the gooey and the firm) and there it was, shiny, stained, alien. What convinced Alex that hiding an engagement ring in a molten soufflé was a good idea?

She looked at his rosy cheeks, beads of sweat glistening on his forehead, his hairy, shaking hands.

"My dear Anna," he began, as Anna licked, no, sucked, the chocolate off the ring, leaving a trail of saliva and specks of chocolate encrusted along with the tiny piqués around the solitaire. "You must know how I feel about you."

"I do," she said, as if reading dialogue out of a book, a clumsy, heavy-handed passage of "foreshadowing." She was aware that she had colluded in something, and here was its inevitable conclusion. If you were going to say no, shouldn't it have been months ago when the plan was being hatched, executed?

"The last year and a half have only proven to me that we are so well suited," Alex continued. He mumbled an abridged list of their activities: their first date that lasted half the night and two bottles of wine, their ski trip to Vermont, where he had to summon a doctor for her sprained ankle, the Rodin show, where she confessed to him that she adored Rodin, their first tender night together, et cetera, et cetera.

In Anna's peripheral vision, the waiters gathered themselves into a cluster by the fake fireplace, wringing their hands, preparing to clap, to send out the celebratory chestnut crème brûlée. One of them glanced at his watch.

Alex stood up, his chair squeaking. He lowered himself on both knees, then shifted, propping himself on the right one. He plucked the ring out of her hands and held it up next to his nose.

"Will you marry me, Anna?" Time, she thought, time could not be ignored.

"Chicken livers, thirty-two," a cook called out from the kitchen, and was shushed. A woman at a nearby table broke into nervous tears. Someone else was pouring wine, taking surreptitious bites of food. Otherwise, it was as black and quiet as outer space.

"Yes, Sasha, I will," Anna whispered. The clapping was hearty, diners kept sending over glasses of champagne. And the crème brûlée, when it arrived, was delicious, creamy, the perfect brittle blanket, you could barely taste the chestnut. Hence, the proposal, the chocolate ring, the expected conclusion. The end.

3

THE GREAT RUSSIAN SOUL

We cannot continue the story of Anna K. without tackling the issue of the Russian soul—*velikaia russkaia dusha*. Much ink has been spilled on it, no one can adequately articulate what it entails. It is generally agreed that the term is hazy and amorphous, an exclusive gift for the suffering Russians. Does it have anything to do with bitter cold? Communist timetables? Policing grandmothers? The addictive qualities of vodka? Wars fought with little training, shoddy clothing, and primitive equipment? An affection for murderous dictators? Ambivalence about the Westernizing innovations of Peter the Great?

Fyodor Dostoyevsky called it the "Russian disease . . . an indifference toward everything that is vital—toward the truth of life, everything that nourishes life and generates health." But is there truth to any of it, or is it just a story, a myth created to justify one's suffering?

Does it have something to do with this *toska* everyone talks about, an irrepressible longing for the Motherland, a misty-eyed nostalgia for God-knows-what, God-knows-when? And what happens to the Great Russian Soul when it is transplanted? Can it flourish in Rego Park, Queens, for example?

The Russians around Anna had their own—immigrant—interpretations of the phenomenon. To Anna, this was what the Russian soul in America looked like:

1. Shopping Extortions: In department stores, a Russian friend encourages Anna to clip a $200 price tag for a Fendi scarf and surreptitiously exchange it with the $35 sales tag belonging to a Nike sports bra. Why pay more?

2. Rebuke from Strangers: How often has Anna found herself scolded by Russians in public places? "Maybe if you hadn't wandered away, *devushka,* you wouldn't have lost your spot in line," being an example of leftover schadenfreude that used to be exercised in millions of lines around the Soviet Union.

3. Suspicion of Positive Sentiments: In Anna's observation, Russians avoided voicing praise, presumably to ward off the evil eye. If the young Anna Roitman received compliments from a Russian adult, chances were either she had lost a significant amount of weight or they lacked a Russian soul.

4. Indifference to the Enjoyment of Others: How often had Anna overheard exceedingly loud conversations, say, about a friend's abortion during a Met performance of *Don Giovanni*? If Anna tried to shush the two women, she would inevitably receive an earful.

5. Fondness for Politically Incorrect Jokes: Anna could never understand the mysterious proliferation of *anekdoty,* passed via Internet and retold around dinner tables, skewering impotent men, mistresses, dissatisfied wives, alcoholism, peasants, excessive stupidity, old-school communists, Chapayev, Stalin, Putin, Georgians, Bukharians, Jews, lesbians, and other non-"Russian" personages. Anna immigrated to America at a young age, and therefore the humor of the punch lines passed her by completely.

Et cetera.

Perhaps this was the result of the Russian soul's transmutation—its Sovietization, its immigration. Or, more likely, this was the only slice allotted to the Russian Jews (just called "Jews" in Russia), while the good stuff, that special concentrated essence Dostoyevsky spoke of, would be saved for the ethnic Russians, the real Russians.

It seemed that Anna K., for all her Americanness, might not be an owner of a *velikaia russkaia dusha*. She woke up optimistically to a new day, tried to take pride in small accomplishments, rarely voiced criticism to family and friends, to lovers (much less to strangers standing in front of her at a checkout line). She began interactions with new people on a platform of politesse.

Yet, Anna decided, shards of the Russian soul might have lodged themselves inside her, unwilling to be removed. She loved to drink, even if it often made her combative and depressed afterward, for reasons she could not pinpoint. She had a fatalistic binary mentality—things tended to be wonderful or terrible; there were few nuances to her failures. Like a child, who builds castles with the aim to destroy, so Anna was tempted to topple her own best efforts—a hard-earned employment contact she didn't follow up on, a phone message from a promising romantic prospect ignored until it was too late. She didn't believe or didn't want to believe in therapy as a cure for any of these ailments. Most damningly, even at the height of her pleasure—splashed by sun on a beautiful spring day or in the middle of an engrossing activity requiring all her concentration—she was engulfed by an overall feeling of doom. The Russian soul had come to claim her, extinguishing all that was sanguine and buoyant, all that was American inside her, leaving only the Siberian Steppes, the crust of black bread, the acerbic aftertaste of marinated herring, the eternal, bleak winter.

At least that was what she told herself. Her Russianness, her immigration, had given her the license to tell that story.

4

SHOULD SHE BRING IN DOSTOYEVSKY?

Waiting for Alex K.'s train to arrive at Penn Station, Anna decided that she would revel in her newly solid life—after all, there was no reason to deny the pleasure of certainty, of routine, a finale to those energy-consuming dramas of the single life. The predictable dilution of every former relationship—the first moment the guy withdraws into himself, not to be coaxed out; the nights he is too tired to see Anna, insisting on sleeping in his own bed; the "Look, this isn't working" if she's lucky, the lack of returned phone calls if she isn't. Kisses, thinning, drained of passion. How much armor can a single young woman accumulate before she puts down her weapons?

An older man stood next to Anna playing the accordion; was that a Ukrainian polka, a song her father used to sing to her as a child? Anna could not remember. She watched the man, the few coins in his hat, the way he squeezed the folds of the accordion, a striped scarf wrapped around his neck. He seemed to be playing primarily for himself, as if the music yanked him back to where he came from. Anna's father had played the accordion in Russia—why hadn't Americans embraced that instrument? she wondered.

She glimpsed his face in the crowd, one instantly recognizable from that of many meaningless heads: his particular smile, wide but lopsided, the scent of cigarettes and coffee on the coat. The approval in Alex's eyes as he skimmed Anna's form, the open shearling jacket, the silk blouse, the black pencil skirt.

"*Moia dorogaia* Anna." He kissed her, quickly, on the lips. Did anyone say those words in the exact way that he did? The singular way he dragged out the word "dear" in Russian, how melodious: *dorogaia.* There was no American man who could hit the precise nerve of nostalgia with that word.

"Wait right here." He left her with one bag and went to find his colleagues. This was what normal couples did, Anna thought, pleased. They performed rituals for one another, parceling out their hours, there was a neatness to it. A conscious choice made: *You, you will be important to me.*

A train pulled into the station and secreted its passengers. Anna closed her eyes, feeling the rush of bodies stir the air around her, the corners of objects, of knees and elbows grazing her. When she opened her eyes, only a young man remained, listening to the accordion player strike up a fresh round of "Balalaika." He was dressed touchingly like a student in a peacoat, a book under one arm, his backpack on the floor between his legs. His eyes were magnified behind rimmed glasses. He lingered, darting glances at her.

She knew what she looked like, a heroine of a French film, perhaps, enveloped in black. Not pretending to read, protecting herself with nothing but her coat and her thoughts. He was staring at her. She stilled her mind, forced it away from scenarios she would have played out in the past. If her life had the narrative qualities of a book, how would their meeting unfold? Simply, she decided, they would be fused by a mutual look. There would be no need to speak. The man peeled two dollars from his wallet clip and dropped them into the man's hat.

"From both of us?" he called out. His smile was something confident and unshaking. He reached into his wallet and pulled out one more dollar. "Musicians in the subways, well, they're overlooked, aren't they?"

"Yes. I mean, the song," she said. "It has some significance." She tried to sound regal, indifferent, like her expected image, but it came out high-pitched, inelegant.

"Oh?" Two strides and he was beside her. She noticed his tattered paperback was dappled with yellow Post-its across the spine—*Notes from the Underground*. His face was smooth, unlined, soft, serious, a cleft in his chin. And it occurred to Anna that there was nothing, now, she could do with all that. She would have to forget his eyes—the color of autumn grass, green giving way to brown.

"It reminds me of home." So she would play the immigrant card, after all, the story that never failed her, the story that always sucked them in. But now there was a kind of heightened desperation in returning to the same old ploys of seduction; this time, she wanted to exude authenticity.

"Really? Did you come here from Eastern Europe? I thought I heard a Russian accent." She didn't answer; it was too easy, after all. He said, "Were you on this train too? From Chicago?"

"No. My fiancé was. He got on at Philadelphia." There, she said it, the word that cut the path short.

They stood together for a minute, listening to the accordion player. This man seemed unwilling to move from her side. He put his backpack on the ground, shifted his book to the crook of the arm closest to Anna. Should Anna enliven the conversation somehow—should she bring in Dostoyevsky? (Anna saw he had written *Nihilist?* on one of the Post-its.) For the first time since the proposal, Anna experienced a rumble of disappointment.

The man seemed to have made up his mind. "David." He stretched out his hand. He smelled, marvelously, of nothing. The clean absence of smell.

She took it, squeezed its cold fingers. "Anna Roitman." The train from Philadelphia pulled away, leaving them, linked together, on the platform.

By the time Alex found Anna, this David was gone, magically heaved into the crowd, leaving a faint trail of himself as though he had never existed. She looked for him in the crowd as Alex took her arm and steered her upstairs, across Penn Station, to the cab queue. "Didn't I talk about nothing but my soon-to-be wife the entire trip?" Alex said to his colleagues, both of whom Anna had met before at the Vodka Room; they wore enormous gold pinky rings and sucked in air after downing a shot. No one responded; they believed it to be a rhetorical question.

The four of them stood outside in the sputtering rain, moving up the line, until the next cab was theirs.

"To Queens," one said, adjusting himself beside her; she was sitting on the sash of his raincoat.

"But not for long," said Alex, his hand entwined around Anna's neck. "After the wedding, we'll be looking on the East Side."

Anna stared out of a window pummeled by rain. She felt ill; squashed in a cab with foreign male bodies, the sour smell of the upholstery. No matter how hard she tried, Anna couldn't suppress her fear of what she had relinquished, the not entirely pleasant "we," decisions made around her. She thought of green eyes, stylish spectacles, the well-worn book in his hands. He had not asked for her number; it went exactly as she had imagined, all subtext, very little text. She thought of the Woody Allen film (*Manhattan,* wasn't it?) in which he and his younger girlfriend ate Chinese food directly out of containers, the simple act of watching a black-and-white movie together on television. With Alex, there would be no tank tops, probably, and no sweatpants either, no eating out of containers—he was a plate man, a man of thick cotton T-shirts. The cab lurched to the right, switching lanes. But what did Chinese food have to do with it? she thought. During winters, for example, she preferred French stews.

The younger pinky ring said, "So, I'm at the Millionaire Fair in Moscow, right? And this one guy buys a diamond-studded cell phone. He's wearing this Rolex or whatnot, his diamond cuff links, and says his plastic cell phone was the one thing that didn't match. He says he has to buy the phone to make it match."

The men shook their heads, in contempt or envy. Anna couldn't be sure but suspected the latter.

Cabs and cars snaked before them, a long, red, wet blur seemingly without end.

"Comrade passengers, I suggest you relax back there," the cab-driver called out in Russian. "We got long ride."

After a while, Alex began to nap, his head falling slightly to the side, onto the shoulder of one of his colleagues. The man made eye contact with Anna, a conspiratorial smile—he'd been married for seven years himself, and this was pretty much the way it was most of the time: unpleasant snores, unpleasant smells, the screech of your name, the demands. But he would say nothing to this semi-young woman, this pale, haughty woman whose English was far better than her Russian, who, for some reason, had decided to take on the fifty-six-year-old bachelor Alexei K. for life, despite everything.

5

THE CONDENSED LOVE STORY OF ANNA K.

Anna had always had crushes on her teachers. All she needed to see was a man striding to the front of the room, books under his arm, a scarf wrapped around his neck, preparing to address the class, and her heart would be captured at once.

She could never forget her first day of school in Russia, a national holiday, waking up to know that millions of kids were doing exactly what she was doing—accepting flowers from relatives, being walked to school for that very first meeting, the music, the speech from the principal. All those kids, in their polished shoes, their white pinafores. Heaven.

Her first love was Tovarisch Alexei Petrovich Grushin, her first-grade teacher in Moscow. Picture the future Anna K. sitting in the first row, her pencil case neatly aligned with the right edge of her desk, her quad-lined workbook filled with jostling numbers, her two braids held in place by white chiffon ribbons. What was it about Grushin? He was no great looker. He was balding, but proudly so, his thick eyebrows masking a genuinely kindly face, a face that could be animated into passion by small, attainable pleasures: a glass of strong black tea, a chicken dumpling, the sight of a woman's pink skin after a hot shower.

Later, Anna would imagine all these details about dear Alexei
Petrovich, but back then she just wanted to give him the right answer.
She would rattle off, "One, two, three, five, seven, eleven," and then
sit back, flush with pride, basking in his approval. "Very good, Anna
Borisovna, very good," he would say. And wasn't Grushin the one who
pinned Anna with her very first October pin when she was becoming an
Octyabryonok? Wasn't it his hand—trembling, for fear of pricking her
with the sharp point—that clumsily attached the red-gold star, Lenin's
face in its center, to her prepubescent chest? Wasn't it Grushin whom
her parents invited to the Roitmans' communal apartment for dinner, the way he thanked Natasha for every crust of bread and praised
Anna to the skies—the neatness of her handwriting, her perfect fives
in every problem? Anna sat to his right, passing him the bowl of garlic
potatoes. In the Soviet Union, it was so easy to please a man.

After the Roitmans immigrated to the United States, it was never
the same. Here, the first day of school was no longer special; parents
plunked their kids in the schoolyard and went straight to the office.
Her teachers were unattractive women or, if attractive, they were
young and distracted, their own neediness directed outward. The men
varied. Anna was happy to note that her Russian accent and freshly
scrubbed, nectarine smoothness attracted their attention at once. She
was always the first to raise her hand, answers at her fingertips. The
teachers called her "Ehna" and tended to want to do special things
for her.

Mr. Stevens, for example—portly, young, idealistic—explained
compound adjectives to Anna after class, hovering over her and an
open book in the hallway as kids ran past them to their classrooms.
"Blue eyed," he said, "is not the same as blue-eyed."

"I understand," the hushed twelve-year-old Anna agreed, her
breath caressing those thick, slightly crooked fingers gripping the textbook. "Like blue-eyed girl."

"Yes," he said. "Yes."

Mr. Horowitz taught Anna to serve a volleyball not with her wrist—
stinging, red, and swollen afterward—but with the palm of her hand.
World history teacher Mr. Miller blushed as he went over the details

of Russia's 1917 Revolution, then the ensuing civil war, terror, gulag, Lubyanka. They sat in adjacent school desks—his, a leftie—touching arms, their heads inclined. "But you must know all this already, right?" he would say, even as Anna shook her head. No, how could she possibly know all this if no one had taught it to her?

"Watt is the unit of power?" the physics teacher, Mr. Fried, would joke, waiting for the right answer. "Yes," she would reply, giving him what she knew he wanted. And of course there were many others: Messrs. Lawrence and Hoffman and Lee and Monroe—all more luminous than the American boys around Anna with their stutters, their scabs, their ketchup-stained sports jerseys. And they didn't know what to make of her either, a brooding young girl wearing dark colors, staring out windows, reading, always reading.

It was only in Queens College that Anna started to realize that she was so busy pleasing all her teachers, she had no idea what she wanted to do for herself. Junior year creaked around and there it was—major-selection time approaching with Anna still under the thrall of last year's Shakespearean scholar, Professor Watling, and Proto-Renaissance art history expert, Mr. Heyraud. ("And look at the dress on that Madonna": Heyraud's ecstatic, French-tinged voice sliced through the dim lights, the sensuous colors.)

Anna tried doing research at Career Services, an unassuming brown house on the edge of the campus, where she flipped through heavy black binders. Inside, university graduates talked about what they did in their offices all day. They would "solve problems," "manage teams," and "interface with departments," their testimonies spilling over with bluster and bravado. She signed up for an appointment with an advisor, who told Anna that a writing class might unearth her secret desires. Who knows what you'll find out? she said from behind an oversized artificial fern, pushing glasses up the bridge of her nose. She shoved the course catalog into her hands.

Anna checked the course listings for the fall. Yes, a man would be teaching creative writing this semester—and a Russian man at that, a Zubovsky.

The class was small, just twelve people, more girls than boys.

Zubovsky made the class create a circle of their chairs so they could all see one another, but the collective focus was always on the front of the room, directed at the teacher. Anna wished she could say this Zubovsky was the best-looking man she'd ever seen, a worthy successor to all the men who came before, but that was not the case. Zubovsky's round head was not integrated with his slight, angular frame; Anna could tell he barely reached five feet tall. He spent most of the class in his seat, one leg crossed over the other, winding a pen around each finger. He wore a three-piece suit and had a small trace of an accent. He was a nervous, first-time professor, evident by the long pauses, the rapid eye movements, his reluctance to disagree with student opinions.

They took turns around the room telling the class who they were. Anna's speech became particularly long and rambling. I'm from Russia, she told the class, holding Zubovsky's gaze for as long as possible. He listened attentively, a whisper of a smile on his simian face.

During Thanksgiving dinner, Anna told her parents that she had selected English as her major. Twenty relatives, internally flambéed on vodka, sat around the table, waiting for Anna's parents' reaction. And Anna found herself wanting to hurt her parents, because if they had stayed in Russia, wouldn't she have had a clearer focus for her life: some babies on the way, a budding career as an engineer?

The Roitman table was the Russian interpretation of the first American meal—parsley-dusted potatoes instead of yams, two roasted chickens (pregnant with apples) instead of turkey. Anna's father squinted at her.

"What career is good with English major?" he asked. "In the Soviet Union—" he began good-naturedly, but the relatives broke in to remind him as if he had forgotten that there was no Soviet Union, and thank God for that. Another round of toasts broke out.

It is time, Zubovsky said, to write a short story. This was the moment in the semester the class had been dreading, having satisfied its creative impulses with brief vignettes, with lists of favorite childhood toys, descriptions of their most vivid birthdays.

Last class, Zubovsky had circulated Anna's piece to all the students. It was set during a New Year's when she was eight years old and still in Russia, and Father Frost came to pay a home visit. Of course, even at that time, she'd known it was her father dressed up in a beard, a ridiculous fake white fur collar, holding a plastic bag filled with walnuts and a mauve one-eyed bear. When Anna asked for Snegurochka, his sexy young niece, his government-invented partner-in-crime, he told her that this year he was traveling solo. Anna's mother was being fired that very day for having applied to emigrate, a traitor soon to have her citizenship taken away, a betrayer of her country—they should have known not to hire a Jew. But Anna did not include this in her cozy memory piece, which the class loved. More ethnic details, the class sighed, more food, more indigenous scenes.

But no matter how much Anna tried, she couldn't get Zubovsky's attention. He appeared to be besotted with Janice, a quiet blonde whose flowery writing had been deemed publishable by the class. Her mouth was shaped like a cherry and as she announced that she had already written her short story, her shirt slipped a little to reveal a pale, dimpled shoulder.

Zubovsky handed out one of his own stories as an example. It was called "Baba Yaga" and appeared to be about the end of his marriage to a voluptuous but shrewish Russian woman. He is not yet over her, Anna thought as he read the whole thing out loud, moistening his lips with his tongue, clearing his throat from time to time. In the story, the protagonist is tall, towering over all the other characters, until he is consumed, piece by piece, by his wife. As the class listened, Anna watched Janice's face. She was looking down at her slender hands, her rounded pink fingernails, taking deep, even breaths.

"To write a story is to learn about yourself," Zubovsky said when he finished reading. But Anna didn't want to write a story. In the library, she looked up Zubovsky's name in the online catalog. There she discovered that he had written only one book, called *Russian Hauntings*. It sat on the shelf, new, its spine crisp. The cover was ornate, decorated with folk characters, sorcerers, and demons, but inside, Anna found conventional stories—basically fairy tales updated with Russian immigrants. Fearing mediocrity, she closed the book and returned it to where she'd found it.

On her way back to the bus that would take her back to Ninety-ninth Street and her parents' apartment with its smell of salmon soup, Anna tried to forget the book, its leanness, its paucity, and imagined something thicker hidden in his drawer, Tolstoyan in scope, erudite, historical. On the bus, she pictured Zubovsky grabbing her after class, pushing her against the wall, lifting her by the slope behind her knees, wrapping her legs around his waist. He would address her, brusquely, only in Russian. In return, she would consume him.

The next morning, Anna realized she had dreamt about Grushin. The dream was washed of all color, like the black-and-white pictures with scalloped edges the Roitmans had brought with them from Russia. What would he look like shuffling around like the other elderly immigrants, with a fedora, a cane, arthritic legs warmed by a wool plaid blanket? And what would he talk about—his emphysema, the pulsating ache in his hips? No more strings of numbers magically exuding from his mouth, no more "very good, Anna Borisovna."

"How is English major going?" her father asked. They were eating as usual, the table full of food; most of it would be thrown away. At the supermarket, her parents stocked up on a mountain of supplies, savored the process of replenishing that empty box of tissues, the sliver of soap, the moldy brick of cheese.

With an English major, there were many practical applications, Anna explained. She could be a journalist, an editor, a teacher. But as she spoke, none of those possible futures felt tangible to her; they were simply words she could translate into other words. She took a bite of carrot cake.

"Even if you do get a job with this major, you can always live with us," her mother said, pushing the plate beneath the cake, catching some of the falling crumbs. "You can live here for as long as you like," she said, patting Anna's hand.

. . .

Zubovsky's office was in the basement of the English department, in
the corner of a badly lit labyrinth. Outside his office was a shantytown
of students, some standing, some crouching on the floor, waiting for
the professor to tell them about themselves. Anna joined the line.

"He's very supportive, isn't he?" one girl standing next to Anna said.
"He really listens to you, and he's not fucking boring like the others."
Anna smiled until the girl turned away. For good luck, she wore her
hair in two braids; the hairstyle gave her a sense of control.

The line went slowly as Zubovsky spent time with each student,
the door closed, murmuring on the other side until the student was
exhaled from the room, wearing her own secret smile. Anna looked for
Janice, but she was not in this line.

At last, Zubovsky waved Anna in. She closed the door herself and
sat in one of a pair of chairs, legs pressed together, knapsack neatly
resting on her knees. The office was mostly bare, but there were some
personal touches—a tiny cactus on one side of the desk, a calendar of
movie posters, and a shelf of Russian literature, cataloged chronologically (the Chekhovs, then the Gogols, all the way up to *Russian Hauntings*). His desk was pressed against the wall. Zubovsky heaved himself
into a swivel chair and crossed his legs. Anna waited for him to speak.

"Anna," he said, clasping his hands together. They stared at each
other. Finally he turned to look for Anna's story, "Rusalka," among the
stack of papers on his desk. The story had come to Anna in a spurt
of inspiration. When she'd flipped through Zubovsky's book, she'd
noticed that the rusalka was the one mythical character missing from
his collection—that siren who lures men to a watery grave at the bottom of the lake. A woman, wronged in life (an early death of some
kind, a betrayal), returns in her afterlife to claim the souls of men. She
is strong and beautiful, God is she beautiful—more beautiful than Janice could ever be—with thick, luxurious tresses, pudding-soft curves,
sweet dimpled spots that no man—stumbling, lost, alone—can resist.
In Anna's story the rusalka finally acts, winding her slim arms around
the teacher, learning from him for eternity.

Peeking around Zubovsky, Anna saw red-penned etchings in the margin of the paper. *Very good, Anna,* she glimpsed on one page. *A nice image.* In the past, how much pleasure those words would have given her! But now they felt hollow, not enough to fill her. She wasn't a writer, that was clear, but she could love one.

He put the story down and turned to Anna. Even though the teacher's name in the story was Grushin, she could tell Zubovsky was uncomfortable. He shuffled in his seat, running his fingers mechanically through his hair. He had a faintly Slavic face, round and monkey-like, the back of his neck dotted with stubble.

"Anna," he began again. "This is a fine fictional effort." He pronounced her name the same way her parents did, patiently, the same long tender "A" for "Ah-na." There was no Ehna in this room. Somebody knocked on the door; Anna ignored the sound and allowed her own name to wash over her, embracing her. This was the first teacher who was just like her, forced to churn out fairy tales to make sense of his life. Their story was the same story. Her body was taut, humming, ready to claim him.

Before he could open the door to his office, to release her into that unfathomable, indifferent hallway, Anna placed her hands on Zubovsky's shoulders. He seemed paralyzed with surprise; his eyes were wide, unblinking. She gripped his cheap, itchy sweater and leaned in to kiss him. She cradled the back of his head with one hand and pressed her tongue into his mouth. Heaven. Before he pushed her away, Anna could hear her knapsack hitting the floor between their feet, the thump resonating with her like a bell, like coming home, like that first-day-of-school Moscow sound that summoned every schoolchild throughout the land into the red, glorious building of education.

6

THE MARRIED LIFE OF ANNA K.

Fabergé Russian Restaurant was located on a side street, discreetly removed from the traffic of Brighton Beach Avenue. (Did you think a restaurant like this would mingle with your common Nationals, the Rasputins, the Catherine the Greats?) Tucked away around the corner from a pierogi stand and a florist who also sold brand-name sneakers at a steep discount, the restaurant had no sign, just a neon egg blinking hot blues and purples. Outside its tinted front doors, men in sunglasses smoked, waiting for a Mercedes or a BMW to park. (Where did they park the cars? This was no suburb with parking lots and multilevel garages. No, here the streets were plugged up with cars, parked nose to toe, some even squeezing themselves before fire hydrants. But nobody asked—this was the covenant between the Russian restaurant and its guests, and more often than not, the car was returned with no visible memory of its last six hours.)

Fabergé was famously hard to get into, boasting imperial service and a superior Russian-French kitchen. *Where is the French part?* an uninformed guest might ask, scanning the plates of Salat Olivier, vinaigrette, herring, and smoked fish. Ah, but it was everywhere, from the bottles of Merlot on the table, the hors d'ouevres (rather than *zakuski*) that peppered the lazy Susan, the coq au vin (easily mistaken for roasted *kuritza*) glistening as the centerpiece.

Like other Russian restaurants in the area, Fabergé's main income came from special events: birthdays and bar mitzvahs, weddings and anniversaries. All the musicians needed to learn was the name of the man or woman of the hour. Would they sing, "Happy Byorsday, Leon?" or "Congratulations, Tania and Misha"? The parties operated on a strict prototype, with a single script, food and vodka and thumping music layered on top of one another. Sentimental ballads would be timed with the hors d'oeuvres, raunchy disco songs with the skewered meat. Then the show would erupt, with ladies sparkling in sequins, kicking legs wrapped in fishnets. The show tended to draw its inspiration from homespun Gogolian villages or the imperial Pushkin era when princesses and poets spoke to each other in heavily accented French.

The wedding videographer, a stocky Georgian in a shiny red vest, scanned the bounty on the tables, waiting for the young women with their décolletages, their swaying-to-ABBA asses. Their necks drowning in perfume, earlobes drooping with rhinestone earrings. He shot the band as they warmed up onstage, "Anya and Sasha" printed in red on a silver banner behind them. Beneath the banner, the videographer captured the bridal table, the chairs regal in their white-netted plumage.

The guests began to arrive; those delectable women shed their furs, slipping off coats to reveal freckled shoulders, veiny wrists, half-moon hips. The more money these Russians amassed, the more obnoxious they became, the videographer thought; they refused to make eye contact with him, as if they'd never worked as electricians or seamstresses when they first landed, as if they'd never taken on extra work for money, tinkering with broken clocks or slicing open pumpernickel bagels.

And the videos, nothing he did ever pleased them. They wanted more sophisticated dance music, more jump cuts (hey, he did his time in a Tbilisi film school), and no aimless scenes of dancing. They wanted a reality television show—the baby pictures of the bride and groom, two pudgy lumps of dough placed side by side, giving the impression that they had been reaching toward each other since birth. Then they wanted a shot of the couple's first meeting place (a depressing shish kebab restaurant, a bench on the boardwalk); inevitably they wanted the movie to offer a supporting role to the parents, the lovable family spinster who had introduced them or somebody's half-senile babushka, baking spinach pies in her miniature Ocean Parkway kitchen. Who did they think he was, Spielberg?

The groom was old, the man thought, following Alex as he conferred with the Fabergé proprietors, passed rolls of bills from palm to palm. But the bride was no spring chicken either; the videographer had scrutinized her picture. This one had a certain *je ne sais quoi,* a mysterious quality, she commanded attention, but there was something guarded about her, ill at ease. Why was she marrying this putz, then, this puffed-up peacock? But then she looked to be on the wrong side of thirty-five, and that explained a lot. In his day, a twenty-six-year-old woman was considered an old maid, but here, ach, what could he say? He was just happy he no longer had to drive a cab.

Now, if he were twenty years younger, *that* would be the woman for him. His lens had found Katia Zavurov, Anna's cousin. Katia looked to be in her early twenties; she was dressed in a green velvet sheath, her brown hair framing a generous round face. But it was the kindness of her expression that grabbed the videographer's attention, her eager kisses of greeting, the way she listened to the old ladies with rapt attention, never looking bored or scanning the room for someone more interesting. But there was a sadness in her posture; he was a professional, and could discern these things immediately.

The videographer noticed another man, who looked to be around her age, staring at Katia just as intently, but never quite having the heart to cut in on her conversations. Instead, he loitered by the winding staircase, gripping his flute of champagne, glowering through thick eyebrows, until his friend called him, "Lev, come look at this one!" and he was pulled away. Ah, youth, the videographer thought, you couldn't pay me to be that fumbling age again.

The videographer moved to Katia's right side until Katia looked up from the old lady and, finally, a smile was his, full-lipped and unrestrained. But the man had work to do and he reluctantly moved on, taking his place near the chuppah; his feet ached from running around all day, picking up equipment from Senya's place, his suit from the dry cleaners, because God forbid his Lena might anticipate anything in advance of when he needed it.

The band broke into a delayed rendition of "Sunrise, Sunset" and the bridal party walked down the aisle, the groom's mama, his papa, then a younger, more awkward version of the groom and his tweezed wife, and finally the groom, his chest pushed forward as though he'd just swallowed an entire *kuritza*, bones, thighs, and all. The lovely Katia and her parents. The music paused, then swelled with importance. The guests craned their necks toward the back, a few even put down their forkfuls of smoked salmon.

Flanked by two relatively stout, unimpressive immigrants came the surprisingly tall bride, and the videographer's steady hand wavered, causing a dip in the image. He cursed to himself, then made a mental note to edit the curse out. She was setting the pace for her parents, walking perhaps a bit too quickly. Her dress was strapless, presenting a real pair of shoulders, neck as haughty and long as the swan of the ice sculpture melting behind her, curls tumbling around her ears. The videographer could sense the rest of the guests around him stop nibbling their *zakuski*, no, excuse me, rather, hors d'oeuvres. A stillness permeated the room, an exhale.

How could I have preferred Katia, the videographer thought, when here, why, it is obvious, the bride is far superior? But his thoughts made him depressed, he could see something in the bride's expression, the way she looked at the groom. Was it resignation, an ember of fear, perhaps? The videographer scurried around the chuppah for a long shot of the pair. From this vantage point, everything was lovelier, framed and centered, the flowers, the lace of the veil, the bride's white-painted fingernails.

Who was he to judge, the videographer thought, was it better with him and Lena in those early days? Why, they hardly knew each other when they came together on the wedding night, and he had been such a romantic, all those Victor Hugo, those Dumas vixens in his head; he

certainly didn't expect his bride would eventually climb into bed slathered in face cream, hair in curlers, those pendulous breasts let loose
beneath an oversized floral nightgown. But it didn't take him long,
did it, to get used to all those uncinematic tics of hers, the way she
picked her nose when she thought no one was looking being one glaring example. But still, they'd traversed oceans together and the way
she looked at him when their son visited from Baltimore, surely there
was something special in that dear look, sly and affectionate, two gods
who created the most perfect being together. And then they rested.

"*Opa!*" To his horror, the videographer snapped back to the glass
already broken on the floor, a shot he missed, my God he would have
to do some creative editing to make up for this! He would have to rifle
through his archives to insert another groom's foot. He stepped aside
as the married couple, the mamochki and papochki, and the charming, rosy Katia retreated back up the aisle, only to return again as the
wedding party of Mr. and Mrs. K.!

From then on, he was strictly on cue, he did not miss a single
shout of "*Gor'ko,*" did not miss a single "sweet" kiss that responded
to that "bitter" plea. He got a few reaction shots to particularly moving toasts, especially one given by the bride's father—who knew that
little man would burst into tears and have to be escorted off the stage
by his wife and the mustachioed female singer? And he recorded
every second of the restaurant's signature show—half-naked women
in handkerchiefs and folksy bikinis gyrating their way out of oversized
Fabergé-style eggs.

But he always returned to the bride, now in the middle of the hora
circle, now sitting in her chair, buoyed on the shoulders of half a dozen
men. With one hand she held on to the bottom of her seat, the other
twirled a lacy white handkerchief. Eyelids lowered, she did not smile.
She circled far above the heads of the guests, a seductive white phan-
tom bobbing in the sky.

Alex's vodka-soaked mouth pressed against her own, his uncoordinated
fingers lifted the bottom of her cotton nightgown. He murmured as he

worked, "There you go, that's right." Her breasts were seized. At the wedding, it had felt as though she had watched herself get married from some kind of elevated perch, as if her view of the proceedings was at an angle, almost upside down. What had she felt? A numbed panic, a dulled, paralyzed peace.

Alex peeled down her underwear, his teeth pecked at her skin. She felt suffocated beneath her own hair, his fleshy lips, gentle bites, and all those words—why did he have to talk so much? What was he saying? *Dorogaia Anyechka,* again, *dorogaia,* the word now mangled, stifled. If she relaxed, if she thought of the actor Andrew McCarthy, whose poster she'd had on her walls as a teenager, or even the guy from the train station, it would all be less painful, she was sure.

This act, this thing they were doing felt unlike their past exertions, after other alcohol-fueled dinners or half asleep in the morning. His touch had been pleasant then but temporary. Excellent sushi or steak frites would be delivered immediately afterward and later, whatever else she craved. She had somehow managed to forget the sex entirely, the sushi had been so fresh, so velvety. Here, his touch was jabbing and belligerent, insisting on itself.

She readjusted herself, turning her back, her face unnaturally wedged between two pillows, but it wouldn't be long now; she could feel a mindless desperation to his movements. Her hair caught on the metallic links of his watch wristband and with one hand she tried to reach behind to free herself.

"Anyechka," Alex groaned. And afterward, he was still there, taking even breaths beside her, mouth wide open. They were in Alex's house in Kew Gardens Hills; the streetlight haze filtering through the window illuminated gifts and envelopes, open champagne bottles and ribbons strewn all over the furniture. Nothing is forever, Anna assured herself, but he was her husband now, and it still meant something, even now at the beginning of the twenty-first century, when so much else felt fragile, temporary. She had made a choice, and she would swim around in it, find her footing. This was the way of weddings; it had been time for her to make a choice and she had made it. Choices were what people made. Why should Anna be any different? She lifted her head from between the pillows, wresting her shoulder out of Alex's grip. Her wedding dress lay across the carpet, limp and lifeless, like a deboned fish.

After the wedding, life folded itself into neat packets and Anna found that there were few empty hours to fill. There was the move to the Upper East Side, the decoration of their two-bedroom apartment— auctions at William Doyle, SoHo showrooms. The three-part couch against the wall, facing the plasma screen TV. And afterward, when the apartment was assembled, the K.s established their daily routine. She would come home from the publisher first and start rustling up their dinner, or they would meet at one of Alex's favorite restaurants. By the time he appeared, Anna would have dived into a basket of bread or bowl of olives. Future dinner plans would be made over dessert, inserted into their BlackBerrys.

"We have dinner on the eighth at that new place, that Perry Street one, tickets to *Spamalot* on the thirteenth, a dinner party on the fourteenth," Alex said, peering into his phone. The restaurant was choked with attractive, manicured lives. Anna saw them refracted in oval mirrors, in the crystal wall sconces, the marble top of her table. They were the kind of women she imagined she would one day be—sleek hair pulled away from their faces, wearing ambitious, unstructured tops, bored expressions.

She plugged the plans into her own BlackBerry, a gift from Alex, even if later she would transfer all the data into her paper planner. When the sommelier came over, Alex engaged him in a debate on digestifs.

"I love this guy," the sommelier joked, whispering to the waiter to fill the K.s' glasses with two extra inches of cognac.

They sat with their coffees and drinks, Anna fighting a plummeting sensation. She did not resemble those around her—gesticulating with their hands, nodding at their companions, noses bobbing in the steam of their dishes. Anna felt no curiosity, no suspense at what lay ahead for her beyond this moment, just a dull sense of existing. The bill arrived and Alex slipped his credit card between the leather folds. In the cab Anna let her head drop back, already pounding with alcohol, her stomach churning with lamb and panna cotta.

As they slid up Madison Avenue or across Seventy-ninth Street, she wasn't sure where she had been anymore; the stores already closed, the night's possibilities exhausted. Her doorman, Mike, had been replaced by the night guy, she noticed sleepily. The elevator was slow, passing the lobby to first drop down to the basement. A young woman stood against the wall, her hair pulled back into a ponytail, gripping her late-night laundry, and Anna watched her stand there, the plastic hamper balanced against one knee.

In bed, Anna tried to read Trollope, but gave up. She felt a kiss on her shoulder, and she allowed her body to slacken. Her pajama bottoms were pulled down, pooling around her ankles. This time, she found that so much depended on her attitude. She was being nibbled, as though a vanilla wafer or a buttered sliver of toast. But her mind returned to the woman in the elevator. Alone, she probably was now, reading a novel in the laundry room while her clothes did somersaults. She recalled being in the laundry room of her old Chelsea studio— heat emanating from the dryer, speeding toward the end of her book, wondering if she would finish the drying or the novel first. Racing upstairs with her warm clothes, immediately slipping on socks straight from the basket, she used to stir trail mix and honey into a container of Greek yogurt and finish her book. She would imagine it was she who was the heroine, willing powerful lovers to prostrate themselves before her, allowing them to sob their love to her in the middle of a rainstorm, at balls, inside carriages. But now, as Anna remembered all this, she wondered if her dreams had been thrilling, or if they had concluded by her pushing those imaginary lovers away. How did those reveries end?

No, Darcy, it cannot be, she would protest, while the man clutched her by the wrists, begging her to change her mind. The man would always be an amalgam of soldier and great writer, a combination that made sense at the time. He would fight for her in the present and write about her afterward.

But Anna, is there no other way? His knees would be splattered with mud, the stars of his gold war medals poking into the skin beneath her corset. But she would yank her hand back (he, kissing it all the while), hop up in the carriage, and allow herself to be carried away by the cantering horses. There he would be, poor Darcy, or whoever, receding into a black dot in the misted-over window (having chased the carriage for a mile or so and now lying sprawled on the wet earth). Then the nineteenth-century Anna would be free to burst into tears, wringing her handkerchief until the carriage stopped before a new man. Yes, Anna decided now, on East Eightieth Street, lights out after her husband finished loving her rather hastily; even in her unbridled fantasies, happiness had been difficult to conjure.

Like most Russian men, Alex K. was a mama's boy. Every other weekend, he dragged Anna to his parents' house in Kew Gardens. They were stylish where her own parents were frayed; even at home his mother wore tailored suits, clip-on earrings, the father his V-neck cashmere sweaters. In the background, the cleaning woman bustled around, answering the telephone or returning from walks with the Shi-Tzu. Their house, with all its order, didn't feel quite real to Anna.

Alex's mother's fingers were always moving—picking lint off Alex's jacket, wiping invisible fingerprints off glass surfaces, refreshing the water in the flower vase. When Anna helped his mother set the table for dinner, the woman engaged Anna in girl-to-girl chats about the hottest vacations spots (all the Russians were going to Croatia this year, last year Johannesburg, the year before, Sardinia).

"I don't know anything about that," Anna would be forced to admit. "Personally, I've always loved Paris."

"Well, yes, of course, Paris never goes out of style." His mother would examine her daughter-in-law. If left alone for a minute, Alex's mother would think, she would probably sit in a corner and read or stare out the window. A strange girl his son married. Was that an adult way to interact with in-laws? Paris, for God's sake? As clichéd as it gets.

His father, an owner of a successful limousine conglomerate, loved talking traffic. The Henry Hudson, he was always saying, always the Henry Hudson, never the FDR. Always the Battery Tunnel, never the Brooklyn Bridge. Of course, there were always exceptions: the Sunday of Gay Pride Parade (those naked *golubye*) ruled out the Henry Hudson, and the Battery Tunnel under construction with its single lane, don't even think about it. Coming back from the Hudson Valley or Woodbury Common, Alex would dial his father. *Saw Mill, Papa? Triborough Bridge? Is this the best way to go, or is there a better route, a faster road?*

Alex and Anna took vacations to St. Thomas or Italy or Munich with Alex's colleagues and their wives. On vacation, the groups naturally divided into men and women strolling down some scenic, cobblestoned *strasse* arm in arm, discussing how to make money or how to spend it. Anna would be the silent one, absorbing the opinions of others—they were all so confident, so certain of never being challenged.

"A cuckoo clock," someone would say, and the group would pause in front of a shop. Or else they would all take the English-language bus tour of the city, watching foreign life on the other side of the frosted glass.

She would be the one to wake up at seven a.m., to meet everyone else at breakfast after a solitary stroll around crumbling European bridges, always returning with a memento in her purse—a disintegrating rock, a leather journal. She knew the other wives were suspicious of her; what pleasure could a woman take in solitary walks? they wondered. Wasn't every experience enhanced by communal participation, by the validation of a fellow witness?

And so went a year of Anna K.'s marriage.

The only person in whose company Anna took real pleasure was Katia. She enjoyed Katia's simplicity, her admiration; she knew that in Katia's eyes, Anna was the epitome of style and sophistication. It was lovely to be worshipped, to see your idealized self refracted through someone else's gaze. If she were not Bukharian, Katia said she would have retraced Anna's life steps: her apartments and boyfriends, her provocative clothes, her intelligence.

But she was Bukharian, and thus had to pour her energy into dreams of marriage. Once she was married, Katia promised to stock the refrigerator with a different homemade meal for each night of the week, varying the fish and the meats. One evening she would serve a side dish of braised cabbage, another okra. She would clear out a space for her husband to work, inserting herself into his line of vision only to bring him a sweetened tea or a pastry. Anna tried to explain to the girl that marriage was not like that, it was more like the layering of memory—a buried impulse resting on top of a fresh wound, one annoyance recalling another just like it. But Katia wasn't yet ready to hear it; as a marriageable Bukharian girl, it was all she had to look forward to, and after a while, Anna realized the fragility of this fantasy and stopped sharing her own truth.

Bukharians remained exotic to Anna, even if her own mother had been an exiled Bukharian in Moscow, so happily Sovietized that she had no desire to return to Uzbekistan. Just weeks before the Roitmans emigrated, Anna's uncle took a trip to Samarkand and returned with a sultry, dark-skinned eighteen-year-old bride, Katia's mother.

Bukharian Jews. How could they be just like us and so not like us? Anna had wondered while still living with her parents in Rego Park. How could they be so pious, so earnest, especially compared with Russians whose post-Soviet cynicism drowned out religions, politics, nations? She used to monitor the Bukharian Jews strolling home from synagogue, while she and her girlfriend were on their way to buy ripped jeans or used Journey tapes. Those families, clumped together, making their slow progress up the street, the girls in modest skirts, whispering among themselves. New York City was just across the bridge, gleaming in all its modernity and promises of vice, yet for Bukharians it was as distant as Afghanistan used to be. They had no idea that they should be buying jeans, ripped, just so, in all the right places.

When visiting her Bukharian relatives, Anna would see the women on food and baby duty, the men with their glasses of cognac, how primitive it seemed to her then. Later, of course, a year or so into her marriage, Anna would come to envy the Bukharian Jews with all their boundaries, so clearly demarcated, when her own were tenuous, shifting, murky. Vaguely, without fully realizing it, she would come to appreciate the power of a shared narrative, with its sacred ideals; without them, an immigrant is lost, stretching toward a mirage that, once seized, immediately disintegrates.

One Saturday a month, Anna and Katia met to go to a museum and have dinner together. Anna loved to listen to Katia's raw thoughts on art, her preference for muted colors, yellows and light greens, her love of bucolic scenes, of still life, of rococo. She refused to see the lascivious embedded inside the painting, the French gentleman looking up his companion's skirt as she swung in the air, for example.

"What a pretty scene," Katia would say. How simple it was, Anna thought, to find beauty in what had been carefully arranged for its discovery.

This Saturday, they were at the Guggenheim to see the "Russia!" show. *Nine hundred years of masterpieces,* the posters said. The lobby teemed with Russians, other New Yorkers, and tourists. Naïveté encased inside a globe, Anna thought when she saw Katia in her orange coat, her brown leather gloves. She was at a time of life when the novelty of adult expectations collided with the leftovers of childhood. They kissed each other like always, appraising one another quickly for new accessories, weight loss, a different cast to the skin.

While waiting in line to hand in their coats, they asked after each other's families. Anna sensed the girl had something to tell her—Katia's terse answers, the way she gripped her coat, the tautness of knuckle, told Anna she was holding something back—so she waited with her own news. They decided to begin at the bottom, to circle their way up, to skip the ruddy canvases of socialist realism.

The icons were astounding, the gleam of them, the sheer size, as well as the tapestries of the shroud of Christ with their silk and gold and silver threads, but Anna had always felt that as a Jew, most of Russian history was inaccessible to her, as if she had been shoved out of its way. In the Russian language, one was either a "Russian" or a "Jew" (one annihilated the possibility of the other), and this show only highlighted the exclusion of the Jews. And now, as an immigrant and a Jew, she could only be one of these awed Americans, ogling the work of a foreign country.

She heard snippets of Russian conversations. "What did you expect? It's the usual: Stalin, Lenin, blah, blah, blah." "Now, when I saw this at the Hermitage, that was an experience. You can't compare the Hermitage to this museum, so white and ugly." Or "This Kabakov guy is really pretty clever, looks just like our old room in the *communalka*, doesn't it?" Anna did not remember if she had ever been in the Hermitage; her mother insisted that she had been there as a little girl, but this Guggenheim was all she knew.

Then Anna glimpsed Ivan Kramskoy's *Unknown Woman*. A late-nineteenth-century painting in which a woman stares at the viewer from one side of an opulent carriage. Her expression halted Anna, and she lay a hand on Katia's back to still her in front of the painting. The woman was dark-skinned (Jewish?), hair pulled back, her face the only part of her body exposed to the gaze, swathed as she was in a fur-lined coat, a white feather affixed to her cap. She appeared to be looking down from behind half-hooded, glistening eyes, the space beside her on the carriage conspicuously empty.

"She does kind of look like you," Katia whispered, looking from the painting to Anna. "Except you, my dear, are much paler and much happier. She's more of a depressed version of you."

"Look." Anna pointed. "Who do you think she is looking at?"

Katia didn't answer right away.

"I think I may be in love," she finally said.

"I'm pregnant," Anna replied. They stood there, under the gaze of the unknown woman, staring into and through each other. It took them a few minutes to extract themselves from their own revelation and respond to the other's news. They hugged, leaning into each other's warmth, submerged in each other's perfume. Katia was forced to clutch around Anna's waist, gingerly, so as not to press too hard. But Anna was the first to pull back, to turn away from the unknown woman and Katia. Her own story suddenly felt hacked off; instead of a future, Anna could envision only a tree stump.

Later, after they had finished viewing the entire show, before Anna was forced to cut the queue to the first-floor women's room to violently throw up, the two women went to the museum shop, where Katia bought a stack of Hanukkah cards and secretly, as a future gift honoring their closeness, honoring the moment they had just shared, the Kramskoy postcard.

7

THE CONDENSED LOVE
STORY OF ANNA K., PART II

Everyone has had a young, unhappy love affair in their twenties and why should Anna K. have been any different? If anything, Anna K. was genetically predisposed to unhappy love affairs. Wasn't it she who consumed *Wuthering Heights* no less than fourteen times (not counting the six times she watched the Laurence Olivier/Ralph Fiennes movie versions)? Wasn't it she who wrote tormented notes to bucktoothed, freckled Nick Moynihan in seventh grade, tore them up, then Scotch-taped them back together? Listened to Billy Joel's "She's Got a Way" lying on her bed with the lights out, her eyes closed, then got up to rewind the tape and listen to it again? And again? Who saw herself in Natasha, in Margarita, Jo, Catherine Earnshaw, Elizabeth Bennet, all those heroines the novels would refer to as "plucky"? Who was certain that her ineffable Russianness set her apart in America, made of her a romantic heroine doomed to a sweetly tragic end?

Wasn't it she who stood alone at high school dances, in her black turtlenecks, her layered black-taffeta miniskirts, in her first pair of patent high heels that would make her insteps hurt for days? There she stood in those dimly lit gymnasiums, alone at the windowsill, looking out at the great dark cosmos, certain that her mysterious apartness would lure Seth or Michael or Jacob to seek her out. "You're not like the others," she imagined them saying as they approached her, taking her hand and leading her onto the dance floor, swaying to the melancholy strains of the Cure. But in the end, the boys were content enough dancing to their Huey Lewis and the News, their Eddie Moneys, with their Jennifers and Susans, their Heathers and Emilys. Who needed different anyway, who ever said different was good?

And in the sleepaway creative arts camp in the Adirondacks, thirteen-year-old Anna did not yet comprehend that all the boys rejected her flirtations because they were grappling with their sexuality. After afternoon rehearsals for *West Side Story* or an evening activity of a Chevy Chase movie, she would walk back to the bunks with a Seth or a Michael or a Jake. Instead of a kiss (which Anna prepared for by consuming breath mints, practicing with her fist inside her sleeping bag, having signed up for Slutty Pamela's lecture, "How to Kiss Good"), Seth/Michael/Jake would stammer, blush, build small mountains of pebbles with his Converse sneakers. His cheeks would be smeared with pink.

"I would like to," he would begin. "It's just, well, I can't."

"Why?"

"I dunno. I can't explain it. You are pretty and nice and . . ."

She would turn away, leaving him sapped of all color under the lights illuminating the bunks. Boys and girls would disperse around him, to their flashlights and comic books and secret stash of Mallomars, to their own private longings.

"So what happened?" Pamela would ask, slipping the scrunchie from her permed blond ponytail, pulling her Benetton T-shirt over her head. "I saw you out there. Any action?"

Later that night, Anna would sneak out onto the dock in her nightgown and stare at the ghostly peaks of the Adirondacks. If Seth/Michael/Jake was not meant for her, there would be another, one much more sensual, profound. He would have brown hair that curled beneath the collar of his shirt, wear small round glasses, read Tolstoy or at least Dickens. He would imprint deep kisses on her lips, hold her head between his palms as he kissed her. She waited for him every summer, scanned the new kids hopping off the bus with their duffel bags, their cool mullet hairdos and Iron Maiden jackets, but no Darcy alighted, not then, not ever.

And didn't she need Darcy to liberate her, to erase the memories of all those immigrant traumas of grade school? In fifth grade, a freckled bully threw a rock at her face. "Commie," he screamed, right before he flung the rock, until suddenly Anna felt the impact, the wetness, a dull pain in her forehead. The grimacing doctor mumbled incoherently as he stitched up the gash, providing little comfort to the young Anna. Teachers looked past her as if she had not yet formed into a human being, as if she were mentally deficient—her inability to understand what went on in class gave her a perpetually surprised expression, eyebrows stretched taut in concentration.

For weeks, it seemed, she knew just a single word in English, "No." And it did feel like the most useful word she could learn because all social interactions carried an undercurrent of menace. But it could also backfire. Her favorite lunch of pizza, the one pleasure she looked forward to all week, would incur the materialization of the very same freckled bully—"Do you want your pizza?" he would taunt, phrasing the question to accommodate her one English word. "No," she would whimper. The pizza would be yanked out of her hands.

The girl who sat behind her in biology class, pressing her foot into her backside, confident that Anna wouldn't respond. The kids who tripped her as she made her way to the back of the bus. The girls who peeked over the bathroom stall as Anna crouched, mortified, frozen in mid-pee. Soon she learned to keep it in all day, to explode in relief when she returned to the safety of the apartment. What an easy target she must have been throughout grade school, just pre-perestroika—naïve, pigtailed, Soviet.

"Your accent, slight but still there. Where are you from?" she was asked repeatedly, then and later. Always a reminder that she was from anywhere but here, as if yanked out of a lineup of pretenders—her performance the least convincing. "From Russia," she would be forced to answer. "From Moscow. From the former Soviet Union." But she was only trying to order a spinach salad, rent a pair of bowling shoes;

why, even in those innocuous situations, did she have to be from some-where?

And while all this was happening around her, if Anna closed her eyes, she could call up the particular Moscow air, the kind of aggres-sive cold that pummeled her in the gut as soon as she stepped outside in December, the precise oranges and reds of the Turkish rug hanging on their bedroom wall, the grainy texture of a sausage-shaped dessert that had to be kept in the freezer, the hidden candies inside the folds of the New Year's tree, the smell of chamomile.

Eventually, all those details would become useful, the negative charge of her identity neutralized and switched to its opposite. In college, and beyond, her Russianness would be an asset, the signifier that would set her apart from others, that would lend her a distin-guished glow. "She's a Russian immigrant," they would whisper about her, respect and awe in their voices, the derision, the hatred all gone, smoothed away by the passage of years.

After college, after the horrible Zubovsky incident (he had pushed her away in the most unromantic manner, squealed something about the loss of his job), there were men who were drawn to Anna's Russian soul. Bespectacled men emerged in New York out of the cloisters of colleges like Oberlin, Hampshire, Swarthmore, Reed; these men were Philip Roth/Updike/Nabokov (sometimes Henry Miller) disciples who finally saw her as the heroine of their future, unwritten novels. It was as if she'd stepped right off the pages of their favorite books, her fur-tive glances, her well-chosen silences, the way she wore black, picked at her whole dorade, drank only plummy red wines, ordered in French if the occasion allowed. And Anna, freed from her parents' apartment, from the dreary noncampus commuter anonymity of Queens College, was ready to become their muse.

Perversely, she turned away the obvious options—sturdy young men finishing up residencies at Mount Sinai, Armani-clad indepen-dent movie producers, Wharton business school students with one foot inside a banking career. The smoother the sheen, the less it interested her; its value would only deteriorate with time, she had assumed. But against all logic, one after another, the bespectacled broke her heart—

left for life-changing jaunts teaching English to schoolkids in China, Southeast Asia, South America—and when they returned, settled into grim domesticity with plain, undernourished Vassar alumni. What did they leave Anna with? A few badly written stories in literary magazines, utterly unworthy of her, where she made her fictional appearances under names like Olga *(Olga!)* or Larissa; unread copies of Evgenia Ginzburg's war diaries. They never sat still, never committed, were always on their way out; too quickly, they lost interest in creating her, molding her onto the page.

There would come a time in her relationship when ordering in French, wearing high boots with a short skirt, no longer had its effects. Her particular magic would become more and more condensed. "Oh, Anna," he would say, sipping his coffee. Outside the window, over his shoulder, Anna would be able to glimpse happy hordes of her contemporaries making their way to the subterranean bars on Waverly. "I don't think I will be as happy without you," he might add, a parting kiss gently applied to her forehead. Sometime afterward, the Vassar alum would make her appearance in his life.

And the stage for unhappy love affairs was set. Enter: Peter Roberts. A man who never went by the name Pete, who drank Pabst Blue Ribbon ironically, who cradled a woman's entire head when he kissed her. Whose torso was appealingly stringy, like Keith Richards's. Who considered himself a breast man with a heart. Who lived in the East Village. Who hailed from the Upper Peninsula ("UP") in Michigan. Who called American politicians "fascists." Who turned silent when he listened to early Leonard Cohen.

Who first saw Anna at a party in a crowded Chelsea apartment. The hosts? Who knows? A young literary agent with a handful of clients in MFA programs, her husband a graphic designer who played the banjo. Anna was sitting by herself next to a table on which stood an enormous glass bowl filled with blue tortilla chips and a jug of cheap wine. People were stumbling over her legs when they wanted to turn the corner into the bathroom. She was wearing leather pants, a pendant lay between her breasts, what else did Peter Roberts, part-time IT consultant at Citibank, need to note while making his way to the bathroom?

He halted before the specter of Anna, and without introducing himself dropped to his knees and commenced to recite the only passage from "Ode to a Nightingale" he knew by heart, the most visceral part in his opinion, involving those beaded bubbles, that purple-stained mouth. When he finished and she had still not said a word, he felt a bit foolish. To cover up his nervousness, he proceeded to eat a tortilla chip, crunching it loudly, corners tumbling to the floor. It turned out that he did not need this last flourish—Anna was in his bed within four hours.

The next morning, they argued about which bakery had the freshest croissants. He sprinted to Tartlet, around the corner on First Avenue, and returned with still-warm croissants—some plain, some drooling with chocolate—and two cups of lukewarm coffee. While he was gone, Anna looked around, snooped, really, through his bookshelves, crammed with travel guidebooks and poetry and paperback novels, phone bills spilling over in one corner. She found he cooked with cumin, studied Spanish, liked Hitchcock, and hadn't cleaned his bathtub in a very long time.

It was the best coffee she had had in a while, microwaved in one of Peter's cracked wholesale mugs. She hadn't bothered to get dressed, had wanted to feel a shirt of his on her skin, and soon it was evening, so they rented *Persona* and ordered tikka masala. Peter traced her collarbone with his finger, sketched her naked ass with a crayon: "There's something about you," he said, the planets colliding behind her eyes as he said "it."

He left her messages at Random House—where she worked as an eternal sub-rights assistant—four times a day in the first month, then two, then one, a year later. She signed him up for creative writing classes at the New School and after his class met him for a drink at the Cedar Tavern, that legendary literary haunt. She felt she gave him enough material from her life for a handful of novels.

They went to northern Spain together, and as soon as they landed, it became clear that Peter spoke no Spanish at all and refused to ask for directions, so it was up to Anna to get them from point A to point B, to order them olives and octopus salad and espresso, to check out of their pension in San Sebastian.

How his hair gleamed in the sunlight, though, the way he crossed his corduroyed legs, the way he said something with the utmost seriousness, the downiness of his arm hair. The ways he loved surprising her, tiny packages hidden in the unlikeliest places: behind the toilet bowl at the pension he had wedged a box containing a bright silk scarf she had admired in one of San Sebastian's glitzier boutiques. The secrets he wrapped up for her, the ones he withheld for special occasions.

They sat on the beach, a half-munched loaf of bread in one hand. Bare-breasted girls were wrapping up their towels for the day, fastening their tops over their heads, shimmying into cotton dresses. Peter and Anna watched them lazily, nibbling at the remains of their picnic, gulping from the same cheap but delicious bottle of wine. The evening stretched before them: dinner at eleven, a jazz club where they would complete getting drunk, where they would intertwine legs and tap their fingers in unison.

"Just one more year at Citibank and I will have saved enough to go to Southeast Asia," Peter said, spitting an olive pit into her palm. And there it was, in every relationship, there was that moment: Will it be an "I" *or* a "we," an "I" *and* a "we"? The sun dipped below the horizon.

"What about your writing?"

"What about it? It was a fun class, sweets, but you know I'm no writer, I hate writing. I'm a traveler. I gotta see things."

No matter how many croissants they ate, how many poems he recited, how many concerts they stumbled out of, tasting cigarettes on one another's tongues, Peter would always be yet another "I."

The next day, they took the train to Barcelona. For the first time, Anna took no pleasure in the train ride. They read their own books, paying no attention to the Basque countryside.

"You are my Russian princess, Anna," he used to say, usually after making love. Their eyes open, nose to nose, exchanging breaths like volleying back and forth a tennis ball.

8

VASILISA THE BEAUTIFUL

This was Lev's fifth wedding this month and still not his own. Just last weekend he had attended the K.s' wedding, though he no longer remembered how his family knew the K.s, who were not Bukharian Jews at all but from Moscow. The Pinkhasov wedding, his best friend's, was held at one of the usual places on Queens Boulevard, just a stroll from the homes of most of the guests. An American driving by might consider the restaurant's brown-paneled facade closed off and shady, not realizing that to enter the place was to discover a red-carpeted staircase, fake crystal chandeliers, cascading velvet curtains, mirrored walls. And a Russian-language band celebrating the marriage of yet another Bukharian couple.

By now the dancing was well under way; the slightly intoxicated Orthodox rabbi fled the room when the female singer took over the microphone. Once a famous opera singer in Russia in the 1960s and '70s, she was here crooning sentimental Soviet ballads, Bukharian folk songs, and hits by the Bee Gees. Lev was sick of it, and worst of all, the quality of the girls being seated next to him at weddings these days was quickly deteriorating—this one had eyes spaced too close together and the underside of her jaw was dotted with acne.

"So what do you do for a living?" She uttered this original, scintillating question. Lev barely brought himself to look at her—a flat, banana-shaped body camouflaged in sheets of silver taffeta.

"I'm a pharmacist. I do not repair shoes. Is that what you want to hear?" he said, regretting his tone because really she was just a kid. But on the other hand, maybe it would teach her a lesson, force her to be less predictable in the future if she wanted to stand out in a swarm of marriageable women.

On dates, Bukhi women always asked the same questions: How much do you make? Do you own a house in Forest Hills? What kind of car do you drive? It was unsubtle, unromantic. Lev saw them mentally calculating right there at the restaurant after he gave them his answer. Gripping their martini glasses by the stem, thinking, Will I have to shop discount? Will I have a cleaning lady? Will I have to work if I don't want to? In the French films he loved, women never let on those kinds of thoughts; they were soft and yielding in their high heels, in their clinging blouses.

Oleg waved to him from the dance floor and Lev rose to join the hora link, breaking up a chain of cousins, his hands slick with sweat. The music grew more frenzied, the circle revolved faster, the groom's father gestured for Lev to help lift the chair. He disconnected himself from the circle and hoisted one side of the chair against his chest. The guests started to clap, and as they bobbed along with the chair, Lev noticed Katia Zavurov, the one he had silently branded Vasilisa the Beautiful years ago, alone at a front table, clapping mechanically, a single beat behind everyone else. Her hair was pinned in ringlets on top of her head, thin but shapely arms half covered by lavender silk sleeves. When they first entered the restaurant and saw her standing by the bar, Lev's mother said that after what happened, it was amazing that she dared show her face here at all.

"*Opa!*" Oleg's father said, as the bride grasped the other side of the handkerchief. "Now there is no escape! They are tied to one another!" The men cheered.

Lev thought of the bachelor party at an Austin Street bar the night before. Most of these men were buying Oleg drink after drink. The air had been smoky and stale and Lev had felt nauseous.

"I'm gonna crack her in two. The little virgin won't know what hit her!" Oleg had boasted to Lev, red-faced and bloated from beer and vodka. One of his hands was clutching a glass filled with some kind of clear liquid, another was wrapped around a local girl coerced into the middle of the group for a tongue kiss with the bachelor.

The young bride waved the white handkerchief, doubled over in her chair from giggling, long strands of dark hair falling out of her pearled clip. From his spot below the chair, Lev could see Oleg's left hand directly above him, veined and muscular, pointing him to where he should go.

The following day, when Lev got home from the pharmacy, he found the *svakha* in their living room sipping tea with his parents. The woman wore the same outfit every time he saw her, a floral hand-kerchief around her head, a roomy housecoat with buttons down the front. Spread out on the table were snapshots of girls. From where he stood, Lev could see that some were cradling cats, others wearing graduation caps, posing in front of fake fireplaces. Lev took off his coat and hung it up in the hall closet. The *svakha*'s wool coat seemed to fill the entire closet and emanate a scent of raw fish.

"Well, the situation is not good, of course," the *svakha* said, raising her voice a bit now that the object of her disdain was within earshot. Lev walked into the kitchen and removed pan lids to taste the carrot pilaf with raisins. "He has waited so long that all the parents are asking questions. How long can I keep them at bay?"

The *svakha* was one of the best, her success rate reported at ninety percent. She would have retired long ago if it wasn't for the intrica-cies of Lev's case, she said, but now she's personally invested, it has become a matter of pride. A nice pharmacist like Lev must not be abandoned to sleep cold and alone, without the warmth of a wife, for another winter. The *svakha* drank her tea strong, thick, almost black. One of her bottom teeth was missing.

"Levchik," his mother pleaded. "People are talking about us. I know, I hear them, and it's killing me that it should be about you. Why don't you make us all happy and choose one? There are still so many lovely Bukharian girls left."

"Yes," the *svakha* said, a trembling finger in the air for emphasis. "There is no reason to think Ashkenazi yet. It has not reached that point. Lev is still only twenty-six years old."

His father was silent. Lev knew he sympathized, but did not approve of standing out in the community—to be different was to bring on the evil eye—and in a few weeks or a couple of months, he too would lose his patience. The *svakha* reached for another slice of pound cake, store-bought on 108th Street. "One is as good as any other," his father said finally, his voice raspy as though used for the first time that day. "Lev is just stubborn. It's all those French films he watches, thinks life is like that. A romance, right, son?"

In the kitchen, Lev scooped out a bowl of *plov,* slathered a cube of butter across the top, and ate it just like that, standing up in the living room, leaning against the wall, ignoring the stray, tumbling grains of rice his mother would have to sweep up later.

Of course, Vasilisa's name was not really Vasilisa. This was a private name Lev had wrapped around the more ordinary Katia Zavurov. From all the Russian fairy tales he read in childhood, he recalled only the figure of the softhearted Vasilisa the Beautiful, who managed to outwit her evil stepmother and Baba Yaga with the help of a magic doll. When the stepmother envied the girl her transcendent, golden beauty or Baba Yaga tried to enslave her, Vasilisa would feed her doll and ask her advice. The doll would perform Vasilisa's chores for her, rescue her from life-threatening situations, and, eventually, bring her into contact with a handsome prince who made her his bride. Lev's favorite part of the story had been when poor, generous Vasilisa would offer her doll all the scraps of food she'd squirreled away, while she herself remained starving.

There used to be something of Vasilisa in Katia Zavurov. Her complexion was not olive like that of many Bukharian girls, but creamy white, like sour cream. Her brown hair was tinged with lemon, her almond-colored eyes fanned by feathery eyelashes. She spoke little, but it seemed to Lev that behind her silence he would find smoldering nuances. Her existence proved that there was no need to look outside the community for a wife; she was one reason Bukharian Jews would continue to prosper in this country. He would glimpse her every day in high school—her fresh, un-made-up face, her careful steps, her neat book bag weighing down one side of her body—before she disappeared into the student throng.

Like Lev, his Bukhi friends could not wait for the final bell to ring, to get the hell out of that depressing building where teachers could not pronounce their names, where the Hispanic gangs insisted they prove themselves. They would wait for their pack to gather in front of the flagpole to which a quivering American flag was affixed. Then, at Oleg's command, they would all head toward Queens Boulevard and Austin Street and scatter into the blinking lights of the Continental Movie Theater, tease their brothers and uncles at the barber and shoe repair shops, buy their mamas some flowers, or sneak a swig of beer at one of the bars.

But while they ran into other Bukhi kids from Forest Hills or from the religious schools, Vasilisa was rarely among them. She was at home studying, her friends complained, pouting their red-lipsticked mouths, spraying their bangs in the lobby of the movie theater. These were girls who smuggled makeup in their bags, girls who tweezed their eyebrows even if it was strictly forbidden to look good for anyone but their future husbands. These were the girls who told their parents they would be having coffee with girlfriends but then transformed themselves in diner bathrooms. Predictably, these were the girls who were drawn to Oleg's animal swagger, his erratic charm. On several occasions, one of Vasilisa's friends had slipped into the back of the theater with Oleg, emerging with her jean jacket unzipped, her lips bare, grotesquely outlined in magenta.

The girls disgusted Lev, especially the ones who knew they had something to bring to a marriage: a beautiful face, a father who held power in the community, an interest in earning money but also keeping the house in pristine condition. Lev had felt that Vasilisa was the only girl he could admire, unsullied in her homework, intelligent and elusive like Anna Karina or Anouk Aimée.

As he prowled Austin Street with Oleg and the rest of his friends, Lev secretly calculated that he would only have to wait a year or two at most before he could enter her father's barbershop for a haircut. Then, when the man handed him the mirror to check his length in the back, Lev would rise, take out a bottle of fine cognac hidden in his backpack, sit the man down in his own chair, and tell him that he would never have to struggle again. He would take care of his daughter, his Vasilisa.

But then, one June afternoon, they all met at an Italian café. There were five of them there from their *tusovka,* including Lev and Oleg and Ruben, sitting around harassing the young Russian waitress. She was cute in that light-eyed, pale northern Russian way but hapless, mixing up drink orders and apologizing and then making it worse by hovering over the table and wringing her hands—an easy target, in other words. It was then, while staring at her receding ass, that Oleg said, "So, guess what I did last night," his eyes fiery and round, and blurted out the story. Lev's chest collapsed.

And Vasilisa the Beautiful transformed back into Katia Zavurov, a fleshy, defiled human, no longer his future wife. Afterward, there were hushed rumors that it was all a lie, fabricated after Katia rejected him for a date, but Oleg's story was the only vocal one and Lev couldn't get the image out of his mind—the supine Vasilisa the Beautiful, her magic doll pressed to her side, beneath a stabbing Oleg.

Flanagan's was so crowded that Lev had a hard time finding his friends. After craning his neck for a few minutes, he no longer bothered to say "Excuse me," but pushed his way past damp backs, beer spilling on his shoes. It was early in the evening and the conversations around him were humming, gathering speed, the laughter of girls punctuating the ends of sentences. That morning, a week after the wedding and the lavender body in the front row still fresh in his thoughts, he had looked up Katia Zavurov's pharmaceutical record. All the Bukhi families came to the pharmacy where he worked and he had no trouble locating her name. Her doctor had prescribed her antidepressants, it seemed, but she never came for them.

Oleg waved over to him from a corner booth and Lev slid in next to Ruben, a pitcher of beer standing, half full and urine-colored, between them on the table. Lev steeled himself for the stories. He did not want to hear about the honeymoon, about Oleg sticking it to his bride standing up in the elevator on the way to their Marriott suite. About forcing her fingers beneath his bathing trunks as they lay sunbathing. About taking her from behind in the water, ignoring her protesting hands slapping his beneath the waves of the ocean. Oleg dwelled on the bride's surprised expressions, the O's of her mouth, how she never realized that all those things were allowed. A few times, she had actually wanted to consult with the rabbi over the phone, and this made Ruben spit the beer in his mouth back into the glass.

"My new wife has been at home making *baksh* for hours now, in case you guys wanna come over," Oleg announced. He was wearing one of his many forest-green shirts, which brought out the unusual hazel of his eyes. One of his early girlfriends made that observation and he had been wearing them ever since, the collars slightly turned up, the buttons opened just enough for the hint of his chest hair to peek through.

Ruben was finally engaged, to an eighteen-year-old Bukhi girl. He had never had much luck with women; as a manager at Bukhara Express, a local shish kebab house, he was always passed over for more lucrative prospects. He was not handsome, not *delovoy,* he did not own a business, no car. Again and again, he was politely thanked for the date, and nothing more. Go younger, he was advised, the ones in their twenties are jaded, materialistic. And good thing he did, Ruben had said, after announcing his engagement, *my Nina is a lamb, never asks how much I make.*

"It took her a few days to get used to it and now she loves married life," Oleg said, lingering on the word "loves." The wedding ring looked heavy to Lev, but it made a hollow sound every time Oleg picked up his glass. When Oleg reached for a cigarette, the ring appeared sunken, carved into his flesh.

"She loves it, huh?" Ruben said, finishing his beer in a single gulp. "I can't wait."

"Just make sure she's a virgin, man," Oleg warned.

"Are you crazy?" Ruben said, ordering another pitcher from the waitress. "That's the first thing I asked Ninochka when we went out. I'm not taking any risks." Over the last few years, Ruben had developed a stoop; his head jutted out from his shoulders, lending him a crowlike intensity. Lev tried to remember the boy who generously waited for him to jump off the seesaw first, who stood in front of the ark reading earnestly from the Torah, but couldn't. All he saw was the small black hairs sticking out from inside Ruben's ears.

"You're next, man." Ruben turned to Lev, finishing the remainder of his beer in a single gulp. "You better pick someone and stop fucking around."

By the time the waitress returned with the pitcher, Lev found himself recounting a raunchy joke his father told him the other night. "What's a woman good for?" it began, but Oleg was distracted, glancing at his watch, undulating a quarter between his fingers, so Lev never made it to the punch line.

Lev no longer thought about Samarkand. His memories were impressionistic at best: the tugging feel of his mother's hand dragging him through the fragrant marketplace, the sticky air of summer, the hallucinatory feel of walking down narrow cobblestone roads, claustrophobic car rides past miles of prickly wheat fields. Later he would see pictures of turquoise mosques, their cupolas majestic and swollen, and he might as well have been gaping at them as an American tourist. The Jews did not live in those pictures in guidebooks.

Now, other than food and the occasional Bukhori expression, he no longer knew what made them so Bukharian. But each Bukharian wedding was celebrated more ferociously, more chaotically than the one before—the whirling, interlocking arms, the hoarse voices, the empty bottles of Georgian wine. At each wedding, the reminder, a warning to the unmarried, that Bukharians are uniquely capable of preserving traditions, for didn't they flourish in the most inhospitable of areas, among Muslims and Soviets, ethnic Koreans and Chinese? In other words, we dare you to get yourself an American bride, we dare you to murder your own future people.

At each wedding, Lev imagined himself as the groom, but then, his mind would wander to the following day, waking up with a hangover, his eyes squinting at an anonymous, non-Vasilisa wife beside him. A wife who would have demands, who would cover her breasts protectively when he tried to slide her top over her head, who would nag him when he came to bed at two in the morning, neck sore from an Eric Rohmer double feature. If he were Oleg, it would look very different—his wife would be shedding her clothes in impatient desire, engulfing him with supple arms—but he wasn't Oleg. The idea of the everyday allotted to him frightened Lev, but then later he felt foolish. Who was he to put himself before the community, to chase rainbows when he should be planning for the future? What made him any better than his friends? Who was he?

9

THIS DAVID

Serge K. was a rather self-contained six-month-old baby. He would bawl during any transition, between sleep and awareness, food and its removal, his tiny fists helplessly flailing at his sides. Most of the time he stared at the ceiling, as if studying it for tiny flakes or patterns.

Alex insisted on naming their son Sergei, after his beloved grandfather who died of Alzheimer's at age seventy-eight, but how could a child named Sergei have a shot at a prestigious Manhattan preschool? No, Anna decided, at the very least his American name would be Serge after Serge Gainsbourg, her favorite singer. Maybe Serge would grow into his namesake's offhand sexiness, his guttural appeal, though at the moment there was nothing low-pitched about him.

And she tried to love her new son, Anna did. Some nights during the first month, she stood over his crib, waiting for him to wake and demand the food pouring out of her breasts. Afterward, she went to bed, finding shed hair snarled on her pillow. She played with Serge on a blanket, rattling toys and blowing into his belly button. Her favorite moments with him were during their strolls; he tended to fall asleep after a block or two and she was left alone with her thoughts.

At thirty-nine, she felt too old to scamper, her swollen breasts and lumpy belly weighing her down. She mourned the loss of her body, the swift fading of color. When Alex reached for her in bed, it felt like yet another tugging of skin, another invasion. But the baby continued to insist on his own simple goals. And it was fluttering within her, this love, but still inaccessible to her.

Their new live-in nanny, Stasia, announced Katia's arrival. Katia smelled of outdoors, a place with which Anna was increasingly trying to reacquaint herself. How mature the young woman was becoming, Anna thought, watching Katia on all fours beside Serge, her skin really settling onto her bones. How wonderful to be that young again. Katia put down a box on the floor, a BabyBjörn carrier.

"From my family," she whispered, tugging Serge's feet, to which he responded gamely, kicking them closer toward Katia. "Aren't you the cutest thing?" Serge Gainsbourg in the background was crooning of Bonnie and Clyde.

Later, Anna had Stasia put the baby to nap and took out some knitting. Other mothers had told her about the soothing, tethering power of knitting, but Anna had not yet experienced any of these symptoms; she was too restless to be going row by painstaking row, endlessly weaving a yellow-and-black-striped sweater Alex would never wear.

"So what is the news with your young man?" she asked Katia, pouring her some tea, arranging a plate of Payard éclairs.

"I think I've finally exhausted my parents. They're going to say yes to the match. Very soon, I can feel it," Katia said.

Anna put down her knitting and poured herself a cup too. She understood that Katia had been somehow disgraced in her community and according to her parents, at least, no Bukharian boy would consider her. And there has been this young man waiting in the wings, this David Zuckerman, Jewish in that bland American way no doubt, but it seemed the clock was ticking. Katia, already twenty-five. Anna always found Bukharian customs draconian, terribly repressive of women, probably influenced by living beside Muslims in those incomprehensible countries like Uzbekistan and Tajikistan. She was just happy her own mother had had the good sense to stay in Moscow and meet her father.

"So I think it will finally happen this New Year's. I think he'll finally propose. There is something about him—you'll see when you meet him—the way he pretends not to need you, there's this aloofness, right? It's because he's headed for great things, he's so smart, Anna. He will be a great author or politician. Every great author needs a wife, doesn't he? That loyal person he relies on when he leaves his office. Maybe that'll be me. Why not, Anna, right?"

Katia saw that Anna was not listening. She was silent for a moment, and then altered her tone. "You will come to my parents' party this year, won't you, Anna? I want you to meet David. And bring little Seryozha, my parents would be thrilled." Anna smiled that classic Anna nonsmile, where only the narrowing of the eyes gave any hint of its presence.

She picked up the plate of éclairs and offered it to Katia, noticing her cousin had gained a little weight, but it still suited her, it filled out her youthful, oval face, added depth, dimension.

Anna sipped her tea. Her first party. After the hellish pregnancy that turned her body into an unrecognizable appendage. The first three months, she had not been able to move more than five feet from a toilet, then the swelling of the limbs, feet so engorged she was forced to pad around in Velcro slippers all day. The doctor prescribed a month of bed rest with the droning TV, and there was nothing to do but watch all those depressing Apex Tech commercials, the slobbering women on daytime talk shows, toll-free phone numbers blinking from the bottom of the screen. And cable, even worse! The dreary reality shows, with their artificial narratives, their lack of shame, the women in their cheap clothes, their trite epiphanies.

And even worse, tolerating Alex's relatives, with their talk of miracles and the joy to come, the sunflowers and lilies and white roses they brought, with their overpowering fragrance. She had to remind Alex to throw them out when after a few days their stalk corpses browned and expanded in the water.

The birth, oh, God, she didn't want to think about that. Pain she could not have imagined in her wildest nightmares, her pulsating body out of her control. Why didn't she opt for the scheduled C-section? As if her organs were being shuffled about, ready to burst. Alex discreetly waited out of sight; maybe he sensed that her screams were partially aimed at him.

When it was over, there was nothing inside her, nothing left for the baby. They handed her a rubbery red creature, its fingers grasping at the air, its head bent back, eyes sealed with her juices. He was placed in her arms, she was called "Mama," everyone around her expecting cooing, tears of happiness.

"Take him," she said, and turned away from it all.

"Let her rest." She was left alone.

The first weeks, she couldn't perceive the difference between night and day. Every morning, she would slip on the same cotton house robe, its hems gray with dust. Half asleep, she would lift her son, proffer a breast. Anna tolerated breast-feeding for one month until they hired Stasia. She needed herself back already! All those Manhattan mothers and their breast-milk guilt—had there ever been children who blamed their cognitive deficiencies on the lack of breast milk? Anna was convinced this renewed obsession with breast milk was yet another ploy to tether mothers to the crib. Even Serge was happier after formula, no more frustrated cries after futile tugging at her breasts.

Only last week, she had recognized her body for the first time. Yes, the breasts she remembered right here, the thighs were no longer two eggplants rubbing against each other. Her hair began regaining its former thickness, the swelling in her hands was almost gone.

Katia wandered into the other room to peek in on the sleeping Serge. If she only knew the truth behind what she was looking forward to, Anna thought. And now this New Year's party would be Anna's first chance to wear a dress, to put on some makeup, to wax her eyebrows, to prod and arrange herself into some kind of appealing package. She would go to the gym every day until New Year's, she would regain this year of her life, she would be mesmerizing, the old Anna.

"Of course I will come to the party," Anna called out. "I'm dying to meet this David, the man who will make my Katia so happy." Katia tiptoed back. The women found each other's hands and stayed in that spot on the couch until early evening. They had so much to discuss, what with Serge's physical changes taking place almost every day now, and according to Katia, their old Rego Park neighborhood was under-going quite a renaissance. Anna sipped her tea until it grew cold, Serge hiccupping in the next room until he was silenced.

The Zavurovs always held their New Year's celebrations (or post-Hanukkah, as they called it, because the rabbi would hardly approve of celebrating this most secular of holidays, this little piece of Soviet-invented nostalgia) in a minor Brighton Beach establishment called Chagall, and this would have to be the site of Anna's return to her full premarital glory.

She scoured Bergdorf's and Barneys for the perfect simple dress, the hardest one to find, after all. She could tell that Alex was pleased to see her reinvigoration. He asked about her daily purchases and even accompanied her on one trip, though he barked at his colleagues on the cell phone the entire time. At home she modeled for him several dress options, because she always doubted her own taste.

"Magnificent," he said about one. "Not quite right," about another. Her middle was shrinking; she could now stuff herself into a girdle and achieve the appearance of a flat stomach. Only in private, when she slipped off the control top, did her lumpy stomach reappear. But the mirage would hold.

Alex reached for her in bed, a stealthy arm around her waist, cup-ping her breasts—but no, she would pretend to be asleep and freeze in that position until she heard the sigh, the rollover. All she could think about was the party, the way they would all look at her, at Anna K. resurrected from the Hades of motherhood.

1 0

―――――――

MA CHÈRE COUSINE

For Katia, December 31 was a day of exquisite torture. For hadn't David practically promised to ask her father for her hand in marriage on New Year's Eve? No, she could not be mistaken, when the lights went down in the Metropolitan Opera House and *Evgeny Onegin* was about to begin, didn't David pull some feather out of her hair, didn't he look deep within her as he flicked it off? Didn't he say, with a special emphasis, that he could not wait for the new year?

The new year. She would admit this to no one, but lately Katia had been thinking of nothing but sex. It seemed to her that everything around her was infused with sex: the way clothes fit men's bodies on the street, the suggestive shapes of mangoes and persimmons. Her own ability to touch and feel shapes was heightened—Katia had become aware of the sharp edges of books, the cold smoothness of linoleum, the ridges inscribed into David's palm. At night, she took off all her clothes and followed the suggestions of girlfriends; it was okay, they said, as long as you thought about your future husband.

During the day, as she answered the telephone at her father's barbershop, she watched hair being snipped off men. She watched shorn hair fall on their shoulders, the way it clung to the back of their necks.

She eagerly volunteered to sweep up the hair once the customer left, and if he was particularly attractive, she would gather the hair into a heap herself and gingerly lead it into the dustpan. No one had brought out these instincts before David.

She had met him at Queens College, she in her last semester of school and he a young professor of composition. She had gone to the Writing Center to get help with her grammar. There were some hints dropped by her professors that she would not pass their classes, and possibly not even graduate. Many of her teachers were complaining about the poor quality of her essays, entreating "Katie Zaburov" to take English as a Second Language classes even if she was born in this country. She could admit that English was never her area of expertise, she was a people person, not a writing person, considering jobs in hotel management or even retail sales, if her future husband would allow that. The pleasure, so acute in her, of helping somebody find whatever he was seeking.

So there she was, her D papers in her knapsack, waiting for the next available tutor. And wasn't it during the time that the Oleg story spread all over the neighborhood, just because she was the only available Bukhi girl in the area to find him truly repugnant? Yes, she believed it was at that time that it had felt hopeless to even contemplate marriage, when possible matches were canceling appointments with her father, politely saying that the sons had found themselves attached to other girls. When she knew it was a result of Oleg's vicious lies. The lies seemed to add years to Katia's young life, evenings of wanting nothing except to lie in bed, with no enthusiasm for food, for seeing her girl-friends, even for borrowing an illicit *Cosmopolitan* magazine.

Yes, it was that exact time that she found herself sitting across from David Zuckerman, adjunct comp assistant professor and Writing Center tutor. His hair needed brushing, but he had kind lips, an open smile. He called her Katie, and the way he said it, it sounded dear, solicitous, not infantilizing or foreign. Her stack of papers lay at her arm, but he stopped taking notes, as if mesmerized by her speech, the cadences of her accent. He told her a few things about himself: the bitter divorce of his parents when he was seventeen, his plans of becoming a famous writer. He told her about the corpses of his previous literary efforts, his methods of procrastination (playing the piano, vacuuming, purchasing stationery). How he ran in every New York City marathon, the sensation of pushing his body beyond endurance, beyond anything rational.

Katia loved his long, serious face, his uncertainty of where to rest his gangly arms—on the table, beside his chair, should he hold a pencil? She loved the passion dripping from his words—what were Bukharian boys passionate about anyway? Money? The latest acquisition, whatever and whoever that was? There was something beautiful about this boy, a kind of dreaminess, a desire to anchor it, attach it to someone. Almost immediately she understood what this David was seeking. Inspiration. And only after a few more sessions, Katia grasped that she had the means, the irresistible drive, to unite this man with his desires. And they would become hers also, if her parents could allow it to happen.

At first, surprise, surprise, her parents were adamantly against a match with a secular American Jew, but as more and more *svakhas* canceled and boys began to disappear from the front door, her parents became more tractable, more shamed. Her father had nothing to tell his clients, no joyous news, no future plans. With just one more push, Katia knew that all that work would finally pay off; there was a tiny opening within her father for the first time, and if she grabbed David's hand, if she held on to his torso, she knew she would be able to squeeze him through that opening. And it would be a new year, indeed.

After a stroll in the park, they sat over the remains of two cups of coffee, two forks licked clean of cherry pie.

"I want to eat all American things, all those things I saw on commercials but never tried," Katia said. They had to choose: meat or dairy. David was a borderline atheist, but she still revered the laws handed down to her in yeshiva. So it was to be dairy: macaroni and cheese, vanilla milkshake, rice pudding, cherry pie. One straw, two forks. Strong coffee, caffeinated.

They were in a Manhattan diner booth, a shabby one with chrome siding, the pink vinyl peeling on the seats. The embedded smell of onions. They pretended she had just immigrated the day before from Uzbekistan and this was her first introduction to American food. The older waitress was indifferent, borderline truculent, but in the end did not charge them for the pie.

Their jukebox was broken, the windows were steamed up. She was wearing mittens anyway.

"It is so easy with you, Katie. Is it allowed to be this easy?"

She gorged on classic American sweets, matching him bite for bite long after she was full.

Of course, she wouldn't sleep with David before marriage. He understood that from the beginning. Didn't he? His hands had wandered inside her shirts, crept up her thighs. He could never take her no's seriously, what girl still said no in this day and age? She had to explain to him about Bukharian Jews, what they took seriously: modesty, tradition, your father's respect.

"But don't you love me?" he would murmur in her hair. Those sinuous hands, flat palms, neat fingernails. His skin had emanated a herbaceous scent, like the tearing open of mint leaves.

"Why not, Katie? Why not? We love each other, isn't that enough for the Bukharians?" That smile, the push and pull of it. He knew that she wanted to, he could feel it thrumming on her skin.

"In the twenty-first century? In New York?"

Once, his finger had entered her and he argued that sex wouldn't be much different. It was a week before the New Year's party. They were splayed across her couch, while her mother was out on errands— they had whole afternoons to themselves when David wasn't teaching. Their fingers lazily entwined, listening to the wind banging itself against the building's foundation.

"Why not, Katie?" he had said, but she did not hear, *I need you to the point of desperation.* She heard, *You are something to write about.* He had that predatory air at times, her David, didn't he, the air of a car salesman or a newspaper reporter. But then he said, "Who wants popcorn?" And Katia chided herself for her thoughts. He was an artist, for whom work and love bled together. She would learn to accept, to respect that.

"Extra butter?" She repositioned her bra, zipped up her sweater, covering up her red, puckered skin.

"Oh, yes," he said, eyebrow cocked. "As much butter as you wanna give."

What to wear, what to wear? Katia had agonized for weeks. The perfect dress did not present itself until two days before the party, when Katia grew desperate, ran around to all the stores she knew and trusted on 108th Street, on Austin Street. It had to be modest but alluring, it had to finally catapult her from little girl to woman.

She had not even planned on going into Parisian Chic; it felt like a store for those licentious, overstated Russian wives at Russian restaurants, bursting out of their outfits, flaunting their breasts in everyone's faces. Only the sheer terror of having no dress hurled her inside the glass door. She rifled, with little hope, through sequins and feathers, through faux-fur and lace, and as if by divine hand, there it was in the sale rack, wedged between a crimson miniskirt and canary-yellow silk blazer. It was plain cream satin with long sleeves and a high neck, but when Katia put it on, even the saleswoman's raptures sounded genuine. She stood in front of the mirror, picturing David's eyes on her. The satin made her skin appear softer, unblemished, it gave her the body of a pinup, each tuck showing off a rounded hip, a slender waist. There was no doubt about it—Katia looked like a bride.

She had been to Chagall only once, but she already adored it. Smaller than some of the other Brighton Beach restaurants, it was kosher, which was why her parents chose it for this year's party. In the past, they had held it at Cheburechnaya on Austin Street, but at New Year's one wanted to dance a little. To Katia, Chagall was a brilliant innovation on her parents' part, a place both festive and intimate, where her father and David could find a place to be alone and then they would all celebrate, uncorking some champagne a bit early, toasting her future life, the first dance as an engaged couple.

The band was getting the sentimental songs over with, "A Yiddishe Mame" getting the night off to a rather lachrymose start. For a change, Katia had little patience for the grandmothers and aunts, their probing questions, the way they squeezed her middle. Be patient, babushkas, I will have some news for you soon.

How beautiful you look, Katyenka, how grown up! What a stunning dress, Katyusha. Yes, yes, thank you, and how is your Misha and his lovely wife? Well, congratulate them for me, please, a child is truly a blessing.

Katia could barely breathe, was there enough oxygen pumped in here? At the sight of *zakuski,* the herring smothered with cubed beets, the oily surface of the smoked salmon, her stomach contorted. Then there he was, her David, entering the restaurant so sweetly, so ill-at-ease, and for once he didn't look like a student; he wore a dark blue suit, a silver tie, he carried tulips. Katia Zuckerman, she thought.

Katia took the flowers and brought David over to her parents, who shook his hand, my God, the handshake had so much purpose, it was a promise, wasn't it? To speak later, to make decisions. Then she would only have to wait a few weeks to feel his breath on her neck, the kisses on her breasts. She sat David down at their table; he, a little befuddled with his surroundings, the live band, the strobe lights, the cadre of waiters who flitted in and out with more and more food, all that vodka, all those people speaking in Russian, and was Bukharian even a language? He would ask Katia later.

"You look beautiful, Katie," he said, so she got up and ran around relatives so he could see her dress from every angle, the seam that ran down her back, the slight flare at her hips. She felt drunk with herself for the first time, irresponsible. Didn't she too deserve this, the things Oleg tried to strip away from her? She took surreptitious sips of wine, looked at the other young women. No, no one could compete with her tonight.

And then, suspension of breath, *she* walked in with her husband. Even the band seemed to play softer music, because no doubt they were gawking at Anna as Katia was, as everyone was. Anna K. did not walk on the ground; rather, she was transported, as if on a cloud, Aphrodite unleashed in a Russian restaurant. Katia had never seen her look so transfixing. And yet, her dress was, as usual, a simple black, a corset top and a long, form-fitting skirt, a pendant hanging between her breasts. She wore pale makeup and a blood-red lipstick and those curls fell where they could, here and there, untamed. The men froze in their conversations, put out their cigarettes, ran over to say hello, their wives hanging back with pursed mouths, clicks of their tongues. It was disgusting, what she was doing, and having just had her baby, what was she trying to prove? She should be with her baby tonight and not flaunting her body like an aging tramp. That Anna Roitman . . . that Anna K., we always knew she was trouble.

Katia inserted herself into the group around her cousin. She kissed Anna on her warm cheek, wiping away the marks of her own lipstick afterward. And Katia could sense that Anna had recognized her own triumph; she was flushed, not fully paying attention to Katia, except to tell her, mechanically, how good she looked, how becoming that white dress was. And, a bit ashamed, Katia felt she no longer wanted to introduce this Anna to David. She said her hellos and then moved away, leaving Anna to the men and their hungry stares.

She regained her spirits, even rolled up a piece of smoked salmon and pushed it into her mouth. She was relieved that her parents placed the K.s on the other side of the restaurant, at the far end of the wall. She darted quick looks and found Anna seated most of the time, not dancing, but radiating lushness, a shrouded beauty. Guests were paying court, as it were, finding Anna at her table, complimenting her.

Katia turned to find David talking to her father and Seva from the barbershop. She tried to join in; they were discussing digital cameras and Katia allowed her mind to wander, to see if she could read the body language. David seemed tense, perhaps working to make a good impression, or he was having a hard time understanding her father's thick accent.

"Let's dance." Seva dragged her onto the dance floor. She allowed herself to be twirled around. Seva smelled slightly of sliced raw onions, the armpits of his shirt were damp. After each rotation, she tried to locate David and her father. But the floor filled up and bodies obscured her view. One couple left the dance floor, and Katia could see a part of a shoulder, a corner of a knee, but Seva turned her so she was facing the band, in the opposite direction. She steeled herself to break away, to plead exhaustion.

"You're an impressive dancer," she said.

It was then that she felt Anna's arm around her waist.

"Where is he?"

Katia became enveloped in the familiar fig-infused perfume, that low sensuous voice. They weaved past tangoing couples, leaving poor Seva on the dance floor. David stood alone with his drink, watching them approach.

"Je vous présente, ma chère cousine," Katia said, though she had no idea why she felt compelled to do it in French. Never had she felt so young. She saw their faces perform a kind of leap (had they met before?), then Anna stretched out her hand. They were practically the same height, and Katia felt tiny by comparison, craning her neck between them.

"Yes, I've heard so much about you," Anna said. "You're the writer."

When Anna was confused or rifling through her mind for a piece of information, she had the habit of tugging on her curls, lost in thought. She tugged them now.

Her mother called Katia away to say hello to a distant aunt living by herself in Far Rockaway, the poor dear, we never do get around to visiting her. And each day she is forgetting more and more. Why are all these people speaking English? she asked me just the other day. Come, Katyenka.

Katia allowed herself to be led away, but she never took her eyes off Anna and David. She knew him, yes, she did, she knew him well enough to read every sign. She knew what his gestures meant, the way he tipped his head to the right, listening to Anna intently. Every time she looked back, they were still rooted to the spot. She watched David lift a bottle of wine off the table and pour Anna a glass. He handed it to her by the stem, holding it just a second too long, as if to verify that it would not come crashing to the floor. From his face, she could tell they were talking about books, books Katia had not read but Anna probably had. Nabokov novels no one had heard of (more obscure than *Lolita,* even Katia had tried to hack away at that one after David mentioned how much he loved it). Maybe David was trotting out his beloved Brodsky or that Polish Szymborska. Why else was the usually shy David so translucent, practically trembling with charm?

Katia looked around for Alex K., but he was lost in conversation with another man. Should she draw his attention to the scene, or was it not her place? Turning back to them, Katia recognized the old Anna K., the one whose existence she had always known about but denied, her small, peaceful actions of flirtation, almost unobtrusive, the invisible ways in which she controlled a man's attention, then swallowed it whole. In the past, Katia had admired this quality of Anna's, her enviable composure. Didn't Katia have the smallest crush on all that, if she were to be entirely honest?

But there they stood. Why, she was almost as tall as he was, and they were leaning into each other. Was the music too loud, was that why they had to whisper? Why did the momentum of their conversation generate speed, whirring, one picking up where the other left off, sentences left unfinished, unarticulated? He nodded, he kept on nodding, agreeing with her, nodding, while Anna appeared composed, polite, even. But Katia read the pinkness of her cousin's chest—it was this that gave her pleasure away, her deep, red enjoyment in the conversation.

Was it then, right then, that Katia became certain that there would be no more conversation between her father and David, not tonight, not ever? Still, at that moment, nodding at the elderly aunt, who was lost in her own memories of her dead husband, of her nightmares of approaching Germans, her collective farm distinctions, Katia continued to hope.

It did not seem possible, no, it was her own imagination, she was being ridiculous, paranoid. And yet. And yet.

1 1

BITE BY BITE

I t began, as these things tended to, with tiny excuses, pretenses, and posturing, deceptions that could be interpreted otherwise. The borrowing of a book—*Pnin,* to be exact—the exchange taking place at an Upper East Side café, its walls yellow and cheerful, its staff sleepy on a weekday morning.

She had called David on a whim while taking Serge out for one of his walks. She and Serge strolled around the Whitney Museum, her son bundled in three layers and a wool jacket. But despite the cold, Anna was reluctant to return home. Seeing the poster for the Edward Hopper show, she was gripped by a desire to know what David would have thought of it—she, for example, had felt no sadness at the isolation of the artist's figures. To be alone in an empty room—a situation incomprehensible to the average citizen of the Soviet Union—certainly that was a kind of privilege. She found herself envying the figures in the canvases, their freedom, their ability to remove themselves from the judgment of a community, from family and needy lovers. The museum's brochure, though, said the viewer was supposed to feel quite the opposite.

When at the exhibit, she had had no one with whom to share her thoughts. Alex had been three galleries ahead of her, speeding toward the exit, and that persistent Nadia and her husband Zhak were disagreeing loudly in Russian in front of *Summer Interior.* She had wondered what David would make of the underwearless woman on the floor in the painting, the bedsheet stretched out beneath her.

When she called from her cell phone, on her walk with Serge, David had been surprised to hear from her and seemed eager to play along with her ruse—that she wanted to take *Pnin* out for a test drive, a book he had raved about at the New Year's party. And he waited for her at the coffee shop, already halfway into a cup of coffee by the time she arrived. He wore a wool sweater, simple, gray.

"When you're done, tell me what you think," David said, pushing the thin green paperback across the table.

His hair was damp and mussed on his forehead. He stared at her with the same intensity she remembered, his eyes, behind glasses, the same dim shade of green.

"A teacher of mine turned me on to it. It's not the first novel you think of when you think of Nabokov, is it?"

"No," she said. How could she be doing this, she wondered. There was no innocence in this, this forced encounter. She could barely focus on his words. Outside the window, people ran, holding objects over their heads.

"Do you remember it was raining when we met at the train station too?" she asked.

"The train station?"

"Penn Station, remember? The train from Chicago?"

He appeared genuinely confused. Anna waved over the waiter and ordered a mixed-berry muffin. She didn't know where to place her hands. On the table, they looked to her like claws.

"We met at Penn Station?"

"Never mind, never mind. So, *Pnin* is really your favorite Nabokov?" When it arrived, its bottom slightly burnt, she realized it would be one of those disappointing muffins in which the fruit was clustered on the surface of the crust.

"I love Nabókov," she said, careful to pronounce the author's name the right way, the Russian way. There would be no Nábokovs between them.

"His wordplay."

"His wit."

"Your favorite scene in *Lolita*."

"It would have to be . . ."

"Yes."

"The minute he knows . . ."

"She's never been his."

Anna could see he was a cream guy, not a milk guy, he ate his cookies thoughtfully, he gripped his mug around the middle, not by the handle. He flicked crumbs off his sweater perhaps a bit too self-consciously. His fingernails long but neat, clean. Those unthinking actions were wholly his.

When the bill came, Anna offered to pay and David simply said, "Thank you." An entire muffin was consumed. Bite by bite. She realized that she forgot to mention Hopper, but no time seemed right for inserting him. David did not remember her in the shearling, in the train station. How, then, could she expect them to agree about Hopper? She watched the waiter clear off David's plate, his empty coffee cup, wipe his scattered crumbs onto the floor. David's eyes were on hers, as if the man did not exist.

"I had a nice time," he said. "I feel like we think alike about so many things."

"Thanks." The vapid response, attached to none of his words, made her flush. But she had been considering the same thing, the way this man could finish her sentences, how erotic was that sensation of gulped-back words. His lips would be like Spanish clementines in the winter, she decided, firm but yielding, sweet.

It was just talking, Anna told an invisible judge, as she rushed home to Serge. A simple pleasure, to speak with an intelligent person. To think about things other than diaper changes, feeding schedules, deals sealed at Alex's work. To let loose those pieces of the brain fermenting for lack of use—after all there was literature to talk about, music, film, travel, ideas. Is there room for the comfort of routine and the wild beating of the heart to coexist in a single life? Anna wondered. Can the two live together in Yves Delorme sheets, tucked inside a classic six?

Her doorman, Mike, waved to her, but Anna knew she looked disheveled compared to her usual compact self. She waved hastily but thought she saw something in the doorman's face. His greeting was not extraordinary, but wasn't there a certain pique, a vocal dip to the way he said, "Good afternoon, Mrs. K."? Hadn't Mike seen everything? Women running out in the mornings without their children, coming home sans shopping bags, warm cheeks, beret, unbuttoned coat. Was that really so unusual compared to the more violent daily dramas of his job?

In the apartment, she clasped Serge to her, and he squirmed and fussed in her arms. Stasia stood on the other side of the crib, holding the bottle with her arms crossed, with that dour Eastern European look of disapproval. Or maybe it was a consequence of the extreme oval nature of her overplucked eyebrows. The nanny must have understood her inner state because women always intuit when embraces are born of guilt.

But why was she overthinking all this, Anna thought, putting Serge down, why was she tormenting herself? She should have never quit her job, tedious and saturated with office politics as it was; she no longer had enough to do. The child began to bawl, his hands extending toward Stasia.

Anna went into the kitchen to pour herself a drink. My goodness, she thought, it was only talking. Proof, though, that her narrative still sprouted strands, still led to places unexpected. The vodka was crisp and spicy gliding down. Anna wanted to remain at the center of the story.

The things that bothered Anna about Alex: the way he invited his friends over for dinner parties without giving her advance notice being one example. He loved showing off a particularly aged and rare Rioja, to socialize, to buy and show off his purchases. How she grew to dislike the pleasure he took in compliments—he rocked slightly between heel and toe, his hands in the pockets of his pants, nodding his approval, as if the guest should be flattered for sharing the tastes of his host. Did he even love the art he bought? Anna didn't think so—this blue palette will look lovely in the bedroom, his art advisor told him, the image of the hawk, so masculine, belongs in the study.

And the people he invited over! They could talk about real estate for hours, money markets versus bonds versus CDs, praising some guy who skirted the system to make millions, cashing in on Russia before it was too late, before Putin began the crackdown, began tightening the governmental control over private profit. And their wives, even worse. Baby clothes, jewelry, blabeddy blah. It was like the nineteenth century over here; didn't male and female concerns overlap these days?

Almost three years of marriage, and Alex seemed to have lost all enthusiasm in the ritual of the romantic dinner. Even now, their anniversary had to be spent with his friends. Anna busied herself in setting out quiche, marinated herring, mushroom tarts, in painstakingly chopping chives. She kept the dishwasher running; the guests expected a new plate for every course. And it was a relief to bustle around, it prevented her from thinking. Because she felt like a gnarly thing, neither on the male nor the female side of the conversation, her own thoughts flying far above them, out the window.

They spoke a Russian-English patois, Americanizing their Russian, Russifying their English. The women dressed themselves and their men and the result was bright pinks, pinstripes, matching necklaces and earrings, manicures, thick, visible lip liner. Gold was favored over silver, chunky pieces that screamed out for attention. They brought cognac with them, cakes from Agata & Valentina, out-of-season blackberries.

Anna's job was to serve the food; Alex's, the wine. Why did she feel a stranger to the clarity of her role?

"Please, take a bit more," she urged. "Mashenka, you haven't eaten a thing." Mashenka was an interior designer who had recently founded her own company in Moscow. Interior design was a relatively new profession in the land of worn Persian carpets, porcelain elephant knickknacks, and utilitarian furniture. The first impulse of the newly rich was to anxiously transform their apartments and houses into Greek temples and Trump-like marble palaces. Mashenka's job was to return understated taste to people who had acquired too much too fast, who equated minimalism with the impoverished past.

"I've eaten plenty, Anna, please, no more," she was saying. "So I had to convince Petukhov to take down the Doric column, put away that horrible gold Baroque dining table, and introduced him to Eames and Noguchi."

Everyone nodded in sympathy, for didn't they go through similar phases themselves at the first acquisition of leisure money? Weren't there photographs hidden in yellowing albums that attested to their own lapses in good taste—those gaudy carpets with red and yellow Mondrian-type squares, vases shaped like skyscrapers, gold-tinted stairway railings? An easy shorthand for, *We've made it.* Now they were relearning to say the same thing in more subtle ways.

"A bit more wine?" Alex offered, interrupting their reveries. "Isn't anyone going to say a toast to the happy couple?"

They drained their glasses. Anna began the process of clearing the table. Forty is the new thirty, they said, but she felt no more than sixteen, the eternal ingénue, all those talents and possibilities still rapping at the glass. In the pocket of her apron, Anna kept a folded piece of paper with David's phone number; on her night table, for weeks now, lay *Pnin.*

"Anyechka, where do you get those airy *pieroshki*? Do you get the Samovar to deliver?" the most imposing of the wives asked, lurking in the kitchen. If there was one woman Anna feared, it was this one, this Nadia Gubnitsky, with her blond bouffant and thin, coral-plastered lips. Who watched her carefully throughout dinner, who patted the tablecloth with her napkin when Anna clumsily tipped over her own wine glass. And Nadia's husband Zhak practically slurped Anna's décolletage with his eyes.

She thought of her own parents, sharing two chicken cutlets and fried potatoes in Rego Park. An open jug of Manischewitz. So she left all that behind, and now what? When she was forty, her own mother had no time for idle reflections. She had arrived in New York seven years before with no English, a fifteen-year-old daughter to occupy her.

At last, the first of the guests started to leave, setting off a chain of yawns. Alex distributed the coats, his complexion swollen with wine.

"I would like to see more of you," Nadia said, already across the threshold, her hand on Anna's. It was a command, not a request. The large coral stone on her ring reminded Anna of her own bare fingers.

"That would be wonderful," Anna said through gritted teeth, shutting the door.

The things that bothered her about Alex: he let her brood. It was best for women and children to overcome their own moods, he believed. None of that coddling, that insincere consolation Americans loved so much. None of that "It's going to be okay, honey." So no hand touched Anna K.'s shoulder as she stared out the window, or wrapped herself around her pillow, or cried in the shower. She would hear him moving about in the living room, lifting books off shelves, flipping past programs on the remote control, delivering an awkward monologue to their son. Creating an ozone layer between himself and her emotions.

After they fought, there would be no conversation, no verbal attempts at reconciliation. Truce would be declared when one or the other reentered the domestic routine—when Anna placed an egg on Alex's plate, when Alex brought home orchids or a toy for the baby. For a few moments, both would be pleased, enfolded in harmony and gratitude. Until Anna extricated herself to go for an evening walk, making brief contact with other people by passing them, gulping in fragments of their sentences. Other lives, other paths, would be less enticing if she could only shrug off the fact of her immigration, if she wasn't convinced that she operated under different standards. But she returned to the same romantic, unrealized story, and again the world felt thick with intrigue, fierce with dappled colors, a world she could have attained if she had only been more patient, if she had not given up quite so quickly.

———————

YOU'RE OLEG'S FRIEND, AREN'T YOU?

Oleg's wife took away the remains of stuffed cabbage and brought them three steaming glasses of tea. It was Sunday—Lev, Oleg, and Ruben having gathered together on Sundays for over ten years now, and Lev was happy to see that marriage did not interfere with their tradition. He began to think that it was time for him to give up on Vasilisa and seriously start looking around for a wife. After all, the latest rumors circulating were that Katia had been this close to marriage, the Ashkenazi American practically proposed, but then it all somehow fell through. No one had seen Katia around the neighborhood for months.

Oleg pushed his chair away from the table and exhaled, offering Lev and Ruben cigarettes out of a gilded, lacquered box they had never seen before. The wife sat down with her tea—Lev could see that after pouring all of their glasses, her own contained only several teaspoons of liquid.

After a year of marriage, Oleg was becoming rounder, enjoying his food more. His wife too had developed a slight heaviness in her hips, and Lev wondered if she was already pregnant. He remembered her as a giddy but religious girl who wore long plaid skirts but hopped on sidewalks, braids swinging. During the meal, she remained quiet, slic-

ing one thing, refilling something else. Once, Oleg called her name
three times before she started, her chin resting on a fist, her mind
clearly in a faraway place.

When she went into the kitchen to wash dishes, Oleg shrugged,
lighting a cigarette. Marriage was a shocking revelation to Bukharian
girls, Lev imagined. All they knew were the flowers, the brief courtship, the ring, the mystical concept of their one *bashert*. Their heads
were swirling with the attention, everyone was bending over to please
them. Then one morning, they were no longer little princesses and
things began to be expected of them. Cooking, cleaning, the spreading
of legs. The members of the community had all turned to celebrate a
new bride-to-be.

Oleg inserted a new CD by a popular female Uzbek singer and as
the music started to pulsate out of the amplifier, it was as it had always
been—the three of them layering words over one another, enveloped
by cigarette smoke, heads muddled with vodka. Oleg got up on the
sofa to sing along, using the vodka bottle first as a microphone, then
a guitar. Steam was drifting in from the kitchen, but they ignored its
tendrils, it did not exist for them. The music had a dirty electric guitar
sound, the singer's voice growling, seductive. Oleg belted out the lyr-
ics, baying the chorus at the ceiling. Of course Oleg's stories couldn't
be lies, Lev thought, grinning, jumping on the couch to play backup
with a glass candle holder. Oleg did not need to lie. It had been his
own fault for having named her Vasilisa in the first place.

The doorbell rang, but Oleg continued to play guitar, his spine
curved backward, his face grimacing with effort. Ruben joined in on
the pillow cushion next to Lev, playing an imaginary synthesizer in the
air. On the third doorbell, the wife (Svetlana, he really should call her
by her name, she was the reality, after all) emerged from the kitchen.

"Boys." She smiled, seeing the three of them on the sofa. She wiped
her hands on a towel and answered the front door.

"Who is it, Oleg?" Ruben asked, choking with laughter.

The bride returned to the room with the girl from Oleg's wedding,
the one who'd sat next to Lev, the one now introduced as Irina. After
she took off her coat, Lev saw that she was wearing a navy blue pant-

suit and from a distance her acne was barely noticeable. Lev turned down the music, returned the candle holder back to its place on the bookshelf, and shook her hand, aware of the beads of sweat suspended on his upper lip. After the introductions, they returned to the table, the conversation slower, at a higher pitch, threaded by a staccato string of feminine chatter. Cherry preserves were brought out along with a honey cake, a delicate china cup was filled to the rim with white sugar.

Oleg and Ruben drank their cold teas, eyes lowered into their saucers; across from them, the two women sat shoulder to shoulder. Lev felt at the center of their expectations; they were waiting for him to act. He looked at the girl who had taken over the evening. She was pouring cherry preserves over her cake. The makeup on her face was heavily applied, her eyebrows thin and overplucked.

"So, I hear you like French movies. *Aimez-vous les films français?*" she said to Lev, her accent clunky and consonant-heavy, and there was silence again. The girl, triumphant, a virgin, sat back and took her first bite of cake.

"I don't know if I'm unhappy because I'm not free or I'm not free because I'm unhappy," Jean Seberg said in *Breathless*. Once Lev left the theater, he could easily have paid for the next show and watched it all over again. What was it about that movie, the way the same scene could look so different from moment to moment, here a shadow, there the full splash of daylight on Seberg's nose? The way the two main characters spoke to each other, as if they were both stretching the same piece of taffy with their teeth. Lev loved that insouciant movie.

And outside, on Houston Street in Manhattan, the humidity made all the moisture accumulate in places where flesh rolled over flesh. Lev turned right on Houston and walked to the Angelika—there was a four-thirty show starting in just a few minutes; he would have to hurry. And then, after that, he would walk farther down Houston, to Sunshine Cinemas, on the way inhaling a mustard-coated pretzel.

Since the Sunday gathering at Oleg's, it was made clear that he ought to, no, absolutely had to, pursue this Irina girl. She was not without a figure, her hips had a sensuous swing to them after all, her thighs a pleasant roundness. Her father was new to the neighborhood and ignorant of Lev's romantic history; he was some kind of real estate hotshot, just two years in Rego Park and he had already invested in some condominiums on Queens Boulevard. All this was nothing to scoff at.

It was time, Lev's father said. It was time, Lev's mother said. He blindly followed these instructions, mechanically dialing Irina's number and asking her to dinner. He tried to ignore his aversion to the way she seemed to leap to the telephone, the immediate assent laced with a sliver of self-satisfaction, her unappealing laugh, a kind of cynical heh-heh. The night of their dinner, though, he had panicked, rustled up a fake cough and called her to cancel. It had now been two weeks, and he felt the entire community waiting. Would Lev mess this one up too, shame his parents for good?

And what had he been doing during those two weeks? Movies. Movies every night, two a night, sometimes five a weekend, old ones, new ones, especially French ones. He was aware of himself watching the screen, his mouth slightly agape, ready to murder anyone who dared rustle a candy wrapper, who chatted to a neighbor, flipped open a cell phone. "Shut your mouth," he would have to say, loudly but firmly, only once, at the very start of the movie, and to his satisfaction, the crinkling would decrease, the whispers disappear. He could then enjoy his movie.

His parents considered his moviegoing habit to be something like marijuana use: baffling, possibly dangerous. Going to a nice movie here and there with a few friends, with a wife, was certainly understandable, but this solitary obsession, this disappearance for hours at a time, returning home with glazed eyes, distracted, swimming in an alternate universe, were these not all symptoms of grave illness?

No, it was only in movies that Lev found himself. When he was twelve or thirteen and first introduced to the Talmud in yeshiva, Lev had been ecstatic. How one idea could divert to another and still another, one question could fan out to a multitude of other questions.

When he told his parents he wanted to be a Talmudic scholar, they were amused, but not discouraging. Why did he let it go? He wasn't smart enough, he decided, the questions he began formulating were not being answered in the Talmud. Instead, movies took its place. Movies, which opened doors onto more open doors.

Just one more, he would say, and I will know what to do. One more movie and I will let go of Vasilisa, I will ask Irina on a date and begin a real life surrounded by family, by children. But another movie would only weigh Lev down with more doubt. What made the Bukharian way of life better when there were so many other ways to live? he wondered. They taunted him, the French beauties of cinema. They were elusive, filled with desires no man could satisfy. He loved the way they smoked, with their thick eyelashes, oversized rings, slim black dresses. They told him of a larger world he feared, a world he could never enter, possibly didn't even want to enter.

He loved the nuances of French films, the talk that did not directly correlate to the feelings, their slippery ambiguity. And the more movies he watched with now-dead stars, their lives flickering across the screen, now extinguished, the less he wanted to call Irina. No, he would not call her, there would be others better for him, more sensitive to their surroundings, more alive to the moment. Movies, by their very nature, whispered to Lev of death.

Thus emboldened, he would leave the theater, his eyes would become adjusted to the bleating cars, the rushing masses. Lev would think of his mother, her recent weight gain, the new thickness of her fingers, the lines creeping around her mouth. Her new habit of watching TV in the afternoons. It was clear by her roots that she was letting more time lag between salon appointments. And this from a woman who used to be able to coax Dima out of a free pound of Havarti. Could he disappoint her again?

The Angelika was crowded and Lev despaired of getting a good aisle seat. He stood in a long line with his ticket and rushed inside the theater along with everyone else. He didn't manage to get an aisle seat, so he took the next best thing, the seat closest to the wall, so he would not have to rise for errant latecomers. There he would not be disturbed and by the time Emmanuelle Béart appeared on the screen (those tranquil eyes, that pouting mouth, that hair!), Lev would make new decisions about his life.

"Aimez-vous les films français?" Irina asked, taking a bite of her salmon. Did she realize she had already said this to him? Lev wondered. They played it safe, going to a local kosher restaurant whose owner they both knew, who kept sending out free dishes from the kitchen. His potatoes, fried with garlic and rosemary, were delicious and the wine was decent. Lev slightly loosened his tie, watching Irina as she drained her glass and became bolder, more animated. If they got married, nothing would ever change between him and Oleg.

He had been too hard on Irina, Lev decided. Her hands were soft and elegant; she evidently took good care of them. Her breasts were a nice size, just full enough. She wasn't one of those dieting girls who ordered everything broiled and tasteless. It was clear that she participated in her life. And she laughed at his jokes, hearty, rolling laughs, throwing her head back, showing all her teeth. At the door to her apartment, she leaned against the wall and closed her eyes. Her skin exuded garlic and perfume. She was waiting for him to accept their future together, to lean in for the kiss.

"But he was Jewish," Katia told the rabbi. The holy man was playing with his purple ballpoint pen, slipping its cap off with his index finger and thumb and snapping it back into place.

Her father had secured her an appointment with Rabbi Melman, one of the most revered in the community. It was he who wrote the widely read online column "Ask Our Rabbi." He to whom Bukhis could turn for advice—their embarrassing sexual queries, religious rites, dating etiquette—concerns that remained unspoken, even to themselves. "Do I still marry her if I already slept with her?" "Should I not be eating legumes on Passover?" "Am I still a virgin?" "If my girlfriend converts, is there a chance for us?"—all answered patiently, seriously, even if referring some of the more delicate feminine queries to his wife. It was Rabbi Melman who helped Bukharian Jews in this country fight off secular temptations, who remained their conscience, the link to their pasts. When Bukharkians grew depressed, when they wanted too much of what was around them, they turned to the rabbi.

He was younger than Katia had expected for such a famous man. A beard with only a sprinkling of grayish flecks. His wife coming in from time to time to pour seltzer, the screams of his kids wafting through walls. Was his chair elevated on some kind of platform?—because she felt miniature, toylike. He spoke to her slowly but affectionately, as if to a child.

"But he was not Bukharian, my dear. That was the root of all your sorrow. You say you have not been damaged, so it's not too late for you. Stay in the community."

He was right, of course, Katia thought. What made her think she could form a life with an outsider? It was understood that American men couldn't take care of their wives, not in the proper way, the all-consuming, bodily way. Even David had forgotten to open some doors for her; a few times, he poured his own wine before hers, and when did he ever bring her a bunch of daisies or orchids? His answers to her questions: "Where were you?" "Why didn't you call?" became evasive. No, her friends had warned her about fickle American guys and Katia had not wanted to believe that of all of them.

But David had stopped looking at her like he used to, as if her very presence animated his inner world. He was harder to reach, their weekends together no longer a certainty. He stopped trying to feel his way inside of her.

"It's just a busy time of year," he told her.

It had all happened so quickly, just weeks after New Year's. Katia blushed to think of her own plans, her expectations for that night. How would she survive this one?

"Thank you, Rabbi." Katia smiled, for the first time, truly, in weeks. What a good idea this was of her father's, to seek his counsel, to have this great man's acceptance.

The rabbi rose. "Katia, is it? God willing you will find your other half. Your *bashert*. Be patient, dear Katia, and he will come." He opened his door and waved in the next consultation. Entering the spare waiting room, Katia saw couples reading separate newspapers; a few young men alone, fidgeting, started when the door opened. Her father, rising, took her arm. On the way home, they didn't speak.

A Rego Park February. Russian women sliding around in their high-heeled leather boots, *babushki* stamping on snow in gray wool coats. Katia saw a few of her Forest Hills classmates navigating strollers around hills of piled slush. They walked by her father's barbershop, which was still open, brightly lit and cozy; inside, Seva was shaving a man in a suit. They waved to him. Next door, a line of people waited at the counter for Chinese takeout. When the door opened, a puff of sesame air was expelled.

She would be twenty-six soon, Katia realized. Maybe she would gather her girlfriends to celebrate, her mother could cook. When was the last time she took pride in her birthday? When she was sixteen, seventeen? They rounded the corner on Sixty-sixth Road. Before them, a toddler slipped on the ice, and his mother, in her fur coat, scooped him up before he could cry, flashing Katia a conspiratorial smile. At least she was capable of happiness in all this, Katia decided, winding her arm through her father's—simple events with no goal, no meaning apart from themselves.

"Let's take an extra turn around the block," she said.

Her father squeezed her elbow. "A wonderful idea, Katyenka." Passing the entrance to their building of twenty-five years, identical to the condominiums to the right and the left, they kept on walking.

The profile of Vasilisa the Beautiful reminded Lev of an illustration of Queen Esther in his *cheder* textbook. The evil Haman is bowing at her throne, his hands clasped together in devious supplication, but her expression is impassive, her head slightly tilted to the heavens. This was how Katia Zavurov looked as she lingered in the aisle of the pharmacy, scanning rows of imported facial cleansers. The way she reached for a tube, her fingers curved and spread apart, was the way

Lev had seen ballet dancers reach for their partners or French movie actresses reach for their lovers.

When she came up to the register to pay for her tube of cleanser, she smiled the smile of someone who both knew him and didn't know him. In high school, he had been certain she was complicit in his plans, that when their eyes met in the halls, she had been telling him that she was waiting for them to be together. But now that he thought of it, he never did say more than hello, or nod when they saw each other at *shul* or at a wedding. Now she took out her wallet and placed it on the counter.

This was his opportunity to draw her into conversation; they were alone in the store. A car alarm went off outside with its insistent repetitive groan and Katia was waiting for him to ring up her purchases. What would he say? Spitefully, he hoped that her beauty was burnished, but here it was in front of him, as vibrant as ever, soaking up its soil. The phone rang.

He picked up the receiver, cradling it with his ear while he rang up Katia's purchase. He did not know if he had anything left to say to her; as far as his family was concerned, a whore was an outcast. But then, what if that was not the case?

"Lev Gavrilov?" The voice on the other end was low, gruff, authoritative. "This is Irina's father. You have been out with her three times now. What do you think we are, Americans? Either state your intentions or give it up. There are other *kavaleri* waiting, you know. My Irina is a nice Bukharian girl who will not waste her time with frivolous dates that go nowhere."

"Yes, sir." Lev stared at Katia's fifty-dollar bill in his hand, the denomination not quite penetrating his consciousness.

"So, good, then. I expect you to come see me with a proposal or never see her again. I know your reputation, Lev, but I thought you knew better." Lev tried to keep the features of his face neutral, certain Katia heard every word. He handed her the change.

To his surprise, Katia continued to stand there, waiting for him to finish the conversation. As she tucked her hair behind her ears, adjusting a diamond earring, her eyes ransacked his. As soon as he put the receiver down, she leaned forward across the counter and whispered, "You're Oleg's friend, aren't you?" He could barely tell she was crying; her shoulders did not shake and her eyes were veiled by the angle of her face, the shadows cast by the abrasive yellow lights.

Lev was not sure what was expected of him, so he lifted the countertop and came around to the customer side to take her awkwardly into his arms. Her hair smelled like orange peel, her face pressed tightly to his right breast pocket. Holding her was not what he imagined it would be, her snagging breath, her willful posture. As he gently rocked her, Lev tried not to breathe, to remain in the moment, but his head was filled with worries: that someone would enter the pharmacy right then, would see this strange embrace. The Bukharian community was small with big mouths—it would only take two people to transport the news to his mother. How many ladies would savor the revenge, to share news of her son to the area's most celebrated gossip? Who hadn't been greeted by Yana Gavrilov with the words, "Have you heard about So-and-So?"

But no one came in.

1 3

─────────

A GREAT, SLOPPY JOY

She began to dread Katia's frequent phone calls. Shall we do the usual? Katia asked. They could brave the line into the Austrian restaurant at the Neue or they could head farther east to their favorite rustic Italian place. Remember their squash ravioli? And there should be no rain, they say, until later this evening. By the time the first drops come, we would be safely tucking into a bowl of pasta. What do you think, Anna?

"Stasia's sick," Anna said. "A migraine. What can I do when I am trapped here at home?"

"Dear Anna," Katia said. Didn't she sense anything? Could it be that she had already forgotten her David? She no longer mentioned him. "How selfish of me! I can come over and watch Seryozha, and you run errands. Please, *dorogaia* Anna, I can be there in an hour and it would be no trouble. No trouble at all."

"How lucky you are, to be so free."

"But I would trade places with you."

"And I, Katia, with you."

. . .

She reached the point in the marriage where she could watch Alex throughout an entire meal and not feel the urge to say a thing. What could he possibly tell her that would surprise her, that would prove he knew her to her very bones?

"Anyechka, please pass the salt," he said. And she knew he would do just that! Salting her chicken stew (*so coarse*) before even tasting it. There, that was the proof that he didn't—no, never—knew her at all. Anna could make a list, start with the pubic hairs on the soap in the shower, his loud, exaggerated yawns. The fact that he'd never, not once, handled a dirty dish. Should she? Did she dare?

But before she could say a thing, the inevitable reversal; noticing the way he hung her raincoat in the closet, carefully, the scarf draped over the hanger as if it were her very own neck. The way Alex lingered in Serge's room, eventually emerging with the pacifier in his palm. The glass of water, simple and clear and perched on a coaster, waiting for her at her dressing table. The good night kiss on the mouth, still heartfelt if no longer passionate, the protective bear hug, the pleasant scratch of his beard against her back. The panic would return and Anna would not get to sleep for hours, weighing, comparing, crossing out, beginning anew.

Sometimes a gray March day had the power to bring all life to a halt. Windows rattling from the wind and rain, the smudged sky, translucent fog. Inside, half a knitted scarf was thrown over the arm of the couch; a paperback was inverted, its pages creased, on an unmade bed; the bubbling of boiling water; a baby's wail, sharp and predictable in its highs and lows, rang out like a car alarm. Then, silence, the ticking of the clock, muffled cooing in Polish, a pulsating headache. Rain, so much of it, as though the clouds had been wrung out. Silence.

And then her cell phone vibrated. A distinctly American voice. And it was him.

"Anna," he said.

. . .

Century 21 with Nadia on a Saturday, was she mad? Russian women from Brooklyn and New Jersey battling tourists from the U.K. for the last Moschino jacket, the latter greatly underestimating the former's tenacity, their ability to grab merchandise at bionic speeds, to tail the workers returning clothes from the dressing room to the racks.

Clutching a sheer Catherine Malandrino blouse, Anna strained to find Nadia in the crowds. Afterward they would have lunch at Les Halles, where Nadia would encourage Anna, again, to join her book club, to join them for foxtrot lessons. So many required activities, their centers scooped out—the book club where discussion was never about books, the wine-pairing courses where the wine was gulped and lectures on *terroir* ignored—always in groups, gossip about individual members conducted on the telephone afterward.

This month, they were reading *Wuthering Heights*, and the discussion, if one could call it that! They simply could not understand why Catherine wasn't happy in her marriage to Linton.

"C'mon, ladies," Nadia had begun, already tipsy after three glasses of wine. "Who would you prefer? The caveman running around the forest or that nice Linton? This book makes no sense to me. This cheese, Lusyenka, is stinky! I love it."

"The moors are not a forest," Anna had said, too loudly, perhaps, herself having consumed a glass or two of Shiraz. And so the book club ended for that month with someone suggesting a more upbeat title for next month. Jane Austen was called out. Sophie Kinsella. Anna had been forced to practically guzzle that bottle of wine just to get through the remainder of the evening.

In Century 21, summer clothes were arrayed in tropical displays of pinks and limes and yellows. In front of her, so many women, each with her own goal, the hope of the perfect designer discovery for a quarter of the price. The image of herself transformed by her outfit, turning heads as she walked down the street. Didn't it make her look thinner? Taller? Trendier? More sophisticated? And younger, always younger. In the background, the brusque demands over the loudspeaker were meant for a single person but were foisted onto the entire store.

"You gotta try that on in the dressing room," a miserable employee in her Pepto-Bismol-colored apron berated one shopper, the woman's head already submerged inside a Lycra top.

Wandering in the European section and looking for Nadia's bouffant, it was difficult to breathe—no windows, just a concrete slab decorated with clothes. She wondered what Nadia would say if she told her that David made her feel like Catherine from *Wuthering Heights,* that he could read all the invisible inscriptions hidden on her body, that she would take a caveman over that patsy Linton any day, and they were all, all of Nadia's friends, so simple and coarse?

The Malandrino blouse settled beautifully on Anna; confrontationally pink, it made just the right indentations. Next to her, Nadia was wriggling into some kind of complicated kimono dress, too small around her thighs, which were harnessed by a control top. Those would be her thighs too in just five years, Anna thought. Pocked, spilling over.

"I'll see you out there, Nadyenka. I have to get out of here." Anna clipped all her clothes back onto hangers and took her number. Around her, rotating in their cubicles in the open dressing room, stuffing themselves into clothes, were so many women.

"What do you love about me, Sasha?" If he answers this right, then this, if he doesn't, then that. It was breakfast, the harsh light of morning, a possibly sour day was before them.

"What do you mean, Anyusha?" So many ways to parse the hours, and Anna, just wanting to get back into bed. These days waking up held little purpose, if only to hear *his* voice, *his* thoughts.

"Just this. Tell me exactly. What do you love about me?"

"I don't know," he said, plunging his spoon into the flesh of a hard-boiled egg. He appeared to think. "That's a strange question isn't it? You're beautiful, obviously, sweet, a wonderful mother. Why are you asking?" Their china pattern, Anna noticed, those fussy yellow flowers, had been the wrong choice after all.

"No, Sasha, no reason." Then it was to be that, just as she thought.

She forgot that a vacation was planned for the summer; this year it was to be Corsica. She could see it already—two weeks on the beach with Nadia, on a boat with Alex and Zhak, the same meal night after night, the four of them shaded by olive trees.

"I just don't feel comfortable leaving Serge," she told Alex on the phone. He had started traveling for work again, and the major decisions of the past three weeks were made over the phone.

"Why?"

"He's walking now, colliding into everything." She had been shopping too much recently; her clothes, with tags attached, were scattered across the bed. "Maybe I'll change my mind. But for now."

She loved Alex's disembodied voice, deep and soft, when he spoke to her through cables and wires from long distances. How she feared to lose him when he was this far, how she missed the concept of him.

At Housing Works, she found David in the back by the café counter, running his fingers along the fiction paperback spines. He was wearing a striped shirt under a trench coat, which gave his lean shoulders the appearance of more heft.

"You changed lipsticks," he said when he saw her.

"You grew your hair," she said, reaching in for an awkward cheek kiss that hit somewhere on the neck below the ear. "It's curlier when it's longer, it coils around the bottom of your neck." It *was* curlier, David's hair, when long. She *had* changed lipsticks. His every word was now a caress, dripping with multiple meanings.

They pretended to look at books for a while. At the podium, employees of the bookstore were setting up for a reading. A few people were already sitting in the rows of aluminum chairs, pointing at a young woman in the front, who was staring straight ahead, gripping a roll of manuscript pages.

"Where should we go?" Anna asked. It was yet another rainy day, and in indecision over outfits (casual slacks or jeans? she settled on jeans), she had forgotten her umbrella. The front windows were covered with an opaque film of rain.

"I thought we would stay for the reading," David said. "You see her?" he pointed toward the young woman. She was pale, her black hair in a bowl cut with severe bangs. "I know her from my writing program, from Sarah Lawrence. I promised. You don't mind, do you?"

And she didn't, though a tiny flicker of consciousness told her that she should, that she might want to. But Alex would be away until the following morning, and it was only seven o'clock. So many hours remained to the evening, and she had never been here before, had walked by but never been inside. This was a universe that had been closed to her, but for David it was his own.

The rows were filling up, so they found a seat in the middle, toward the front. During the reading, David leaned forward in his seat, watching, almost unblinking, the young woman he knew. Anna felt a surge of compassion for him, for his unbridled ambition, for the desire she could feel palpitating near the surface of his skin.

She heard none of the reading, her mind floating along the cadences of the words. The excerpt the woman read was linguistically intimidating, each sentence choked with barely digestible words. It was hard work, to enjoy this. *When will it be you up there?* Anna wanted to ask David. *When will you be a great writer? Will you be able to, with your words, make me come to life?*

After the reading, David bounded up to the front, presumably to offer congratulations. She watched him push his way through the circle of admirers and stand beside the author, his shoulders slouching, head bobbing. Anna would ask to read his work; she could root herself in that way—from reader she could move on to protagonist.

They walked around the corner to a Cuban place, where they had to wait outside for a table. They stood on Elizabeth Street, David holding a broken umbrella over both of their heads. Every few minutes he ran into the restaurant to monitor their place on the waiting list. They stood close together, huddled beneath the umbrella, commingling the steam from their mouths.

"Have you seen Katia, then?" she asked casually.

"No, not recently. I mean, it's been a while." He looked away, focused his attention on the restaurant interior. She knew that it had been a bad idea, what she said, and wanted to erase the surface, to begin again.

"Look, right over there, an open table. I think that one's ours."

She felt a hand around her waist.

"For warmth," he said. And they were called inside.

After dinner, they walked arm in arm, talking about the places books took them. David said when he read *The Chronicles of Narnia*, he tried out all the closet doors to make sure they didn't lead to other worlds. Anna read *The Lion, The Witch, and the Wardrobe* in her first American apartment, having created a treehouse out of four chairs and a sheet.

When they arrived at the subway entrance, she took his elbow for another block, then extended their time together by walking up to the next subway stop, then the one after that. In midtown, she jumped in a cab quickly, to avoid lingering awkwardly by the open door. Frightened of going home, of how she would feel about being at home; it was like dragging oneself out of quicksand. Try to float, wasn't that the way to scramble out of all that suction?

A text message on her cell phone, "What R U doing?"

"Thiking about you," she replied. Alex strolling in front of her, her mother and father on either side. Her galloping heart, lumbering thumbs on the tiny keyboard, misspelling in her haste. Pressing "Send" and joining the group, lacing her arm through Alex's. *Look how happy they are,* her mother exclaimed, pinching her cheeks.

No, she couldn't see Katia that Saturday to go to the MoMA. Why not? A million reasons. The time of year, her son, driven mad by errands.

Who had time for museums these days, for squinting at canvases over people's heads? Squeezing oneself into human semicircles to scrutinize dreary biographies of the artist? The curators always seemed to select the most uninspiring information—the artist's prizes, his newfound interest in color, his use of the palette knife. Never what Anna wanted to know—how often he was depressed, the extent of his parents' neglect, which regrets haunted him, what gave him the right to ignore his worldly responsibilities, to choose art for his life.

This time Katia did not protest. (Did she know?) Each phone call, as if air were slowly trickling out of her voice. But over the years, hadn't it become increasingly difficult to be the object of Katia's admiration? As long as Anna could remember, at every family function, she would find little Katia at her side, praising her dangling gold earrings, her handbags, the cut of her clothes, her "effortless" style. Always asking to hear stories of Manhattan as though it were a distant dreamscape and not just over the Queensboro Bridge. Katia would fetch her cocktails, press her head against Anna's shoulder, arms around Anna's waist.

To think about Katia with any clarity, without a roiling stomach, Anna had to sever the connection between David and Katia in her mind. Guilt: what Anna K. didn't allow herself to feel.

But what if Anna K. were to be honest with Katia? She would say that she couldn't see her simply because her cousin was young (so many emotions wrapped up in that one word), so lovely. Her cousin still had years in which to expand, while her own years were becoming more compressed every day. Being around her was beginning to feel impossible; her cousin, after all, was still so enviably, so vivaciously, so heartbreakingly young.

Seryozha spoke his first words, according to Stasia, that very day, just an hour ago, in fact. "Dada," Stasia said he had said.

Anna had run out for a perfume refill and had a hard time believing it had really happened. "Show me," she said, still in her coat, leaning on her knees before her son.

"Show your mother," Stasia urged the boy, but he cried instead, burying his face in Stasia's bosom, battering her with his fists. He was long overdue for his nap, but Anna waited. Just tears but no words. Any chance he would say "Mama?"

"Go, go, Anna Borisovna, I don't think it happen tonight."

Anna, frozen in place, almost took her coat off. Let him wait, she thought, this is my son, for God's sake. She stood, her hands folded together as if in prayer. Crocodile Gena was singing quietly on the CD; the room was permeated with the scent of baby powder. *"Pozhalusta, dorogoi, skazhi 'Mama,'"* she begged. Seryozha puckered his mouth as if in protest.

"Fine, don't say it," she said, knowing she sounded petulant, childish herself. Why wouldn't he do it for her? Surely he saw her more often than Alex, who was living out of a suitcase these days.

"I'm leaving, Stasia." She lingered, refreshing lipstick. If he says something, anything, I won't go, she thought.

She arrived at the bar forty-five minutes late and David still wasn't there. Anna ordered a glass of red wine and gulped it down, crying uncontrollably. The young bartender, sturdy chest, death's-head tattoo imprinted on his wrist, was stealing nervous looks in her direction. One other woman sat in the place, pretending to read the newspaper. She was waiting for somebody too, checking her cell phone every few seconds. It was still light out, the days were getting longer. Anna ordered another, forcing herself to slow down, to taste the grape. My son, she thought. What am I doing? In the kitchen, someone was frying something, she could hear the hiss of the griddle, a scalding crackle of oil punctured by the sound of clinking glass. The door opened and she spun around, but it was the woman's companion, another young woman, her hair damp, shivering. She heard the smacks of kisses, the shedding of a wet raincoat, the scraping of chair leg against hardwood.

"Just one more glass, please." The bartender nodded.

As she took her first sips of this third glass of wine, she felt a tap on her shoulder. "I'm so sorry." His eyes were narrowed, mouth open. "I thought the F train would never come. And how could I call you from underground?" He took in her tear-streaked face, bent down and wiped her cheeks with a cocktail napkin. His sweater smelled faintly of smoke.

My son . . . But she stopped herself from saying it, realizing she had never mentioned him before. She had been afraid it would cast her as older, maternal, stripped of sexuality.

"You're late," she said instead, allowing a new set of tears to drizzle, perhaps to glisten, down her cheeks.

"Anna." He stroked her hair, but Anna sensed that the touch was pleased, a new confidence vibrating through his fingers. She saw the novel in his hands—she couldn't make out the title—and felt herself calm down.

He paid for her drinks and they left, walking the three blocks to his place. She kissed him before they made it up the stairs to his apartment, by pressing up against him on the stairway. His rib cage, his narrow hips, were pinned beneath her and his skin felt cold, sharp to the touch. Her mind, for once, was blessedly free of all thought.

Inside his small apartment, they inhaled one another; her hair smelled of charred wood, his of mint and clove cigarettes. Black currant lingering on her tongue, they exchanged purple-mouthed kisses synchronized to some Cirque du Soleil soundtrack. *Alegría?*

One sleeve got caught on the other's zipper, and they abandoned it to its fate on the floor. The first unveilings: of breast, of belly, inner thigh. One body long and lean, a smattering of reddish-brown hair, the other fleshy, round, and substantial.

So many couples falling in love would attest that their memories became sharper as their feelings deepened; they realized they were able to call up every detail of their beloved's features, the clothes he wore on a particular night, the patches of hair, the way he shivered in sleep. For Anna it was the opposite—love had always fused specific details into a vague, clouded mass. She tended to forget the words, the actions, the gestures, sometimes even the face disappeared in her mind, all obscured by the monstrosity of her own feelings. A great, sloppy joy.

She remembered to call Stasia and tell her she would be spending the night at her parents', and submerged herself again in the foreign bed, beneath a puffed, purple comforter. Was it too early to ask him how he felt? Yes, she decided. In the dark, she could only see the whites of his eyes.

In the morning, she zipped up her cardigan, kissed him on the forehead. He remained curled in bed, a wide grin, his arms wrapped around a pillow.

"You're wonderful," he said. She silenced him with a kiss, wishing his words were more original somehow, writerly.

She let herself out onto the unfamiliar street and glimpsed a bakery. Leaping around the water puddles, she waited in line behind a tourist couple clutching the Zagat guide and bought herself a cupcake with vanilla frosting. How delicious it was, the cake still warm, crumbly. She ate it outside, thinking about the movie she would tell Alex she saw in Queens. An obscure Chinese film, she decided, slow and lyrical and ending in death. Nothing he would ever want to see. Anna licked the frosting off her fingers and hailed a cab.

1 4

LOOK FOR ME

Their first date was arranged for a Thursday night. Katia agreed with Lev that it was best to meet in the city, away from the Forest Hills spies, who would purchase gossip along with their avocados the following morning (a practice in which his own mother was directly implicated, so he mentioned this night to no one). Lev switched shifts with the other pharmacist, who usually worked the earlier hours, but the morning dragged; each time he looked up at the clock, the minute hand was paralyzed between the same dreary numbers.

All day, Lev felt the world rotating around him while he blinked at it, unmoving. When a doctor called in a prescription, Lev wrote down *Allegra* instead of *Alavert,* and had to call the doctor back to verify. Once he took a credit card but left the receipt fluttering in the machine, until the customer said, *"Nu?* What's the matter with you, young man?" He tried channeling Jean-Paul Belmondo, who never would have been this nervous, who would have smoked a cigarette and popped his convertible car open, waiting for the girl to slide up beside him.

If only it was yet another ordinary Bukhi girl. An Irina, whom he had left crumpled at her door just a few days before and then sprinted out of the building, too ashamed to face the father. "You lied to me," she had said, and Lev hated being the guy that women said such things to. "You are lovely, really," he had mumbled, only making her cry harder. But that couldn't be helped.

The last movie Lev watched, Krzysztof Kieślowski's *Red,* with its alternate realities, its missed opportunities, the luminescent Irène Jacob, cemented his decision. He would not mess with fate—it would either be Katia or waiting, for what he did not know, but a wife he couldn't get rid of would make his life unbearable. So when the clock finally spat out five p.m., he ran home and dressed himself entirely in black—pin-striped pants, a black button-down, a blazer—and prepared to find out which way it would go.

On Austin Street, everyone else was ascending from the subway, determined to put their day behind them, with their laptops and briefcases and hardcovers under their arms. Lev looked at himself in a reflective Baskin-Robbins window, combed his thick, unruly hair as best he could. He grabbed the best-looking cluster of lilies at a bodega on Austin Street and, shoving against the crowds, made his way into the Seventy-first/Continental subway station.

By the time he handed the flowers to Katia, who was already waiting for him outside Turkish Kitchen on Third Avenue, in her white earmuffs, her *Doctor Zhivago* winter coat, Lev was completely at peace with himself. He was charming and confident in a way Oleg would never have recognized. He kissed her calmly on the cheek, escorted her inside, held her handbag as she slid into the booth.

"I love the cold weather," she said. Lev found her preference for winter charming, and they spoke about her affection for the color white, for crisp, unblemished clothes and Saturday afternoons, mere hours before the finale of the Sabbath. Her every word stilled his breath.

He ordered more food than they could possibly eat, complimented Katia on her dangling pearl earrings, and when the waiter came with the check, he would tell him that they weren't ready to leave, to please bring it back when he summoned him. Which to the waiter's, and to Katia's worried father's, dismay, he wouldn't do for another two and a half hours.

. . .

Lev's father looked surprised when Lev entered his shop in the middle of the week. Without telling his parents, Lev took the day off from work, wandering past Forest Hills High School before hopping on a train to Manhattan. The school had not been renovated since his days there, the flag still fluttering in the breeze. Some kids were playing football on the adjacent field, a couple of them with *kipahs* on their heads. Packs of kids were smoking outside, their backpacks at their feet, and the bell, when it clanged, sounded exactly as he remembered it. From what Lev understood, the kids from the former Soviet Union were no longer minorities; it was they who ruled the school these days.

His father lined up gold necklaces inside the glass display case, arranging them side by side against the black platform. Outside the window, on Forty-seventh Street, Lev heard the honking of cars and the vibrating song of hawkers, spitting out low prices on diamonds, on Rolex watches. His father locked the cabinet with a small key and sat down in a swiveling office chair. He wore one of his old sweaters with gray and black stripes, the one Lev's mother had been trying to throw away for months. His was the face of a man who does not look up from the pavement when he walks, Lev thought.

He grinned at Lev. "I know why you're here. It is your turn now, am I right?"

"Yes," he said. "It's my turn."

He had done research on diamond selection, on the "four C's," but the subject bored him and he soon forgot which letter of clarity was good and which was flawed. In any case, to get the ring without his father was unthinkable. Once a Bukharian wedding plan was put into motion, it was the fathers who took over. When the future groom presented the ring to the girl, the father of the bride-to-be had the right to appraise the ring, make sure his daughter's fiancé was not skimping on the carats.

His father tried to pat him on the back, but the blow landed higher, in the cleft where the neck meets the shoulder. "You're a good boy, Lev, I'm proud of you. Have you already made your mother happy with this news? May you be blessed with a long, happy life together."

He scanned Lev's face as if for scars, signs of manhood. "For ring, I know just where to go."

He asked his assistant to watch the front desk and the two of them walked down the stairs into the cacophony of Forty-seventh Street. It occurred to Lev that his father never asked him whom he would be marrying; no doubt he thought it was Irina, daughter of the real estate mogul of Queens Boulevard. And Lev didn't want to tell him just yet; he realized he was angry, his father happy for the wrong girl, any girl, as if they were all interchangeable. Could Irène Jacob, for example, be swapped for Jacqueline Bisset? No, he did not think so. One had a soulful vulnerability, the other an easy sophistication.

The street was choked by security guards, Russian vendors, Orthodox Jews, tourists pawing the windows. When they reached the diamond store and descended a single flight of stairs, Lev held the door open for his father and followed him inside. As soon as they entered, his father began to speak with the proprietor, newly animated. "Don't even think of cheating me," he warned. Lev sat down in a chair and flipped through one of the *Rapaport Diamond Report* magazines fanned out on the table; his own role was finished.

He decided to ask her to marry him the following Sunday, on an unusually cold but clear and sunny March afternoon. Katia suggested they go skating in Central Park—her mother had been an amateur ice-skater and used to take Katia skating from a young age. It's a perfect day for it, she said, the tourists all dispersed. Lev had never ice-skated before, but he imagined it would be the ideal cinematic moment— presenting a diamond on the ice.

How beautiful she looked, Katia; she wore white again, a puffy coat, earmuffs. Her lips were waxy and slightly chapped, she kept running over them with her tongue. She wore tight, stretchy pants and in her ears were pearl studs—she was all pink and white and curvy. Lev's throat felt as though it had swelled to the size of a pomegranate.

They waited in line to rent their ice skates, and when they arrived at the front, the goateed young guy informed him that they no longer had any skates in his size. But he recommended the size below—too tight was safer than too loose, after all. On the bench, Lev fumbled with his cardboard-colored rental skates—even when he loosened the laces, the skates still constricted his toes. And when he rose, Katia had to hold his hand so he could steady himself. He didn't want to tell her that the skates were uncomfortable, their stiff tongues marking indentations in his skin. He tried to move, but his legs sliced at the ice helplessly.

The rink was choked with people traveling counterclockwise and Lev surveyed their efforts. Nervously, he watched several rounds of whirring striped scarfs, the red pom-poms of hats. The stronger skaters stayed closer to the center, weaving backward, making figure eights. One young woman tried a few loops, or axels, as he recalled from watching the Olympics.

Lev buried his hand in the pocket of his jacket, worried about the ring lying there, nestled in its velvet box, that it would fall out or he would land on it and mangle it somehow. He considered saving the proposal for another day, a quieter, more private moment, but now, outfitted with skates in the park, he began to suspect that Katia had led him here for a reason, and that there was a heavy air of expectation drooping between them. She was quieter, eyelashes lowered; she had already relaced her white skates several times.

"Go, please go without me," Lev said, holding on to the railing, hoping to regain some sort of self-control. "Enjoy yourself, please. As you can see, I'm a mess."

"You're not a mess," Katia said firmly. She took and squeezed his hand and slid beside him, prompting him back onto the rink, falling in line behind a blond set of parents with their three small children.

If she lets go of my hand first, I won't do it, thought Lev, trying to capture the moment, to consciously seize the extent of his happiness. He was getting the hang of this skating thing; he pushed himself off with one leg and glided, then pushed himself off with the other. He enjoyed the sensation of seeing only what was before him, the rest of the world pleasantly blurry, irrelevant. His ears were numb with cold, but circulation was now returning to his legs.

"Watch out!" A teenager whipped by them, and Lev panicked, lost his footing, and fell heavily to his knees, one hand dropping to the ice to protect himself from injury. Surprised, he looked up.

Katia was firmly holding on to his other hand.

That night, after a private discussion in the bedroom in which Lev tried to articulate love for his daughter, Katia's father cracked open a brand-new bottle of cognac. "Free haircuts for life," he announced, calling for Katia's mother to come out, come out, stop bustling with those beets in the kitchen at a time like this. Lev didn't have the heart to tell the man that he had half a dozen barbers in his own family. What Bukhi didn't?

As they lingered over a generous dinner with all the traditional dishes he loved (a few frankly better than his own mother's), Lev realized he never had a chance to tell Katia that he'd loved her for all those years, that he'd watched her in the neighborhood, how she had been like a private goddess to him. When he had finally pulled out the ring, there had been no words. She had simply looked down while he slipped it on her finger. Afterward, her breath smelled of cinnamon, nipping and spicy.

His eyes barely met Katia's all night, but he was aware of her body. He recalled their awkward but passionate kisses just minutes ago, it seemed, outside this very door: the cherry taste of the inside of her mouth, the dampness of the back of her neck where he rested his hand. Her clipped sighs, the cold tips of her fingers.

But a different woman was at the table, a woman who could cram hundreds of words, it seemed, into a single sentence. She was describing to her mother the exact manner of his proposal (she exaggerated the story a bit for comic effect, painting a picture of a hapless skater clinging to the safety of the railing, a diamond ring materializing from the bowels of his jacket). Then, before Lev could laugh or participate in any way, the two women had already moved on to more practical matters, discussing the details for the forthcoming party, the shopping that lay ahead for them. Their chatter bored Lev, so he retired with

Katia's father to the living room and the two of them made inroads into the bottle of cognac.

And once the excitement settled down within him, Lev became confused at his own mixed feelings. He had expected this outcome, this fulfillment of all his fantasies, would seal those empty crevices within him. And from the outside, it looked like he thought it would—Katia, so gentle, her smile so infectious that random babushkas on the street would smile back at her, almost in spite of their own misery. But as he said all the right things to Katia's father, he wondered why his bride was dwelling on insignificant details, why they were not holding one another, tasting each other's lips, savoring the joy of the present moment. They should be alone right now in a dark room, exploring each other with abandon.

"Do the 'Save the Date' cards really matter?" he called out from the living room. "The cut of the dress, the announcement in the paper?"

Yes, he was told. Yes, yes.

"You will learn," Katia's father said from his recliner chair. "In marriage, Lev, so much will have to matter to you, things you could never imagine. And you'll be paying for all of it."

Lev tried to laugh—hadn't he swapped these kinds of jokes with the boys? But they had never extended to Katia. It was as if his private thoughts were unleashed in the world, defenseless victims of other people's humor. So that was what it felt like, then, to get what you wanted—a kind of letting go.

"I'm getting married," he told his parents.

"We know, we know, mazel tov." His mother had clearly been informed of the ring expedition, and the table reflected her expectation of the announcement. She'd made the *samsi* herself, rather than buying them at the store. The gefilte fish looked fresh too, speckled with dill, a labor his mother rarely bothered with these days. Fresh flowers released their scent into the air.

It occurred to Lev that his mother may have been spreading the wrong news, may have collided into Irina's mother at Dima's and congratulated her, may have let Irina's name slip at the synagogue. Know-ing his mother, it was probably already too late. Poor Irina had prob-ably been receiving her own congratulations.

"It is Katia Zavurov I'm marrying," he said.

"Katia Zavurov?" His mother said it again and again, as though she never imagined this name crossing their lips. "Katia Zavurov?" She had not forgotten the rumors, she said, her tea growing cold, unsipped, in her saucer. Their handsome pharmacist son squander-ing his youth and looks on a girl who'd been around, who was pushing thirty because nobody in the community was willing to marry her? She must be dreaming, surely, tell her she is dreaming.

"She has not 'been around.' It was a rumor, that's all, a horrible rumor," Lev said, blushing. He thought of the Italian café, of his own disappointment, of Oleg's face as he told the story.

"Rumors are always true," his mother said. "They don't start from nowhere. I should know."

She continued. Katia was a tarnished woman and everyone knew it. Running around with American Ashkenazim too, wasn't she? All because of what she did with Oleg, who, by the way, was such a nice boy, married and a baby on the way. Was Lev implying his best friend had lied?

His father kept his thoughts to himself, but he patted Yana's arm. He was relieved his son was getting married at all, and not having sex with cheap American women under the shroud of Manhattan like some people's sons. He poured his wife a drink.

"Relax, Yanochka, drink a little bit." He winked at Lev. "It's not the worst thing in the world."

"But what will people say? To throw away Irina for this one, it's just not logical." Yana sipped her cognac. And the men waited for her to exhaust the litany, to make her peace, to agree to a meeting.

But Katia won them over, didn't she, with her simple deference to his mother, her charming dinner, her well-timed questions to his father about the diamond business. She had read that most of their diamonds were imported from South Africa, was that where all the mining was done? Lev's father was so easily softened; Lev could see him relaxing, stealing looks at Katia when he thought she wasn't looking.

After dinner, she brought all the plates to the kitchen, wiping down the counters, chatting with his mother about the Zavurov family. Every invasive question, Lev noted, was answered with tact and respect.

"A nice girl," his father whispered to Lev when Katia left, "a good, nice Bukharian girl, but don't tell your mother I said so. Tell her later, when she warms to her, when the grandchildren come."

When he walked Katia home, Lev wanted to spin his fiancée around. He wanted to whisk her away, to squeeze her, to devour her. The evenings were growing warmer, and he was struck with the urge to run with her through the night, to climb trees, to take off their clothes and leap into each other.

"They loved you," was what he said instead, kissing her softly on the lips outside her door. Her parents invited him inside, the smell of fried dough, the loud din of the television set, and the spell was broken. Katia waved good night and went inside. On the way home, Lev tried to sprint, but suddenly he felt silly running like that and he was tired after such a night.

And Lev kept putting off calling Oleg to tell him the news. He had always imagined Oleg as his best man, his brother, and now he was not so sure. Why did he say those things about Katia back in high school? What had really happened between them? But Lev decided not to linger on that thought. Instead he flashed to the eleven-year-old Captain Oleg, marching him and Ruben off to war in a single file on 108th Street. Private Lev in his turtleneck and pressed pants, his mother-made lunch in a plastic Waldbaum's bag. Left, right, left.

And then, one afternoon, drunk on the day's first sighting of Katia (really, who could deny her perfect figure, her knob of a nose, the way she ran across the street directly into his arms?), he took her to see one of his favorites, *Une Femme Est Une Femme*. Lev never expressly told Katia what movies meant to him, he felt this way would be more honest, more seductive. He would let her fall in love as he had.

He held her hand throughout the movie, his heart soaring along with Jean-Claude Brialy's. To see Anna Karina singing, in lush color, her every mischievous, coy expression, those eyelashes, my God! And Katia was no worse, she could give Anna Karina a run for her money, Lev thought proudly, pressing his fiancée's hand, watching the pinks and blues leap from the screen onto Katia's skin.

"Nu, i kak?" he asked, following her out of the theater, even if he usually preferred to sit through every single credit, sopping up the last bits of film, while everyone else stampeded around him. But when the screen went blank and the credits appeared, Katia rose with everyone else.

She smiled up at him, wrapping her shawl around her shoulders even though it was unseasonably warm; it would turn out to be a swel- tering summer. "Why did they sing the whole time? Why didn't he want her to have his baby? It seemed a little silly to me, Levchik. I'm starving. Can we have a snack?"

Dinner with their parents was not scheduled for another three hours, so he took her to a bagel place around the corner. As he ordered Katia's everything bagel with low-fat cream cheese, he turned away from her, at least until he reached across the counter for the brown bag with the bagel in it. He took a few extra minutes on the pretext of checking inside the bag for a plastic knife and napkins. He was afraid she would see disappointment in her reaction stamped across his face.

"Where are you? We can never reach you these days," Natasha Roit- man said one November afternoon when Anna answered her cell phone. "You know your cousin Katia is getting married. Have you called her?"

"I know, I will. Mazel tov," Anna said, and she meant it. The Katia problem, snagged and unresolved, had been rotating in the back of her mind. If there was a ping of remorse, her cousin's marriage absolved her. And it hadn't even occurred to her (shouldn't it have?) to wonder if her cousin would forgive her, poor little Katia, who had felt so beside the point all these months. Katia never would have made David happy—it was absurd—she cried at romantic comedies, pored through *Us* magazine at the newsstand, snuck Candace Bushnell novels from the public library.

"Where are you?" Her mother repeated. What should she say? That she was lolling naked on the futon, that David was in the shower? That she hadn't played with her son for longer than half an hour this entire week? That her new Malandrino blouse was currently wedged between two futon pillows when Nadia was probably already waiting for her at the bar at Compass?

"I'm running errands," she said. "Please tell her mazel tov for me."

Later, as Anna dressed, David toweled himself off in the main room. A scar was etched along the side of his stomach. Appendix operation, she wondered, or something else? She ran her thumb up the scar, repossessing marks that she didn't create.

"Don't forget that I'm running in the marathon next Sunday," he said, kissing her hand. And how could she forget? It would be two days before her forty-first birthday. Forty-one, she enunciated to herself. The number suddenly felt fresh and young.

"I'll wave to you," she said, reaching for her blouse. "On the corner of Fifth Avenue and Eightieth Street. Look for me."

His tongue in her mouth was hot wintergreen. "I'll look for you."

1 5

NOT HERS ANYMORE

She had forgotten that Sunday was Stasia's day off. What Stasia did on her day off, Anna had no idea. Did she visit relatives in Greenpoint, that Polish equivalent of Brighton Beach? Did she treat herself to a Broadway play? Stasia was so severe, so fastidious, the way she beat the life out of the bathroom rug.

Anna thought it was so very inconvenient of her to take this day off. The day of the New York City Marathon. Anna had planned to wear a hothouse-red dress, a dress David couldn't miss as he ran past her like some kind of Olympian god, and right there, in daylight, their eyes would connect.

But from the moment Anna got out of bed everything was wrong. A lingering crick in the neck throbbed sorely. She did not feel well-rested, and realized that Stasia would be gone all day and Seryozha wouldn't like it one bit. And then, just as she was considering whether she would have time to drop her son off in Rego Park and return in time for the marathon, Alex told her his business trip to Pittsburgh was canceled and the three of them should spend the day together.

"But it's the New York Marathon," Anna protested. The way he slathered jam on his bread was odious, she thought, leaving red, pock-marked clumps of raspberry jam.

"Then let's take Seryozha to watch them all go by. He'll love it, right, *moi dorogoi?*" Jam, jam, jam, the piece of bread was buckling under its weight. Anna could picture the red dress, still in its wrapping, spread lifeless on the bed.

No, she said, no. What about a nice museum, introduce Serge to *Tyrannosaurus rex*? Too cold to stand outside.

But Alex, once he made up his mind, was unshakable. He used to run, back in the day, or didn't she know? As a young man in Russia, he was just a few minutes short of competing professionally in the two-hundred-meter, just one torn ligament away. He loved the control, relying only on himself, not on the state or other people. He still had a runner's body, he supposed, though the muscles in his legs must have deteriorated long ago for lack of use.

He rose from the table; at least he would still spend a good half hour in the bathroom. "Clean Seryozha off and we go."

She looked down at her son, and yes, the face, so like his father's, round, floppy-eared, was dotted with the yellow of applesauce. She ran a paper towel beneath a faucet and began to wipe his face. Her son whimpered, struggling against her arm. Turning his face away.

Alex placed them on Eighty-eighth Street and Fifth Avenue, pushed his way to the front of the crowd, Seryozha kicking in the stroller. Runners were already whizzing past and Anna was surprised to be able to hear their jagged breath magnified within her. She was calmer once she saw the thick masses. She had had no idea how many people came out to watch the marathon; there were thousands, it felt like, right here on this corner.

Wasn't she foolish for even suggesting to David that he would find her in the crowd while he was running? He should have enlightened her, she thought, now annoyed. (But Alex's revelation unsettled her too; she had no idea he ran, in fact knew little about his Russian life. By not asking, was she missing something, overlooking something?)

It was a chilly fall day, fall the season of beginnings, of changes. New York in the fall was a city renewing itself, making false promises before crumpling in on itself for winter. The wheat-tinted light, the unassuming breeze. All that energy in front of her, those pumping legs. Active life.

She felt immortal, everything in place, husband, baby. She could afford to merge her worlds, to press their lips together briefly, chastely. "You know who's running today? David, Katia's David," she said.

"Not hers anymore, right?"

"Not anymore." Was it this chilly when they left the house? Earlier, she had stepped out on the balcony, had measured the chill by lingering there, her eyes closed. She had not wanted to cover herself with a jacket, so maybe she had willed it to be warm enough, had ignored the grip of cold air. She had assumed she would have the weather, too, under control.

Clumps of numbers flew by, all greeted by cheers. Anna barely had time to turn her head when a new group had already passed. She was squeezed from all sides, men trying to push their daughters or girlfriends in front for a better view. Her husband was growing annoyed, sheltering Serge from elbows and shoulders. She grew tired of the concentration it required to single out her lover from the running hordes. She decided to turn away, extricate them from the crowd, and get brunch; she and David would laugh about it later.

"Shall we go?" she suggested.

It was then she saw a familiar blur, a reddish-brown leg in the air. Its owner was obscured for a moment by a broad-shouldered college student, but then the face she knew popped into view. "David!" she broke out of the crowd before she could even brace herself, before she could understand her own actions. He turned in the direction of her voice and she saw him go down, slipping onto his side. A few of the onlookers were stretching their hands toward him, while runners were performing semicircles to avoid collision. He landed on the ground like a falling branch. The college student type paused and stretched out a hand. David waved him away.

He was hurt, it was her fault; these were the two fragments rotating in her head. She veered around the runners to the time of her galloping heart and sprinted to the form cradling his leg.

"I thought it was you," he said.

"Are you okay? My husband is here." She placed an arm around his shoulders and raised him.

"I can move it. Nothing broken." His arm remained on her shoulder, a stiff weight. "Your hand feels good."

Anna became aware of herself. They limped to the side so as not to impede the runners. "I should go back."

"Will you tell him? Darling." He rose above her, blocking her sun, a smiling shadow.

"I have to go." Tell him? It had not occurred to her. Why would she do such a thing? Her two men were serving different, crucial functions, each making sense as part of a pair.

"Tell him," David whispered, scanning faces for a man who could be Anna's husband. Now that this man had materialized, became flesh rather than theory, David felt a surge of protectiveness. He rarely lost when in the running with another man. It felt impossible to limp away while Anna returned to her comfortable life.

"Tell him, if not now, soon. We can't do this anymore. I need to be with you, write about you." He squeezed her arm. Nothing about his words felt real to Anna, it was as though they were snatched out of one of her books. But he said it—he would write about her—and it was this that filled her with rapture.

She saw Alex's face in the crowd and hoped her reaction to David's fall could be explained away. Hysteria, stress, mysterious moody symptoms whose vagueness, whose imprecision, seemed to be enough for most men as a way to explain female behavior. She would say she was ill, something triggered in her. Caffeine, her mind pressed on, sugar rush, period. David was no longer beside her.

She started chatting as soon as she and Alex were within speaking distance, spewing all sorts of nonsense at the "coincidence." Strange wasn't it, and she had gotten to know him with Katia, and he really was a very nice young man even if it didn't work out. Cheers from the family to the left drowned out her words: "Go, Nelson!" Yet she continued to move her mouth, forced it to make its shapes. Those dinner parties, those dull nights, the terrible avian art came sharply into focus.

But from Alex's horrified expression (the way he contorted his features, it was as if he had a single, unbroken eyebrow), she could tell he knew. His hands gripped the handle of the stroller, his knuckles became white rock formations. Suddenly Anna realized that it was he who had canceled his business trip, who probably never had a business trip to begin with. That uncharacteristic insistence that they all go as a family. She had always underestimated his intelligence, but what if he knew all along and was searching for its evidence? She thought of Nadia, the little ways a woman slips in conversation with another woman. Where were her allegiances?

"Anna, please tell me . . ." His eyes pleaded, helping her with her cues. They were tightly wedged between people, the stroller pressed against their legs. In the stroller, Seryozha was wide awake, blinking past her somewhere, his hands slapping at the confining seat belt.

"It's nothing," she wanted to say. "Calm down, *uspokoisia dorogoi.*" If she was convincing, if she put before him a credible monologue of fidelity, her current borders would remain intact. But a window had opened, a different vista beckoned, with tangled landscaping, a vivid, scorching sun. A Woody Allen movie. Perhaps a part of her even thought of Hopper, of Kramskoy, a woman alone, her delicious solitude. She didn't look down at her son.

"I love him," she said, before she could reel the words back in. Go, she commanded the three words: you're free now to run around in the world, to wreak your havoc.

1 6

REMEMBER THE EGGPLANTS

The first weeks of marriage were nothing like a French film. Perhaps he was naïve, but Lev was not prepared for all the inconveniences. Most simply, she was there, wasn't she, every single day. Did he recall that she talked this much? Could he have foreseen that she would cut the meat on his plate and then, wordlessly, hand over his fork? When he came home to the apartment shared with his parents, his mother knew that he didn't like to be bothered after work. She heated up the food and let him eat it alone for an hour, reading a magazine.

Now he had to account for every second of his day, who came into the pharmacy, where he went on his break, was he too cold or too warm in that jacket, and worst of all, what did he think about? He did not think about anything, he told her, half-truthfully. He let the day glide by. Closer to lunchtime, he ruminated: falafel or pastrami—and really, that was about the sum total of his thoughts for the day.

He did not know how to be with her, that's what it was. They were husband and wife, what did they have to do to make that real? The new Katia seemed strange to him, so eagerly trying to emulate others, to fit herself into a role. She went with her mother to Dima's every other day, stopping by the pharmacy with a snack, a crumbly bizet or a challah. She began getting weekly manicures and insisted she needed a fur coat if she was to show her face on 108th Street. She dressed in bright colors, fuchsias and lemon yellows. His first postmarital credit card bill terrified Lev. Even her tone of voice was unnerving, it developed a new edge, a new flourish, as if she were acting in a play for a large, restless audience.

"Lev, my dear, please remember the eggplants on your way home."

Who are you? he wanted to know.

Rifling through drawers for her lint brush, he found the notes. Tied together by one of her silk hair ribbons—a pastiche of paper. *I miss you already* on a Post-it, Sharpie-thick lines. A ripped shred out of a notebook, sheaves of heavy stationery Lev could not bring himself to open. He was touched by the girlish accumulation of these mementos; strangely enough, he wasn't jealous, but felt protective of his bride. He himself would have hated to pour himself into objects, only to have them stripped of all meaning. He put the packet back where he found it, heartened by her romantic, tragic past.

Lev wondered if Katia knew he had seen the notes, if he had angled them the wrong way back into the drawer, disturbed their shroud of gloves. He could discern nothing specific, but possibly a tonal shift, a spontaneous kiss during a commercial. Silver Hondas gyrated on the screen and Katia was warm on his mouth. And the following day, the notes were gone, and he never saw them again.

Their first fight, the predictable: Why didn't you call me? On the way home from work, Lev ran into an old friend from their high school *tusovka,* back in the neighborhood to visit his parents. Maksim was living in Manhattan, dating American women; he wore the kind of shirt that required cuff links. A polite exchange of facts—Maksim's banking job, a disdain for long-term commitment, a recent vacation to Tanzania—had filled Lev with a melancholy he couldn't explain. He offered Lev his card, on which the name *Max* was printed in a stern blue-black font. Lev asked him if he wanted to get a beer, did he remember old Flanagan's, still serving cheap swill after all these years. But Maksim seemed uncomfortable to Lev, the way secular Jews were around Orthodox Jews. That first instinct—is this person better than I am?—was instantly buried in contempt.

"I suppose you married," Maksim said.

"To Katia Zavurov," Lev admitted, for the first time not taking pride in the fact. He hated what he saw in Maksim's eyes, as if his own route had been predictable and unadventurous. For a moment, Katia didn't feel like a prize. Maksim and his Manhattan life were taunting him. Lev was the first to break away, to wave good-bye and hurry down the street.

Katia opened the door before Lev could fit his key in the lock. "Why didn't you call me if you were going to be late?"

"I ran into an old friend, Maksim Bulatov. You know him, don't you?" He was aware that he had seen this very exchange on some canned-laughter sitcom, in some boring movie.

"It's not like I'm calling his mother," Katia said defensively, look-ing pitiful in her apron stained with sauces, her fingernails black with crushed peppercorn. "I just hope you're telling the truth."

Lev apologized again, but weakly, unenthusiastically. It was the truth, he *had* run into an old friend. *You apologize first and think later, and that's the secret to peace in a marriage,* his father used to tell him. He imagined Maksim on his way back to Manhattan, he imagined the relief of an empty apartment, the crisp crackling of a radiator, and no other sound. But Lev stuffed away these thoughts, crammed them with other undigested ones into the same internal closet.

He and his bride had not had sex yet. A fact he did not know how to surmount. The wedding night, she was already asleep when he crawled into bed; each night thereafter he felt awkward reaching for her. She carved herself an indentation on her side of the bed, an invis-ible border he was too fearful to cross. Just pull the sheet aside, he prompted himself night after night, embrace her. But there was a kind of pleasure to the not-touching, the delaying of the change between them. It was like the opening credits to a movie, the anticipation of dispersing himself inside the mind and body of another.

Meanwhile, a dinner awaited him, with Katia cutting up his food before he could take the first bite. A steak, surrounded by a fortress of *plov*, would lie severed on his plate.

Lev missed Oleg. The last time he saw Oleg was at his own wedding (he and Ruben had kept to their own families; when Lev glanced down at the men carrying his chair, he saw that none of them was Oleg). He missed their get-togethers at overly heated bars, the easy way conversations bent and swayed among the three of them. The talk about one particular girl would lead to a band, then to another girl, another band. Plans, always hazy and to be resolved at some future date. They knew each other so well, the places they could and couldn't go. They did not speak about Oleg's sister, that was well known, ever since she'd eloped with a Haitian law student. They did not discuss Ruben's sexual problems, even if he tossed them out one night, the way he could only climax alone, often fantasizing about the actress who played the rich girl on *The Facts of Life*. Instinctively, they all knew the sensitive areas not to broach, that it was their job to wait and listen, until the guy brought it up again.

The three of them singing in the streets, daring some babushka to stick her head out of her window and berate them; then they would serenade her with some schmaltzy Russian song about death or the passage of time. *"Zhizn' ne vozmozhno povernut' nazad"* was one favorite.

For twenty-three years they had done such things together. "Go to hell," Oleg would say if someone dared call them commies or dirty Arabs. Lev thought they would have made up by now, but there had been no concrete rupture. Was Oleg worried that he would raise the topic of Katia and the past? But they were kids back then, it had been nobody's fault. Lev mourned the only way he knew how, at the movies.

1 7

———————————————

IT'LL BE QUICKEST

The first sensation after blurting
it all out to Alex had been bliss. She was free to claim the fork not
taken in the road, she could finally turn left this time. To feel the consequences of her words, she wandered around the Upper East Side,
bidding silent good-byes to her personal landmarks. To her favorite
restaurants, Donguri and Etats-Unis, to her D'agostino's, the small
liquor store that supplied her with Veuve Clicquot, the crammed café
where she and David had once used Nabokov as a pretext, the familiar faces out on a Sunday with their strollers, their papers, and their
spouses. The satisfying sound of leaves crunching underfoot. When
she realized she was shivering in her red dress, she called David.

"I told him," she said when he answered his cell phone, wondering
at her own calm voice. If she had opened the conversation with hello,
she did not remember.

Didn't he hesitate, even for a few seconds, before he warmly told
her to come right over? Wasn't there a lull in the conversation, a
short pause that felt eternal? All their thoughts, their decisions, were
crammed into those few seconds of silence. And it had not occurred to
Anna that she would have to return, to undo all those good-byes.

"Take a cab," he had said finally. "It'll be quickest." How thoughtful she had found him then, to rush her to him as soon as possible. She came to him exactly as she was, one complete outfit, a purse filled with the most unnecessary things—hand moisturizer, tissues, one gold earring, the other having been lost for days. Just her and her one pair of underwear, that one red dress, low-heeled boots. She knocked at his door, but strangely, it didn't feel like she had imagined it would. The beige paint on the door was peeling, the buzzer disemboweled, metal wires poking out of the wall.

He swung open the door and embraced her. She noticed his unsteady gait, his weight balanced on one leg.

"You really did it, didn't you?" he said.

They held each other, silent, and she felt his beating heart pressing against her own breast. She couldn't get her hands warm, she dug them underneath his sweater, in the folds of his armpits. Their lovemaking was tender and muted, their pleasure hushed. On his body, she searched for safe places.

After they sent out for noodles and Cokes, Anna could not get her mind off his first reaction. *Take a cab*, he had said. Couldn't he have been on autopilot, dazed, suggesting the fastest route of transportation? *It'll be quickest.* Those may have been the first words to pop into his brain. So many explanations and none of them satisfactory to Anna.

They ate the noodles directly out of the containers; the restaurant sent just one Coke by mistake and they took turns swigging from it. She began to feel easier, her former life already years away. There was only the image of Seryozha, blinking furiously in the stroller, that shaved away a sliver of happiness.

Anna changed into a pair of his sweatpants and one of his sweatshirts, and pulled her hair into a ponytail. She knew how she looked filling out his clothes, sexy, verdant, no older than twenty-eight.

"Now you'll have to write about me."

David nodded at his desk, passing the bottle of Coke back to Anna. "Who's to say I haven't already started?"

That night, she couldn't get to sleep, her body felt as though covered by a film of sweat. "Do you love me?" she thought she had asked, if not on the phone after announcing she was leaving her husband, then sometime later, possibly while her fingers gently scraped up and down his arms or legs or belly button.

"Yes," she thought he had answered, but she couldn't be sure. This late at night, she couldn't be sure.

Should she have lied to Alex? Should she have put it a different way? Simply: she had given up when David came along. Didn't, no, shouldn't all lives have that *him*? But as soon as she told Alex, her whole body shivered. She didn't know Alex had been a runner; didn't she owe it to him to find out when he started, what drew him to the sport, what he thought about when he did it? How did he cope when he found out that he would never run professionally?

In bed with David their first night together, thoughts like these jousted in her mind. It would have been useless to engage Alex about his running past. So he ran, she thought, many people ran, didn't they? Cheaper than joining a gym, less of a commitment. And he had grown repulsive to her, hadn't he? The way he signaled his desire for sex—a glass of *eau de vie* followed by a single raised eyebrow. His second-hand opinions, his certainty about everything—many people in their fifties still probed for answers, still felt there was much left to learn. His crime: Not knowing her, not acknowledging that her curiosities took off where his ended, that she would always harbor a fondness for red-sauce restaurants with checkered tablecloths, prefer Oreos to Payard, and bite off the top of a piece of beef jerky without removing the plastic wrapping. Not understanding that Anna rejected the facts before her in favor of characters and situations and myths operating more vibrantly inside her own mind. That she lived most fully not in life, but on the page.

1 8

―――――――――――――

YOUR WIFE AND YOUR FRIENDS

L ev came home from the pharmacy to find Katia stripping their bedroom closet of wallpaper, her hair pulled back by a handkerchief. She was on her knees, scraping and gluing, a small lamp illuminating her work.

"Dinner's going to be late tonight. I just can't get all this done. This old wallpaper's not coming off!"

Katia's face was splotchy, her neck was covered with scratch marks. Tendrils of wallpaper were scattered around her. Lev could barely stand the sight.

"Why don't you get a job? Something you like? You're so great with people, Katia, maybe part-time." He crouched down beside her, the two of them in the closet, pink roses glaring at them from different angles. He had been thinking about this a lot lately.

Encouraging your wife to get a job right after marriage, he could hear the Bukhi chortle, *what would be the point? She is only going to get pregnant.* But for Lev, this was the only solution he could think of for Katia's aimless peregrinations in their little apartment, within the neighborhood. She had no goal, no reason to be where she was going. The restless energy, all that chatter, worried him. It was dangerous somehow.

Just the other day, she bought a poppy cake for guests, then went out and bought another one, claiming to have forgotten the first one. When he pointed out that they now owned two poppy cakes, crammed side by side in the back of the refrigerator, she had burst into tears.

"You don't love me," she had cried. He consoled her, of course he did, but how many times would he be called upon to cradle his bawling wife, to reassure her of his love? And what did that have to do with a pair of poppy cakes?

Katia put down her brush. "A job? I don't even have a résumé," she said.

"I'll help you."

"My spelling is terrible. I barely finished college."

"There are many jobs where you won't need spelling." He freed a few strands of hair from the handkerchief around her head, wound the ends around his thumb.

As she readjusted herself to a sitting position, Katia's foot knocked the lamp cord out of the socket, engulfing them in darkness. Neither bothered to turn the switch.

And so, in that dark closet, only able to make out the other's glittering eyes, they reached out for each other. Katia's tentative touch, so light he could barely sense it on his skin. His wife.

"It's just us here in this closet," he whispered, a little self-consciously stating the obvious. He pulled Katia gingerly onto the floor, stroking the length of her arm. She made a sound—something less than a moan, more than an exhale—and shut her eyes, as though she were responsible for none of what was about to happen.

And so they finally had their wedding night. Pointy shoes bore into their backs, the scent of mothballs, soured perfume. Katia's arms gripping his waist, a trail of throbbing fingerprints, and eventually, a relieved, complicit laughter.

Sex, sex, sex was even better than she expected. Why did anyone do anything else? All Katia wanted to do was feed it, accessorize and dec-

orate it, talk and think about it. They did it again the following morning, slightly differently this time. Katia found her legs could stretch to
the skies, her back sloped, fingers tingled. Silly songs replayed themselves in her head, her back teeth scraped together. She was thirsty,
craved an imprecise juice—a mix of watermelon and peach? Or was
it mango?

Lev left for work, a shy kiss on the tip of her shoulder, and Katia,
still in her robe, cracked an egg in a sizzling pan and consumed it as
soon as it hit the plate, with a sprinkle of salt and a wedge of pumpernickel bread, washing it down with cold tea. Still hungry, Katia cracked
a second, scrambled it and ate it pensively, slowly.

They spent the next two weeks of nights and weekends in bed,
barely picking up the phone. She still insisted on drawn shades, on
rooms draped in shadow, but she was growing bolder, taking his hand
and placing it on her body. He was getting to know the sounds she
made, the exact texture of her hair (coarser, more brittle than he
thought it would be). He didn't want to press the extent of his desires,
he remembered Oleg's new wife calling the rabbi on her honeymoon.
He worried that he smelled of medicine, of chemicals.

No, she said, her nose pressed against his neck, immediately below
the ear, *more like those peppermint candies they give out at the doctor's
office. Just kidding.*

They were submerged in one another, they did not speak, they
groped, familiarized themselves, they established dominion over their
senses.

The first phone call Lev allowed himself to really answer came from
Ruben. With his parents he mumbled that he was busy, and his father
understood, calling him at work instead. Now he was ready for the
outside world. Katia was in the shower; he could hear her humming
some song over the spray of the water.

"Um," Ruben kept repeating, as if he had practiced this phone call
but forgotten his lines; he never had handled disagreements well. Lev
could imagine his friend, having taken the phone into the bedroom,

stuttering into the wall as he spoke. Conflicts confused Ruben, his instinct had always been to patch, to caulk.

Lev said of course he would come out. There was some Russian art rock band, Auktyon, playing at a theater in Manhattan. Did he remember them? The spastic singer with his tambourine, their energy, the young Russian girls who came out to their concerts—voluptuous, blond-haired girls, their breasts heaving to the music? Ruben's brother's co-worker had free tickets—that is, if he was interested.

"I am," he found himself saying eagerly. He would pay for dinner, whatever. Just to be together with his friends again, see where the night ended up. And hanging up, Lev realized this was his first real moment of contentment since his marriage; the confluence of two good events, how one made the pleasure of the other even more acute. He told Katia about his plans when she emerged from the shower, and was surprised at how disappointed she was at the news. He supposed an idyll of sorts had been broken, but he was happy, happy at the normalcy, the balance of it all.

Don't go without me, Katia wanted to say, a sudden, irrational fear gripping her. As if his leaving would erase the last few weeks. She never asked herself why her husband had been friends with someone like Oleg, who was so slithering, odious. His friendship was not to be discussed, she sensed that from the beginning. It was a fact to accept, her job to forget about his role in her past.

And she thought (not without pain, even after all these months) of her former love for Anna. Do we really know what our friends are capable of, the real motives behind their daily kindnesses, the people they manipulate to serve their own happiness?

And seeing Lev like this, a bit distracted, affectionate, eager to leave the apartment, Katia gulped down her protests. Something within her told her to keep quiet. The first wifely instinct? *Let him go*, it said.

Your wife and your friends, two separate entities, wasn't that what Oleg told him right after his marriage? With whom are you most yourself? Lev wanted to know. If he had actually asked this question, Oleg might have told him, with your friends—the things you tell your friends originate in your belly; the things you tell your wife, from the recesses of your throat. No, Lev didn't want to agree.

But not long after his own marriage, Lev realized he would not have a wife who went to French movies with him. Not in the way he watched them, besotted, uncritical. Everything in the frame, the tiny cups of espresso, the old, winding streets, the high boots, morose, open-ended dialogue, fascinated him. That it could be played continuously with not a single alteration, while in real life the details always changed, each moment never to be re-created. Flashes of death and jolts of life united in a single medium, strung together by a lovely, lilting tongue.

And yet, he had no desire to go to France, to trudge through the cinematic backdrop himself, mangling the French language, chomping on macaroons from touristy bakeries. He understood that the movies would always be his and his alone. The icy reserve of Catherine Deneuve, the devastating curves of Simone Signoret, all his. And then he came home to Katia. Before he left for the concert, they found themselves on the carpet, his Katia giggling, pointing out that it was just a few more feet to the bed. When he thought of it this way, what man had his good fortune?

That's what Lev thought as he danced at the bar lining the back wall of Joe's Pub. Listening to the familiar songs of Auktyon, all these Russian kids around them (because they were kids, really, clearly in their teens and early twenties and unattached and Russian, with no religion to tether them, only culture and language and money), Lev felt lucky to be Bukharian. Still, there was something in it, this shared language, originating from the same basic slab of land. He felt a warmth for everyone here.

And now, if he called Katia and told her when he would be home, he could follow Oleg into the night. Would they wind up at that Hungarian dance club on Canal or just get a late dinner at Florent? He looked over at Oleg, who was sipping his mojito, not watching the band or dancing. Ruben was leaning over a tiny brunette, screaming over the music. If only things could remain just like this, Lev thought, buying them all another round.

1 9

MOURNING

Katia's yearly pilgrimage to Fifth Avenue during Christmastime was becoming more unwieldy every year. It felt like there were more tourists on the streets and they were in a shopping frenzy. Waves of bodies bobbed before gold tinsel displays.

From her childhood, Katia recalled Fifth Avenue holiday strolls as magical—the opulent store windows, the men in uniform blocking entrances to boutiques that seemed to have just two or three items, a sole slouchy handbag, one skirt. She and her parents would end their afternoon before the tree that stretched into the clouds.

Now, on this particularly cold Tuesday, it felt overwhelming, even menacing, to thrust oneself in the middle of all these photographing bodies. Still, she promised herself one stroll up and down, a little something for Lev for Hanukkah, and then she would summon all her courage and enter the offices of Outstretched Arms for her job interview.

Did there used to be all that loud music? she wondered as she passed the thumping Abercrombie and Fitch store and turned away from Fifth Avenue, away from Bergdorf's (out of the question for a wedding dress, of course; she'd found hers at Kleinfeld's and ordered a cheaper replica at Masha's on Kings Highway like everyone else). Fighting through these throngs—a gaping couple rammed into her head-on—Katia decided it wasn't worth it; she would find something for Lev in one of the malls on Queens Boulevard. At least there she could control her surroundings; she knew the location of all the stores.

Manhattan, once so desirable, was out of reach and she found she no longer yearned for the myth. Rego Park was fine with her, with its Russian stores and Bukharian restaurants, the trailing scent of spiced lamb on a skewer, ambling *babushki*, arm in arm, heads bowed together— at least it was human, heartfelt.

She was about to turn toward the subway when she saw them coming out of Hermès. How could Katia miss her, that red, laughing mouth, the shearling coat that never would have looked as good on herself? Her arm was wrapped around his waist, her curls sprinkled on his shoulder. He was pointing at something, but she pulled him to her. It felt to Katia that all eyes rested on them, mesmerized by one another, those thoughtless kisses.

Katia attached herself to a high school group on a field trip. The freshly scrubbed, ponytailed girls wore shiny lime windbreakers and seemed to be singing a school chant about cougars. Katia did not turn around; one glance back at the couple would have sliced through her. Her head throbbed as she darted across Fifth Avenue. She could have sworn that, while pretending otherwise, Anna actually saw her.

He used to write in pencil, Katia remembered that. Did anyone write with sharpened No. 2 pencils anymore? He did, in quad-lined French notebooks, organized by a color-coded system: "Movies," "Books," "Ideas," et cetera. When he saw a movie, he dutifully wrote down the name, director, and a sentence or two of reaction. Strange, Katia had thought, she was happy to let movies, art, and dance penetrate her and then waft out, leaving only the faintest trace. She would depart the theater savoring its flavor and then it would be gone, her palate ready for a new sensation. Not for David—who took it all so seriously, with his lists, his case of sharpened pencils.

He also took out the notebooks whenever an idea burst into his mind. One afternoon, while they were walking together on the Queens College campus, she told him a story from her childhood; he loved her immigrant stories, he said he was charmed by their sweet shabbiness.

It was not a crucial story, the one about a stuffed green foot she had won at a small amusement park. The park (who were we kidding, it consisted of three rides, a smattering of booths) was erected every summer inside an abandoned lot on Sixty-third Road. It was the first time she had ever been to an amusement park, and her parents so poor still, so recently American. How guilty she felt at spending their money on silly games, spraying water into a clown's mouth or banging on the heads of beavers with a mallet. But she had been seduced by the spoils of the other kids, clutching with two hands spotted giraffes bigger than their own bodies.

Katia wasn't sure how many quarters it had taken to be eligible for a real prize (as opposed to those fake, unsatisfying prizes like a barrette, a plastic worm, or an eraser in the shape of a soccer ball). Enough quarters for guilt to settle into her joints. At the prize booth the bored teenager took her tickets and counted them. How many they seemed, surely enough for a pastel elephant or one of those shaggy cows. But the guy slapped a flat, forest-green foot on the counter. A foot? Even its five uncuddly toes lacked a cushiness, a tactile sensuality. Katia had tried to hug it, but it had been a challenge, the heel was the only part of the foot with any stuffing.

In the end, she had promised herself to justify this foot, to lavish it with affection, even though (it was a *foot,* for God's sake) it wasn't inherently lovable. When she made her bed in the mornings before going to school, she would tuck the foot under the covers, settle it in, all cozy, on top of her pillow. She named it Moo.

Moo got lost in their first move to a larger apartment, and Katia was inconsolable. Did her mother throw it out to make room for their toaster or other newly afforded appliances? It seemed Katia had grown to love the foot after all, despite herself.

David suddenly stopped, opened his knapsack, took out his notebook and pencil, and jotted something down. He used his knee as a surface.

"What did you write?" she asked.

He kissed her on the spot below her earlobe, making a big show of inhaling her perfume. "Never mind."

She wondered if Anna had access to those notebooks, if she came across an entry that said, *silly foot story for future novel*. Did she know that it was *her* silly foot? Did she know that Katia had left a foot, no matter how insignificant, behind? Leaving behind a foot—a hollow victory.

But she was a wife, Katia reminded herself, these thoughts don't belong to a wife. Especially to a (probably) pregnant wife whose future was finally on the right track. Instead, she prepared for her first job interview with index cards Lev had made up for her (look your interviewer in the eye, firm handshake, express enthusiasm, et cetera) until she was called into the Outstretched Arms offices. I am very good with people, she would tell a hairy-armed Russian woman, and be hired on the spot.

2 0

────────────────────────

SO MANY WAYS TO BE IN
LOVE IN NEW YORK

Anna K. did not fit easily into
her new neighborhood. A neighborhood where the remains of old
Jewish tailor shops were rubbed off the facades of buildings. Where
couples wolfed down burritos on street corners before disappearing
into underground nightclubs. Where synagogues had been turned into
performance spaces or restaurants, anything but synagogues. Spare
boutiques were splattered with brown vintage clothing. Relics of early
twentieth-century immigration—yellowing lace tablecloths, rusty sam-
ovars, mismatched silver—calcified in the window of the Tenement
Museum. A woman in an unironic (even if discounted) Givenchy lace
dress and a fur coat was not warmly received below Delancey Street.

David's studio apartment was above a bakery, its braided challahs
gleaming in the window. She had expected warmth from the owners;
she was frequenting a dying operation, wasn't she? She could have opted
to munch on fashionable cupcakes, but instead she came here straining
to understand a single word of Yiddish. But the owners had decided
they didn't care for her, she was too flashy, they said in Yiddish as she
stood right in front of them, a challah and open wallet in hand. Their
own children couldn't afford this neighborhood anymore. How was it
that all the rules of immigration were being upended in New York real

estate—the children were supposed to have more, but here they were, elbowing in on the Lower East Side, albeit in shearling coats.

Anna would have to buy a new wardrobe in keeping with her new life; she would return to jeans, to discreet cashmere sweaters, but money in her account was thinning out. She bought David a Hermès wallet for the holidays before it occurred to her that she would soon be paying her own credit cards again.

But she had rarely cared about money. David's skin smelled of pastry, like the fresh *rugelach* her grandmother used to bake. The amazement of coming home to each other, of sitting down to meals, of peeling the bedcovers and sliding inside together. They pulled the blankets over their heads, giggled over nonsense. David's nose was cold pressed against her cheek, his hands burned.

At first, she and David had to come to terms with the new temporality of their relationship as if they had to adjust to the real world after months in Narnia time. Instead of compressing their kisses into hours, they suddenly felt the vastness of days, weeks, and months, of no interruption to their togetherness. The sharp aftertaste of pleasure was being replaced by a slow, whirring hum. They began to fill up those extra hours. She would watch him write, pretending to read her own book, but when he found her standing behind him, he would lower the computer screen, take her in his arms, and waltz with her.

They spent money on each other—on theater, impulsive gifts, lingerie, fresh flowers every week. Then one day at Sephora, David turned a perfume bottle upside down and noted its price. "I can't take care of you like your husband did," he said, and the gifts became rarer, the restaurants cheaper, the kisses deeper.

"I don't care," Anna said, clinging to his arm, her head on his shoulder.

He was an adjunct professor and she was forced to come to terms with the definition of "adjunct." That he would probably never have job security at Queens College, his time would be fractured, at the mercy of measly City College budgets. That he would wait every spring for his contract to be renewed. It had been so long since Anna had thought to worry about such things.

One night, as they were strolling home from slurping *pho* at a Vietnamese place, he told her that he was considering going on the academic job market. Anna was thrilled. Surely that meant a promotion, a full-time salary? Yes, he said cautiously, but the most likely job would be in a place like Bowling Green, Ohio, or worse, much worse. But what else could he do with his life? he added quickly. Work for a corporation, like Anna had, engage in chitchat with dim-witted coworkers, planning a six-day vacation years in advance?

"I'm sick of wanting, of thinking about money. I want the freedom to write *and* to pay the rent. All around me, so many have so much."

She had never heard him like this, spittle forming between his lips, running his fingers through his hair, fastening on a clump, then letting go.

"But you'll write a great novel about me, you'll get a job right here." Anna stopped on a narrow street in Nolita; groups of smokers, their heads wrapped in scarves, were watching them. She turned to face him.

"You're going to leave me, aren't you?" Why was it that when winter came, all memories of warm weather were obliterated? Anna thought. It was as if there was always only winter, only dullness and sharp winds. Only desolation.

"Don't worry, my darling," he said, letting go of his own hair, folding her inside his jacket where it was warm. "I won't go on the market. Not yet. One more year won't kill me." Besides, he continued, summer is coming, so many free things to do in New York in the summer—opera in the park, concerts on the Hudson, the pickle festival in the Lower East Side, those ubiquitous outdoor flea markets with their grilled corn on the cob and Peruvian woven rugs—so many ways to be in love in New York.

But an old, familiar feeling began to seep into Anna's blood, a recalled agony. She did not think she would be able to tolerate another departure, not now, not after everything. When they got back to David's tiny one-bedroom, Anna stopped him at the door and began unbuckling his belt.

"What are you doing?" he asked, laughing, running his fingers through her curls. They had left the television on, and Anna saw a cold, flickering light, David Letterman sneering in the background. Anna didn't say a word; she popped button after button until David started to moan, short moans, low. Her son materialized for a moment and she pushed him out of her mind. The shirt came off, the undershirt. Please be Heathcliff, she thought, you have to be Heathcliff.

Deep into the night, she watched David sleep. His back was turned to her, his spine curved inward. She thought of how he enjoyed making flamboyant declarations ("Let's walk around the entire city, counterclockwise"), which he would enter into and abandon halfway through (they made it as far as Murray Hill, found a sushi place for dinner, and took the subway back home). His bursts of enthusiasm, infectious, eventually waned.

In the night, Anna's mind performed calisthenics. If he doesn't love me, what then? What can I expect? Her ear was sensitive to scratching noises in the apartment, to the sounds of breaking glass on the street, to slamming car doors, to David's muttering. Then, just as the room filled with the first slashes of morning light, she fell asleep. *You selfish, ungrateful bitch,* her mother spat at her in her dreams, *we didn't bring you here so you could leave your husband and child for some kid. You're no better than the rest of those post-Soviet sluts.* Post-Soviet sluts? As though her mother would ever say those words.

And Anna awoke, so certain she was still on the Upper East Side with Sasha snoring next to her, Seryozha whimpering in the next room. But in this alien, barely furnished room, there was only the noise of traffic, of young people screaming, the screech of tires. David, it seemed, did not snore.

David, Alex, Alex, David. The comparison of minutiae. The way one man showered, washing his hair first, then the rest of him—fast, bold strokes of soap. The other lingered under the spray, attended to one appendage at a time, immobile beneath the spurt of water, eyelashes dripping, sealed.

. . .

"Why do you deserve a divorce?" Alex asked her coldly. Anna realized she was squeezing the phone receiver so hard, her hand muscles were white with pain. What did he mean? She knew she deserved very little, but certainly one of those few things would include a divorce.

"You're not a mother," he said, pushing in the sword even deeper. "There's nothing in you, air."

"So why not divorce me?"

"You don't deserve a divorce," he said.

"And Seryozha—" But Alex had already hung up.

He refused to see her, but until she hired a lawyer, he would communicate with her through Nadia, who was all too happy in her new role as mediator. They were to meet in the Bloomie's café, a neutral place where Nadia would tell her Alex's demands, would listen to hers. Nothing else to do but trust her; she gripped Anna's life in her hands.

In Bloomingdale's, Anna bypassed shoes, barely allowing herself to linger in the summer collection. Perfume salespeople sadistically coated her in floral scent. The store was brightly lit, as if those aggressive yellows would wipe out the memory of the dreary afternoon beyond its walls. In no hurry, Anna ambled. She had registered here for the wedding, not for the sake of Russians, of course, who always brought money, but for the smattering of Americans, always asking, *Where are you registered?* A strange, futuristic question. Eventually, she would find Nadia's bouffant not in the café, but in the handbag department.

"Only fourteen hundred dollars," Nadia said by way of greeting, holding up a slouchy purse. "What do you think?"

And somehow this was worse than any outraged speeches about propriety and family values. It seemed that no one cared she had had an affair; her biggest crime was acting on it. And Nadia was certain that Anna had made a fatal error, that if she had only stuck with Alex, with her original choices, money would have conquered her unhappiness in the end. Fuck Heathcliff, Nadia implied. If he existed today, he would hardly be an appealing prospect.

Nadia twisted her purchase this way and that for Anna's admiration. The buckle was wide and silver, glinting in the department store glaze. The leather, a deep magenta, looked soft. Anna did not remind her that Nadia already had a bag exactly like it. And Nadia probably knew this already and was saying to Anna, *I can buy two of the same bag. And you?*

They sat down at a table, ordered their cups of coffee. Nadia was wearing a lovely bouclé suit, a string of pearls. A fresh manicure. Anna kept her own hands clasped on her lap. They discussed Nadia's two children, her husband. His business in Russia was trickling off a bit. Putin was closing doors to foreign investors and so it seemed they, too, Muscovites born and bred, were foreigners now. Can't play both sides of the game like they used to; the fringes of the Iron Curtain were already visible.

They talked about Alex, how he had been less garrulous lately, less social, spending more time at home. He was becoming an art collector of sorts. From time to time, he consulted with the head of the Russian department at Sotheby's. It was as if a new Alex were emerging, more in his head, if that was a way of putting it.

"And my son," Anna finally allowed herself. "Seryozha, how is he?" She could still smell him, from time to time, her fingers still reached for his head, soft and downy, like peach skin. When her stomach clenched at the thought of him, she focused on his tempers, on her own inability to handle them. She knew, by their silences, that her parents timidly visited her son.

"This love of yours, I wonder," Nadia said, her head cocked to one side. "Is it really worth it?"

Anna pushed Seryozha away. Her coffee was already cold, and she had hardly touched it. "Nadyenka, we only live once."

"Yes, I see, but your son, and money, these are the things that last. I mean, I'm not talking about an affair here and there, which of us hasn't done that? But to be so foolish as to only think about today. Don't you ask yourself what will happen tomorrow?"

But she had begun looking through the classifieds on the Internet and didn't know where to begin. The last job she'd found the old-fashioned way, an advertisement printed, in consoling black and white, in *The New York Times*. These days, it seemed to her, job-hunting had become more anonymous, less effort leading to fewer results. Would she do copywriting? Marketing? She could market things. Passion, these marketing companies were looking for, experience. Didn't she embody both of those things?

People obviously waiting for their table began volubly complaining about the two Russian women and their interminable cups of coffee. This love, she decided, it *was* worth it. If it wasn't, nothing was, and that was a depressing thought. Why had she spent her entire child-hood and adolescence reading? All those journeys with their preor-dained conclusions, surely they led to something. She wanted to run out of this store, to find herself liberated on Lexington Avenue, but Nadia was at the counter again, ordering herself a coffeecake.

"Are you sure it's fresh?" Anna heard her asking.

His mother lived alone in Edison, a town in central New Jersey. This was one of the few things Anna knew about David's mother. Other things she knew: divorced now for fifteen years, his mother lived in an elementary school recently converted into individual apartments; her name was Lynn; she grew up in Brooklyn, where she met David's father, and together they escaped to New Jersey.

Once a month, David would slink off to Penn Station with a back-pack stuffed with dirty clothes and return a day later with clean, folded clothes and a tuna casserole. It was easier that way, he said, to keep certain parts of his life to himself.

"When will I meet your mother?" Anna would ask anyway. She often pictured herself on a train with David, heading together in a single direction.

"Soon, soon."

She let it go; mothers seemed unnecessary in their routine. The fact that his mother gave birth and raised David was irrelevant to Anna. If Anna gave up her life to be with him, she wasn't so curious about his own. She resisted David's childhood reminiscences about the Jersey

shore, crammed with oily pubescent bodies, or his fondness for Teddy
Grahams and the then-beleaguered New Jersey Nets. Her mind shut
down when he launched into the details of his parents' divorce, his
track team races, his high school girlfriend, whom he affectionately
mused was from "the wrong side of the tracks" but whose description
made her out to be a rather dull-witted bottle blonde with an affection
for Mötley Crüe and acid-washed jeans.

No, she didn't want to know about the blonde or the ones who came
after her. (Katia!) After all, they had all been smooth-faced, wrinkle-
less things, optimistic probably, jarringly self-confident. She watched
him; sometimes his attention would be drawn to a group of loud young
women, sexy in all the obvious ways.

"Do you think they're pretty?" she would ask. She turned to look at
the girls, the flash of their flat, creamy stomachs.

"No," he would answer, the slightest of pauses. "It's what I used to
like." He would draw her closer, inhale her scent. "Before my tastes
became more sophisticated."

She demanded he read out loud to her at night, she balancing her
chin on his breastbone. They read Balzac and Chekhov, and a lot of
others besides: Stoppard, Bulgakov, Woolf. If a visitor stumbled upon
them in bed, he would be hard-pressed to discern whose limb belonged
to whom, legs wrapped around waists, hooked onto knees.

Or they would meet up with some of David's Columbia buddies
who were still at the phase in their lives where they did not consider
their jobs real. Anna remembered that period well, the dissonance
between what you did and what you thought you did. The fact of simply existing in New York camouflaging one's lassitude or indecision,
the fear of one's own ambition, a maniacal reshuffling of schedule so
as to not think, not to make any real decisions. Anna's Russianness
was, once again, exotic, her separation from her husband even more
so. She was exactly the kind of shattered woman a real New York man
ought to surround himself with.

"First Ashton and now David," she overheard one of his friends say
to another. She nursed her martini, pretending she hadn't heard.

"Exactly what we expect from our David," the other said, approving.

Anna was free to play her role. She found that the less she said the better; she would be tended to like royalty from her barstool. Drinks would be carried to her, men would engage her on witty, ephemeral topics. Her comfort was inquired about, her outfits complimented. She was seen as a tragic heroine.

Returning home from one of those nights, wine-addled, jittery, they played a message on the machine from David's father, a history professor at the University of Chicago. From pictures, Anna had perceived a clean-shaven, portly man with a jutting chin. When he played a message from Myron Zuckerman, David would get agitated and snap at her over little things. Could they really afford a new duvet cover? Why did she have such expensive tastes? And the message didn't seem ominous to Anna, the senior Zuckerman's voice drawling, a thick Brooklyn accent in it still.

Let's just enjoy the buzz, she would say, pulling him away from the machine, tearing him out of his own head, let's see who can get their clothes off first. Sometimes David would need coaxing to turn his attention back to her.

"What kind of history does your father teach?" she asked.

"It doesn't matter," he said, unbuttoning the front of her dress. Then into her neck, "I love you, Anna." Even if she sensed that those words pushed other things away, she basked in them, her body opening up to receive them.

2 1

———————

ALAIN DELON. TULIPS. BABY.

His wife was growing by the day. Lev would come home from the pharmacy and another of her features was lost or changed—the plumpness of her chin exaggerated, fingers too swollen for her wedding ring. He knew he should have welcomed all these alterations—it meant his child was being nurtured in there—but he found himself short-tempered. Sex was still hungry, if sporadic.

She had continued to work at Outstretched Arms throughout her pregnancy. She had even studied some immigration law to prepare for her position. What did she do exactly? He wasn't sure, but she said she now had an entire caseload of clients, recent immigrants who would badger her every day: get their nephew out of there, get little Maya out before it was too late. Poisoning one president in plain sight, what would be next, they would say. And even that dictator, no better than the others. And Karimov rigging the office to extend his bastardized "presidency," random arrests, torture. Never any money left for the people, ach, they were all crooks. At least in America the crooks operated quietly, politely, they had the good manners to conceal their crimes.

His Vasilisa, whose features he had memorized over the years, was already, so soon, leaving him. The baby and the clients, that seemed to be all her head was full of these days. "Are you here or in Tashkent?" he would snap at her sometimes. He wasn't proud of acting like this, but he missed Vasilisa. Marriage. Was it this difficult for everybody?

He would be telling her about his day at work or a movie he had seen at the new IFC Center while she was at her parents'. *You see, Katia, Alain Delon is dispatched to Europe to bring back a rich playboy, but he wants his life, you know, he wants what this other man has.* She would nod beside him, he would feel the heft of her at his side, but he knew her mind was elsewhere. "Look at those booties." She would stop and gurgle at the window of a baby store. And what could he do, what could he insist on? Those booties *were* yellow and striped, like bees with holes.

"It's bad luck to buy anything before the baby is born, Katyenka."

"Of course it's bad luck." And she would get those booties, he would tell his parents to buy them for her as a gift. With a baby on the way, he should feel he had made all the natural choices. And yet, why couldn't she reserve a few minutes of attention for his interests? Childishly, he continued to recite the plot of the movie—*he wants this man's life, he wants to be him*—but Katia was picking up a bouquet of pink tulips and poking her nose into their buds.

Alain Delon. Tulips. Baby. These three intersecting ideas haunted Lev all the way home.

"Levchik, can I ask you for a favor?" his wife asked when they let themselves into the apartment. They would need a bigger place; ironically, the best deals in this crazy real estate market lay in those new high-rises, the ones Irina's father had invested in. "I've been thinking, well, it's kind of awkward for me, but I feel like it has to be done right now, before the baby's born," Katia said, arranging tulips in a vase. She was one of those women who had an unerring instinct about where in the vase the flowers should tumble.

A favor? Lev was intrigued; his wife's idea of favors usually consisted of evening trips to satisfy her taste for *vobla,* those unappetizing salted dried fish still littering all the Russian stores or those chocolate-coated cheese balls. This favor was different, he could tell, it involved someone specific; for a minute he was afraid it would be Oleg Pinkhasov and that some unpleasant fact from that old story would be suddenly foisted upon him. Instinctively, he wanted to stop her from saying any more.

"It's about Anna K.," Katia said. Lev waited, hoping she would not mention *him*, because as far as he was concerned, *he* did not exist. The whole situation with Anna K. had been stuffed into a black plastic bag, and tucked away in their basement. Now Katia was foolishly pulling on the drawstrings to release it.

"You see, I have this." Katia waddled over to the bedroom dresser drawer and took out a small postcard. Lev sat down on the couch and tilted it toward the light. A woman stared down at him from her carriage.

"It's by an artist called Kramskoy. Anna and I saw it at the Guggenheim years ago. I want her to have it. It was meant to be a gift."

"And?"

He knew that she and Anna spoke only under the most strained circumstances, the health of a mutual cousin once, a relative's wedding anniversary. Sometimes, he would find Katia looking at old pictures of herself as a child, climbing monkeylike onto Anna's knees.

Anna hadn't shown up at their wedding, but she sent them an effusive card along with an embarrassing amount of money and, as if in an afterthought, a crate of useless kitchen appliances. Her card had had embossed mistletoe on it too. Didn't she realize that she had sent them a Christmas card? Dimly, Lev recalled waiting in a long returns line at Bed Bath & Beyond with an espresso machine and cucumber slicer in his arms.

"Why don't you send it to her?" he asked.

"No, she would think it was cold and that's not what I want. I want her to know I forgive her, especially now that we're having a baby. She needs to know I forgive her," Katia repeated.

"I'm sure she knows."

"No, she doesn't." She explained that she wanted him to bring her the card personally. Lev was incredulous; she wanted him to enter *his* place? It was so unexpected, so unseemly. Why would she force him to do this?

Katia was already unpacking their shopping bags, dipping into one of the jars for a marinated green tomato, which she sucked on noisily. Let me think about it, he thought he said, because the conversation was over the way they all seemed to end, imperceptibly. That was the way Katia ruled the house, subtly lacing their conversations with her requests, then withdrawing, leaving only their sediments. He was helpless before all that was unexplained to him.

"I don't understand money and I don't understand women." Someone said that, didn't they, in a movie? Lately, he had been thinking that his mind had a limited function; it only appeared to travel backward and forward on a single rail. But he knew Katia's was not like that at all; hers shot out in all directions from a glowing inner source.

He watched her for a few moments, the way she consumed that tomato, sipped the pickle juice directly out of the container. It was a wet but warm Sunday, with dinner coming early tonight. Why had he complained to himself earlier? So she didn't care about *Purple Noon*. So she wanted to help people escape Uzbekistan. He would use the remains of the marinated tomato juice to make a dirty martini for himself later, if he was still stressed. And he would allow her request to settle and then he would see. The more he got to know his wife, the more he grew to respect her; perhaps she touched areas he could not reach.

2 2

THE IMMIGRATION STORY

If Immigration was the seminal moment in Anna K.'s life, if it created her, shaped her, as she believed, why was the story itself so hazy? For one, there was no time to prepare; even while her parents were on a two-year waiting list to emigrate, they did not tell Anna about their plans until they were given the green light. How often do children of divorce recall the moment their parents sit them down for the "talk"? But Anna was given no such "talk." In fact, when her parents prepared to leave the country, they gave away their best furniture, stocked up on toilet paper (just in case, they had heard America had a shortage), on Celsius thermometers, and treated these preparations as normal, everyday occurrences.

Anna's things, her beloved mementos from childhood, began disappearing. The mauve bear from Father Frost, the records, starting with the fairy-tale ones and proceeding to her favorite Alla Pugacheva, then the record player itself, the Chukovsky children's book, the rug on her wall, and finally her school uniform, the Lenin pin still fastened to its lapel, both black and white pinafores. Every day she noticed a new omission, a perforation. When she confronted her parents, they were vague. And her possessions continued to disappear.

Later they would tell Anna they were afraid she would blab to her teachers at school; they feared a denunciation, the knock at the door, the interview, some reversal of their application. Later, in school, she would discover that the Russian period in which she lived was called "Stagnation." But back then, everything moved so quickly. The surreal good-bye at the rink (ice-skates still fastened) to her best friend Olga. Did she really say, "See you," to her dearest playmate, to whom, practically since birth, she had unburdened all her childish troubles?

The morning of departure: waking up to fog outside the window, a raw chill, communal sobs in the living room. Waking up to an apartment stripped of all objects. Anna, eyes closed but wide awake, lay cocooned beneath a wool blanket, convincing herself that it was all a story, that she would pop her eyes open and the room would be as it once was. She felt her mother touch her gently on the cheek. "It's time," she said, pulling back Anna's covers.

The silent ride to the airport, cheap brown suitcases wedged between their knees. The slobbering kisses of relatives, gifts and notes stuffed into her pockets. The inspection of their bags, her father forced to part with a heavy box of war medals—they were no longer Soviets and had thus relinquished any rights to Soviet war medals, an official said.

"They were my father's." Her father's hands were still gripping the box. "Three years he fought for you."

Her mother to her father, "Let it go, Boris."

An airplane to Rome, then eventually to New York. A dog-eared copy of *Evgeny Onegin* for comfort.

"My toys? My records?" Anna had asked.

"Gone," she was told. "The old, gone."

Of course, this was Anna's subjective memory of Immigration. Didn't the story, to be fair, go back to her paternal grandmother Raya, whose first contact with America came in the form of a Red Cross package?

In post–World War II Ukraine, not a spare beet to be had, and a woman was on the eve of her marriage. What to wear, with two "good" dresses all worn to threads? And all the money going toward vodka for the wedding, her father a penny-pincher even when there were only pennies to pinch. A special dress, Raya dreamed about, a dress to celebrate that her husband-to-be had returned from the ghetto and the war haunted but in love as ever.

And then—and it only happens in the movies—the Red Cross package from America arrived and practically on the eve of the wedding. They saw it was from some distant Milwaukee-based cousins who had emigrated before the war; Raya had had no idea they existed, these cousins on the other side of the world. Raya, her two sisters, her mother ripped open the brown box with their bare hands, bending back the tips of fingernails with the effort. Inside were glorious swaths of yellow and pink silk.

Raya didn't know, how could she, that the Milwaukee relatives had sent them fabric for a kite, that the children of these cousins loved flying their own kite in one of the parks on Lake Michigan (really, apart from the weather, they felt as though they had moved to Yalta with all that magnificent shoreline). The kids' images of the poor Ukrainian sisters was gray—ashen faces, sack dresses, dirty chins (well, not all outside the realm of truth), and what was the American antidote to all that gray, if not the most colorful kite they could find in the stores?

So, on her wedding day, Raya wore a resplendent kite dress. They exchanged vows before the sole surviving rabbi, her husband suppressing memories of Jews arbitrarily executed before his eyes. Two generations later: Anna. The kite, the disappearing records, the box of medals, the murder of Ukrainian Jews—was Anna K. created out of those Big Events?

2 3

PORPOISES

Silly things dislodged Anna, snatched away her newly found moments of pleasure. She decided she could no longer not see her son, for example. She found that his image, his scent, his staccato cries, had wormed their way into her very gut. She called Stasia, whom she knew would have a soft spot for the role of the mother. And so she began to see him on the sly.

In the lobby, Stasia would hand over his stroller so Anna wouldn't have to go upstairs, face her old apartment, its opulence, its hints of her former self. Stasia was doing this behind Mr. K.'s back, she reminded Anna. The lawyers were wrangling over her ability to mother, her hastily hired lawyer was battling an image of Anna as neglectful, a drunk, a two-timing whore. So she better bring Seryozha back by four.

It was sunny, almost blindingly so, and she took Seryozha to Central Park, pushed him in the toddler swing next to several Caribbean nannies. The dimpled shadows of leaves leapt across her son's face. If he was shy with her at first, he grew attached to her again before long. His hair had grown in thick and curly, strands winding their way, like ivy, around his ears. He fussed only once, when she removed him from the swing. She fed him an oatmeal concoction created by Stasia and bought a hot dog smothered in ketchup and sauerkraut for herself.

She ran alongside him, until he collapsed, exhausted, into the stroller, and then she snapped his seat belt closed, drawing it across his tummy. When he slept, she pressed her nose to his cheek, and Nadia's bouffant elbowed its way into her mind. *Is it worth it,* it asked, *is it worth it?*

To part with her son, that was the worst part of the day, to actively remove him from her. But he came along with the rest of her former caged life. So she did it. She put his little hand in Stasia's, and then she walked away.

She returned home to the message from a woman, by Anna's estimation, no older than thirty. "Hi, David, this is Lauren. Just checking in. I deleted your message by mistake, so let's get lunch." Anna sat with it, replayed it several times, "Hi, David, this is Lauren." Was this woman's tone proprietary, forced, eager? A few more plays revealed none of these, the voice was sincerely at ease and familiar. It was a voice that once cared very much and now the affection was sublimated, repressed, rewoven into friendship. The light outside the window faded and David found her cross-legged in the dark.

He had come home later than he said he would. "What's wrong, Anna?" he asked. She had turned the futon couch into a bed and was rolled into a fetal position, squinting at the infusion of light. He sat down beside her, cradled her head in his lap. Her face was marked with the red, undulating imprint of the pillowcase's scalloped edge, her curls were thick and unruly. He knew better than to say anything more, but he seemed frightened by her appearance, helpless before it. His pats on her shoulders were perfunctory, petrified. She allowed him to calm her down with his whispers and kisses, ignoring their hollow centers. Eventually, her panic subsided. There had been no seed of guilt in his voice, she decided. Not yet.

She knew all of Alex's major romances, but she had never asked David about his serious ex-girlfriends. She knew about the woman who was almost Alex's first wife in Russia, an electrical engineer, who wasn't Jewish and was slightly anti-Semitic in fact, but had an incredibly optimistic spirit and a passion for rich foods. Anna knew about Alex's one

American girlfriend, who left him after reuniting with an old flame at her high school reunion. About a Moldovan single mother and divorcée he had been fixed up with by his parents and whom he had wanted to marry, but she had been skittish, not sure she was fit for another cohabitation. She had a cat too, Anna even remembered, a black housecat with orange spots named Chaplin.

Lauren. A Lauren would be small-boned, light-haired, with delicate features. Outspoken, from a coddling, liberal Midwestern family. A Lauren would have a brisk temper but would reconcile generously. She would call herself a "homebody." She would read the books recommended by *The New York Times Book Review* editors. She would cook, not extensively, but the few dishes she excelled at—lasagna, a roasted rosemary chicken, an Irish stew—would always be outstanding. A younger Lauren would scare men away with her domesticity, her uninhibited, unsentimental acrobatics in bed. A more mature man would see her in her sensible hiking boots, in her apron, among her basil plants and organic cherry tomatoes, her highlighted Julia Child and All-Clad stockpots, and propose. David had been the former, Anna knew.

And now Anna and David were at the stage where they were unfastening the cocoon, letting others into their insular life. They were going out with their friends, and her eyes no longer scanned sidewalks for Alex's parents, the acquaintances who peopled her former life. Hence, this Lauren? Perfectly normal, she told herself. And yet, didn't David become impatient with Anna just the other night? They had walked out of a movie, and their conversation suddenly turned (how? the movie had been about penguins) to the Israeli-Palestinian conflict. Anna had admitted her ignorance of the situation. She had long since stopped paying attention, except when her mother told her about their Russian relatives in Haifa. How could Russians, so apolitical, be happily living in Israel? Yet, according to her mother, they were happy, even with daughters in the army. They had their lemon trees, they spoke Hebrew (amazing, a young Anna had thought; there were Russians who didn't speak English?), they took buses, and they voted.

"Telling, isn't it, that Sharon would do such an abrupt one-eighty?" David had said. "Even he is convinced now that bargaining is the only way to go. And for a while there, it seemed like it would work."

"I-I'm sorry," she had stammered. She had been thinking about something else. "I really don't know."

A pause, a terrifying pause. "But you have all those relatives in Israel, don't you? The situation must interest you." They headed into the subway, the heat clutching at her throat.

"Of course it does." They should have walked after all, they would be fighting for seats with the increasing number of young people going to Brooklyn.

They rode the train to Delancey Street, Anna holding on to the sweaty pole. David took *The New Yorker* out of his bag, his eyes lowered, scanning the print. She had failed, Anna thought, it would have gone differently with Lauren. Lauren reads the front pages, Lauren cares passionately about events that touch her life only elliptically. *How like Anna K.*, someone who knew her might say, *to think only about herself.*

Could she not give in to an irresistible urge to read his e-mail, peruse it quickly, see what names lined his inbox? What if his e-mails were inappropriate, what if he corresponded with people, with women, who didn't know that she existed? She was already on the computer, applying for yet another job she was unqualified for, a job she never would have imagined being forced to do. Unpleasant public relations job, must bring own contacts. Anna K. in public relations? It was ridiculous—she hated "working with people." And the icon just in the lower right-hand corner, the blue *E* of Internet Explorer. Maybe his password was already typed in and she would simply have to sign on, an innocent movement, a jerk of the index finger.

She clicked on the icon and the Slate homepage appeared. There were just a few letters in "Hotmail." She typed the first letters, stopped, typed the rest. His log-in name was there, "pnin76," but not his password. The arrow hovered over the log-in box. But if he wanted to, she realized, he could check his computer's activity history. With this one click, she would catapult herself into hazardous territory. Then he would really snap at her, turning away to calm himself down. He always returned, though, a few kisses at the back of her ear, wrapping her into his chest.

Quickly, Anna closed the page. David would be home soon with Indian food. If she found something out, a suggestive phrase, e-mails from women she had never heard about, she would have to keep the information inside, would have to force spinach and chickpeas down her throat, keeping silent. With that thought, she turned off the computer before she could do anything else, before she risked the certainty of knowledge—the existence of her lover's alternate life.

When David came home, he emptied the Indian food into ceramic bowls, dipping a spoon into the okra, the chickpeas, the rice. Anna poured their water and white wine, she set out the plates and napkins. She watched him now a little coldly, her gaze sharp and clear.

David helped himself to the food first, heaping rice and bhindi masala onto his plate, and began to eat. Anna took a sip of her wine, an overly sweet Riesling, a bad idea with this food. Alex would have served her first, he would have waited for her before he took his first bite. Whatever else she believed of her husband, at least he would have done that. Russian men, Anna thought, finding it difficult to swallow her food, you can't say they don't have good manners. Their mothers beat manners into them from infancy.

She forced her gaze to go misty again, he had paid for this takeout after all, and most other things. After everything she'd given up, Anna K. couldn't afford to see clearly.

The next day, Anna made a decision: a vacation, of course, that was always the answer. Summer was coming and the studio would be stifling. They had settled into a routine: David went to teach and Anna remained at the computer, fruitlessly matching herself to job descriptions. Seeing a new place together would bond them further, an English-speaking new place (no more *hablo españols* with Peter), maybe somewhere accessible by train. Anna called her parents' Russian travel agent.

"*Nu?*" the agent asked. "Where you want to go?"

Somewhere with an open sea. Somewhere that would reflect her green eyes, where David would have nothing but her to look at. Where they would inhale salt and eat rich, buttery foods. Where her lawyer couldn't reach her, couldn't say the words "child custody."

"Alaska," the agent said. "A cruise for Alaska. You won't be disappointed. Dima himself just went—of course you know the famous Dima of 108th Street—and he was in raptures. All my clients love it. You can see porpoises."

"Porpoises," Anna told her mother that night.

"I just hope you know what you're doing," her mother sighed—and she had taken to sighing lately, after the initial shock of Anna's phone call—"I have left Sasha for another man. Please, Mama, don't judge me." Now that she was numb to her daughter's new life, she sighed as if all the pleasure in her own life had evaporated. There was nothing left to boast of, no pride left in her Anna, as if her daughter's plunging train had veered off the rails into an untamed, uninhabited forest. When her friends asked about Anna, Natasha simply deflected—a few vague facts, "she's very busy in Manhattan, you know, but she adores her son," and then, with practiced dexterity, she would twist the talk to the friends' children, an eternally irresistible topic. With Natasha's brother, Anna's name was never even mentioned.

"Porpoises. They signify new beginnings," Anna insisted.

"Be careful when you say this. They do no such thing, Anyechka. Shouldn't you be thinking about custody of your son? When did you see him? You see how much he's grown? That vest we gave him two months ago doesn't fit now."

"Yes, they do, Mama. New beginnings. It will all work out, don't worry so much."

Anna would have to dip into her savings account, the one she had stowed away to share with Seryozha. For each month she had painstakingly deposited money over the course of her marriage, she would now get a gleaming, slick porpoise. On the cruise ship at night, she would stroll on the deck in her long skirts, wrapped in a woven shawl. And David would come up behind her. *There's something about you,* he would say.

Perhaps as a result of immigrant holes in the English language, neither Anna nor her mother knew what a porpoise looked like. In her mother's mind, a porpoise was half turtle, half porcupine, slow and prickly, fat and unintelligent. For Anna, a porpoise was a seal, long-whiskered and -torsoed, reposing on rocks, lazily soaking up the sun with its companion. Of course, both would be proven wrong.

2 4

WHAT DID SHE KNOW ABOUT ARGENTINA?

Lev took a detour on his way to the Film Forum and found himself in front of their door. On the subway, he had stared again at the Kramskoy postcard and thought it incredibly sad, that empty seat beside the woman on the carriage. How touching, this gift from his wife to the surely unhappy Anna K. What could she mean by it, a reproof, a gloating? *You stole my boyfriend and now look at me?* Or a sentiment he could not fathom, a whisper between women?

Now in front of the rusty Hester Street door, he rang the doorbell. It was a Thursday evening, not too late. He hoped somehow to avoid *him,* to say what he had to say to Anna K. and be watching *Masculin, Féminin* within the hour. He remembered Anna K. on her wedding day, but her outline was hazy, his focus had been on Katia, after all, on his own paralysis, his own inability to present himself. Anna K. had a regal posture, he remembered thinking, not a woman who would ever, if not for family connections, cross his path. Something haughty about her, neither warm nor soft even though she had the physical attributes of both. She was an Isabelle Huppert, he decided, an actress who always unnerved Lev.

He rang the doorbell again, a single bell for an entire apartment complex. Should he introduce himself by name or as Katia's husband, his own name probably meaning nothing to Anna? Suddenly, inexplicably, he wished he had paid more attention to how he had dressed today. This gray sweater, Katia told him, was not at all flattering, the corduroys, she said, added years to his hips.

A man his father's age, with his father's early morning, gray-studded stubble, opened the door. In one hand, he held an oil-splattered spatula, plastic, its edges melted and curved under. Lev paused, embarrassed, not knowing how to ask, who to ask for. He knew Anna only as Anna K. and her lover's name, Katia's ex-boyfriend, he had refused to internalize.

"I am here to see Anna, a tall woman, Russian. Can you please tell me if she's in?" How sordid, how very immigrant, his plea sounded to him. He remembered his first days in the country, how his mother had forced him to ask for things so he could learn the English language.

"Go ahead, Levchik, go ask the nice man," she would say, encouraging the red-faced Lev to shyly look up at strangers and ask, "Excuse me, how much does this cost?" or "Excuse me, which way to Avenue J?" and such polite constructions. Later, he realized that his mother had pushed him only because she was too meek to ask herself, that Americans, frankly, terrified her and probably still did. How he resented Katia at this moment for sending him on such an unpleasant mission. "I don't know which apartment, you see. This Anna, she lives here with her friend."

"They're on vacation. I got their keys. Come back in two weeks." The man slammed the door, chewing the remains of a toothpick or a chicken bone. It was all so foreign, so unlike Rego Park. The building looked like it was scrubbed by wind and rain and snow, its bricks discolored, decaying.

For Katia, the day felt interminable. The company meeting, announced weeks ago, turned ominous. The CEO decided that the company would be moving away from rescuing Jews from the former Soviet Union. It seemed they were no longer in need of rescue, the majority of them were already here and the rest? By continuing to mine Eastern and Central Europe so long after the collapse of communism, Outstretched Arms was sucking blood from a stone, the surest path to bankruptcy. South America, that impoverished, not-too-distant continent, now there were some Jews in real need of help.

Russian philanthropists (Katia didn't even know such a phrase existed) adored the South American spirit, the director of development interjected—they loved the music, the style, the dance. They were tired of helping their own people, pale and miserable, corrupt and hopelessly shtetlized. Happy Argentinians, red-blooded and ambitious, just think of the fundraisers. Hire a few tango teachers and Russians would be paying $200 a pop just to get in. At least, that was what Katia heard. And what did she know about Argentina?

"But I don't speak Spanish," Katia's next-door office neighbor, a middle-aged Olga of sorts, said. As if Katia didn't know that. This Olga was always a step behind; at a recent health insurance overview meeting, she ate pigs in a blanket, posed an endless stream of questions to the insurance representative, and then announced that she herself didn't need insurance because she was on her husband's plan. This Olga was disorganized, always asking Katia about company policies even though she had been at the company three years longer.

"Now there'll be a shakedown," she said to Katia. "They'll hire all Spaniards. You're just lucky you're pregnant. You don't really need this job."

But Katia didn't feel lucky. Right now, at this very moment, she could be losing yet another man to Anna, this time her husband. Why had she devised this kind of test for Lev? She didn't know what had possessed her to ask him to see Anna; she probably thought that if he could go there and not fall in love with her, she could have his baby in peace and not picture some years down the line: a birthday party, Anna's black, low-cut dress, her melancholy, alluring smiles. But she didn't expect him to agree to go, and now that he was probably in her cousin's and David's living room, postcard in hand, who knew what could happen? It was stupid, stupid. A stupid idea, a stupid risk, but at least she would know. It was always better to know.

Rising from her chair with some effort, she began to organize her client folders chronologically, filing them away, accordion-style, into the cabinet. Her parents had been a file here too, once: name of sponsor, date of arrival, profession in the former Soviet Union, amount of the settlement loan. Her parents too had been flattened onto a piece of paper.

2 5

_____

LOOK, LOOK!

Anna and David stood in a long line to check into the cruise ship. Around them milled thick groups of people, including, naturally, Russians. Where can one not find Russians in this day and age? Now David could point them out too. He had learned to tune in to their particular intonations, a shrug wrapped inside a sentence.

The line crawled and when they got to the front, a flute of champagne was shoved into their hands, they were made to smile for the first of many pictures. David, a well-trained photographic subject, stared directly into the camera, eyes open, generous smile. But no _petite pomme_ rescued Anna's face; it was caught by surprise on film, later exhibiting a spongy chin, a slumped jaw.

Their room was smaller than any room they had ever seen (and they had the Soviet Union and New York City to compare it to, after all!). One bed spread out in the middle, a dressing table, and a door (to the closet? no, the bathroom). A television built into the wall, a childishly executed painting of an orange sailboat. They propped the suitcases in the narrow hallway, which blocked access to the door, but unpacking would have to be done later. In David's suitcase: two ver-

sions of his manuscript, a novel inspired by Anna, he had said. But
both drafts were giving him trouble, two stacks of print overlaid by
furious purple ink.

Still attached to the harbor, the boat vibrated. But the room was
theirs, it was private, and soon the ship would let go of the shore
and glide away unprotected. And there was the square window, out
of which, right now anyway, they saw pattering feet and duffel bags
dragged across wooden planks.

"Welcome to Serenity Cruises," said the captain over the intercom.
An itinerary would be flung through the slit beneath their door. Bingo,
they could look forward to, trivia games, art auctions, Ping-Pong, sales
on amber jewelry, lectures on the natural world. Great prizes! Awe-
inspiring trips at their port destinations—helicopter rides over gla-
ciers, scuba diving while ogling sea creatures.

*Ride the route where thousands have lost their lives in the search
of gold,* Anna read in the brochure. The Gold Rush Train in Skagway.
It was the only trip that piqued her interest. David was already asleep,
spread out on his back, his elbows flung over his face, forming isosce-
les triangles.

In the bathroom, where a stand-up shower battled for precious
square footage with a small round toilet and sink, Anna washed her
face. "I wonder why Russia never asked for Alaska back," she called
out. He could sleep later, but right now he needed to pay attention to
her.

"Mnmmm," she heard, as she spritzed herself with David's favorite
perfume, applied fresh eye shadow and mascara. Putting her face back
together, as her mother would say.

If she had stayed in Russia, how would Anna K.'s life have been different? To make broad generalizations, she might have had fewer choices.
Are more choices good or bad? Bad, according to Barry Schwartz,
author of *The Paradox of Choice: Why More Is Less.* The mind gets
muddled and freezes, tangled up in options.

Would Anna K. have been happier with her meager choices in post-Soviet Russia? Marriage at the age of twenty-one, living with her meddling in-laws, one decadent dinner a year at Pushkin? Saving up her salary for anything with the words *Dolce & Gabbana* inscribed in it. Or if she was lucky and picked a husband who had the foresight and gumption to seize a chunk of the country's natural resources, she could have been driven around in a bulletproof town car, had her child enrolled in a Swiss boarding school. She would learn to tolerate his mistress, forgive him when he finally returned home with Pucci gift bags. Schwartz would say yes, she would have been happier. There were only two entrées on the menu, she could then say, just two flavors of ice cream, equally tasteless. Her only task would be to choose one.

Choices. The reason many immigrants (at least on the surface) said they took the plunge in a new country. Usually not so much for themselves as for their children. So their children could make choices. What a terrible thing to inflict on a child, Anna thought. With every choice you made, you took responsibility. That it was irreversible, irretrievable, that it would screw tight the lid, prohibit the path to more choices. That out of all those liberating, mesmerizing options you could choose something bony, fetid, barren. And with that decision, you would have inflicted unhappiness (tragedy, even!) with your very own hand.

Choices had never been kind to Anna K. The friends she chose in school tended to perceive her as a temporary, disposable assignment, her first apartment in Manhattan was invaded by a persistent band of mice, the dish she chose at restaurants tended to be the weakest, the one with the conflicting, pungent flavors that canceled each other out. Now that Anna had made her most important choice yet, at moments she secretly longed for: one party, a state-assigned apartment, whatever remained in the grocery pantry, a Lenin figure to worship.

A fact David did not yet know: Anna was very good at Ping-Pong. The sport of choice at Budding Artists Creative Arts Camp, where

sports held not the slightest interest for campers preparing for their
Hairspray auditions. It was there that Anna honed her skills between
rehearsals, before barbecues and dances and egg tosses. It was there
she perfected the spin, varied her game from defensive to aggressive,
learned to mix up her serves, never to reveal her backhand weakness.
Winning every game, she would only cede the table once her arm was
sore and cramping.

On the cruise, she signed herself up for the Ping-Pong tournament.
The coveted prize: one free bingo card. They made their way to the
deck, David standing to the side with videotaping families who were
cheering on their Stanleys and their Rajivs. Neither the players nor
the benevolent Serenity Cruises leisure coordinator were prepared for
the dark-haired woman in a deep blue velvet blazer. Her stride to the
table was meek almost, self-effacing. A rough day at sea made the table
sway ever so slightly and the image of this woman dipped for most of
the onlookers. All they saw were her curls, the curve of her breasts,
her long, pianist's fingers. She volleyed a few minutes with a scrawny
teenage boy, who was overdressed in slacks, a quilted vest, and dress
shoes, and looked uncomfortable as he leapt for the ball. Then they
played for points. The ball almost levitated against her racket.

David watched as Anna effortlessly wiped one person out after
another. If he admitted it to himself, he would say he was surprised at
her competitive edge, with its tinge of malice. Safely, she would volley,
safely, waiting for the moment to slam the ball, to ram it into the table
with force. The opponents, mostly dads and their teenage sons, were
helpless before the onslaught, their hands thrown up in the air. Woo,
they would say with a grin, take it easy, miss, it's only a game.

So she is capable of this, is she? David might have thought, taking
mental notes for the heroine in his novel, or maybe he didn't think that
at all. Who knows how it is with men, their mental system of connections? They could be thinking of anything at all: an ignored stock tip,
an unresolved problem, a cold pale ale, a plump pair of lips, a way to
untangle themselves from a complicated situation.

.   .   .

They were to split up that afternoon, she to the jewelry store, he to the library. She rifled through plastic bags of amber rings, nothing too unusual here, cut in geometric shapes, fastened on clunky, oversized silver bands. Amber was not a stone that seduced her anyway, dull and brown and speckled. A pair of Russian women stood beside her, one pawing through the bags, the other sniffing, "How much amber can you own, already?" Russians loved amber.

The impulse rose in Anna to buy, to fill a gap with a purchase. For a few minutes to experience the heady power of acquisition. But she resisted, she would wait until one of the ports, until David was with her. She would tell him what struck her eye and he would feign indifference and buy it for her later. As usual, she pretended she didn't understand the women's Russian chatter. She was one of them, but mostly not.

On her way to the library, she passed the computer room. On the right side, elderly people were enrolled in a small class on the basics of the Internet. The Australian leisure coordinator was leading the session, patiently demonstrating something with a mouse. But there on the left, David sat between one of the guys she had beat at Ping-Pong and a teenage girl on Instant Messenger. His fingers danced across the keyboard, even though it cost almost $2 for every minute online. Lauren, she thought, turning away from the computer room.

Oh, God. Why would he stay with a forty-one-year-old Russian woman? Anna was suddenly blinded with the simplicity of the logic. Somehow she found herself in the photography room, where people searched for their family photographs, looking for themselves smiling at dinner, slurping pea soup inside hollowed-out sourdough loaves.

She tried to orient herself in the direction of their room. She told herself that nothing had changed, what could be wrong with him checking his e-mail? The art auction crowd was beginning to congregate, and she was pushed aside by blazers with gold buttons, by manicures and velour tracksuits. Was he infatuated with her particular brooding, her moroseness? How long would it last now that her roots had become brittle with dye, her stomach jutted out over her panty waistline? The time she had wasted—one year had cantered into the next. She found herself sitting on a plush love seat, supporting her head with the palms of her hand.

A waiter rushed to her side as soon as she hit the cushions. No, no drink. Though, on second thought, a martini? Drinking always made it worse, it pulled her farther down by the feet. Yes, she told the waiter. A dry vodka martini, extra olives. Already, it seemed to her, men's eyes were skimming past her as she sank into the love seat; no doubt looking for more color in the cheek, the heather sheen of innocence. Young girls walked by, with their tiny purses, trying to act like their mothers. Anna sipped her martini.

When she was thirteen or fourteen, her mother would drag her to Alexander's, a labyrinthine department store on the corner of Queens Boulevard and Sixty-third Road. There Anna would prop herself against the wall with a V. C. Andrews paperback, while her mother picked out dresses for her. Whatever they could afford coupled with her mother's dubious taste usually resulted in rayon or Lycra, in pleats and bows. Baby blues and the kind of pink you find inside a grapefruit.

How could a young lady not like to shop? her mother wondered, irritated. The heat was always cranked up in that store and her mother would have snarled clothes on hangers bent over her arm. The speeches would begin, gathering force in the dressing room. You have to start early, you know. You will have to learn to keep a man's love. We're not like those Americans, in their mannish pants, their form-hiding sweatshirts, let them get divorced. We Russian women are feminine, Anyechka, and look at you, with your sneakers untied and that horrible skranchi, as you call it, on top of your head? A *chuchelo.*

"Will that be all, madame?" the waiter asked. It was the cue for her to leave. She reached into her purse.

Could Anna pinpoint the exact date, the exact moment when she had transformed from a Mademoiselle into Madame? Did it occur one day, the imperceptible shift, that one additional wrinkle that sealed her new identity? Was there a silent gong that signaled the transition, a heavy line drawn, the falling of a curtain?

And now there was no going back to Mademoiselle, to the pink-cheeked innocence of that word, the licenses, the short-term pleasures of a Mademoiselle: knee socks, whimsical hairstyles, light makeup, spontaneous chats with new people, interminable days of summer. No, Anna had married, had borne a son, she had left her husband for a younger man, she had been deeply disappointed, forgotten entire chunks of her past, she suspected people were inherently evil. She was a Madame.

Anna was halfway across the ship before she realized she was walking down the wrong hallway to their room. All these hallways, narrow and identical except for the numbers. She turned around and tried again. Could it be her mother was on to something? That she should have put her energies into seduction, into maintaining the illusion? With Alex, she had almost succeeded. Was her mother happy? Funny how she never wondered before.

At last finding the room and letting herself in with her card, Anna crumpled on the bed. Tomorrow they would be on a train together, she and David, on a train there was a destination, chaos giving way to order. Once, in the nineteenth century, a train was the height of new technology, a promise of modernity. And now? All she wanted was to cup the past in the palm of her hand, to transform it, lend it meaning. Relive the beauty, the once-dangerous power, the optimism of a fast-moving train.

By the time David returned to the room, Anna was entirely composed, and, he would exclaim immediately upon seeing her, ravishing. She wore a thin silk dress, body-skimming, cut off at the knee, her usual simple black color. What David didn't realize: how hard simplicity was to pull off, harder and harder with each passing year.

She was quick to laugh that night, polishing off almost the entire bottle of Cabernet. Her lips were blotched in the middle with red, like a geisha's. She was the first out on the dance floor, the disco lights flickering red on her skin, green and silver splashed up and down her bare arms. He watched her, the gyrations of her shoulders and hips, her dizzying turns, knotted hair dipping between her breasts. There were no other women for David to notice—there was only her, only Anna K.

Strange dreams, one can have on a boat. Viscous dreams, impossible to scramble out of them. Portentous, undefined situations with Anna at their center, in distress. Tasks with elusive solutions. If she could just find this particular shade of lipstick, a brownish mauve. If she could locate that kitten, hiding behind cabbage leaves. If she could only find her way out of the ship and onto land. Composites of different men, their faces and identities jumbled, threatened Anna's body—they shrank her, led her into empty alleyways flickering their sharpened Swiss army knives. They warned her of future disasters. And always in her dreams—the rocking of trains.

They were awakened at six a.m. to see the Hubbard Glacier. Each cruise had its appointment with the glacier and theirs was going to be early. Just can't be helped, folks, the captain cheerfully announced the night before. Anna and David, eyes still heavy with sleep, tossed blankets around their shoulders and climbed onto the deck.

At first they weren't sure which way to look, so they followed the gaze of the cameras, the twittering of the other tourists. And it rose before them, the glacier, hulking and crusty gray-blue, pieces crumbling off and falling into the ocean. The chunks, so small compared to the glacier, still plunged with a loud crash. Every minute, right before them, the icy structure was changing.

"Incredible, isn't it?" David said, now fully awake. He stood behind Anna, put his arms around her, his head sloped down on her shoulder. Even something that grandiose, that immutable, was changing. Funny how she didn't feel forty-one at all; her relationship with time, once so affectionate, lovingly doled out on the abacus, was now openly hostile. How could there be no going back? Anna thought. It seemed impossible that there was no reverse movement, when flashes from the past were so vivid in her mind. She could still recall the acute pleasure of eating a Siamese cherry lollipop, for example, the kind that could be broken to form two parts. Her first step had been to bite through the icy connecting tissue.

Or she could still remember a walk down Park Avenue on a warm summer night with a male colleague from her first publishing job, the question mark that had never really gotten answered. The colleague had sat at an adjacent cubicle, passed her flirtatious notes folded inside his favorite erotic books. Robert Olen Butler's *They Whisper* was one of them, another something by Kundera. It had been just on the cusp of e-mail's invention, when time had traveled more slowly. He had a goatee, wore loafers. One of their jobs was to alphabetize all the paperbacks in the book room, a job they dragged out for months, sitting cross-legged on the floor and reading salacious passages from *Lady Augustine's Secret* or *The Sister Barnacle Murder Mystery Series*.

They had strolled down Park Avenue after an author signing at Rizzoli. Anna had felt warm and hopeful at the idea of a nascent career in publishing. The evening had been cinematic: the reading, the bottles of wine, all those bookshelves, the chic scarves, the literary exchanges. They left together, taking in the city's energy, gossiping only the way the most inconsequential employees in a large corporation can gossip—the author had gotten drunk and invited Anna to return with him to his Hamptons home, when his middle-aged editor was lobbying for that very invite.

After their stroll, they had stood at Anna's door to say good night. She had kept the tone light, allowed him to peck her on the cheek. He wanted to say something, but she left no room for confessions. She would see him tomorrow, then, the author was counting on rights in half a dozen countries. Before she entered the elevator, though, she whipped around to find his head leaning against the windowpane; his eyes were closed, the tips of his fingers leaving marks on the glass. Back then, it never occurred to her to go back, to take his goateed head in her hands, to lead him up to her apartment. There would be so many others, Anna had assumed, who would not be goateed. What happened to him? she wondered. A roomy but run-down apartment in Sunnyside or a return to his hometown of Northampton, a wife, children?

"Isn't it?" David said, squeezing. "Incredible, right?" He was like that; every experience had to be pinned down, still wriggling, with words. Why couldn't he just *look*?

She had never expected it to be so blue, and that was an easy observation to make. "I just never expected it to be blue," she said. "I thought it would be clear and glossy, like an ice cube."

"That's right," he said, pulling her closer. David, for example, had never sported a goatee. "Exactly. It's just what you least expect it to look like."

The day they saw the porpoises, Anna had put on her turquoise headband. It was an accessory that always drew the attention of men, a bright, unexpected splash of color. She knew its power and used it as a talisman, an incantation.

"How lovely," David said when they met next to the swimming pool. The pool was empty of people—it was that cold. "How well it plays against your eyes," he said.

Anna tried to take pleasure in the compliment, but she knew that while she was chasing muffins down with thin, bitter coffee in the cramped dining room intended for late risers, he had been in the computer room, plugging away at expensive e-mail. He had not touched either draft of the novel the entire time, even though the manuscripts' inclusion in the suitcase had meant the sacrifice of some clothing, handbags, and makeup. She expected he would begin to share the passages concerning her; she wanted the heroine to wear this very headband.

The ship's naturalist, over the loudspeaker, had called everyone out on the deck. Her voice was soothing, mellifluous. Porpoises were leaping alongside the ship, she said, one after the other, an exuberant school of porpoises. Anna curled herself over the rail to see them, scanning the water. There they were, not far from the body of the ship, preening, showing off, presenting themselves to the gaze. So the porpoise was a glorified dolphin, she despaired, nothing more.

"Who do you e-mail for so long?" she asked.

Not looking away from the water, he said, "Students, mostly, asking for recommendations." He wore a shirt he was inexplicably attached to, a blue cotton button-down fraying at the sleeves.

A violent wave of anger overcame Anna; her hand flew across his cheek. It left no mark, only the sound of a rubber band snapping. "Don't lie to me," she spat. They stood staring at each other.

David finally reached out his hand. To touch her cheek, pacify her with a caress? But no, he tugged at the headband, pulled it off her head in a single motion. He crumpled it into a ball and threw it overboard. It made an arc and disappeared from view.

So that's it, she thought. That's all he has inside him. He was withdrawing, she could sense it, back into his favorite shirt.

"Directly north, a school of killer whales," the naturalist crooned.

Children, shrieking at their grandparents, pointing: "Look, look!"

2 6

CONTEMPT

A voluptuous Sunday in Rego Park. There was always the chance of running into an acquaintance on the street. Men were out on errands for their wives, taking detours with friends, having a smoke. The stretch of Ninety-ninth Street as it plunges into Queens Boulevard transforms into a stage for the immigrant flaneur. Apartments turn themselves inside out, their residents out to breathe air, to check in with the latest local news, the latest with Putin, to swap notes on the soap opera steaming up their Russian-language television sets. The lazy progress of strollers, moms wearing body-hugging knits, their eight-year-olds trying to stuff their mouths with wads of chewing gum. Clutching a hot *cheburekh* in both hands, lamb juice dripping down the wrist. A plastic Strawberry's bag stuffed with children's clothes, one handle broken. Panting with pleasure, dogs.

A man supporting his hugely pregnant wife, a man who for the first time in all his thirty years feared death.

"Go," Katia said. "My father tells me they're back. Take the postcard." She was days away, hours, her skin distended to its limits. She walked with difficulty. "Do it now, before I give birth. It's important that I know."

"Know what?"

"That I can rest, Levchik. Poor Anna."

Poor Anna? His wife, what did she mean? He would never ask—the domain of women.

Across the street, he saw Oleg walking with his own wife and baby. His friend matched his stride to that of his family, head down to the pavement, hands in the pockets of his khakis. They hadn't spoken since the concert, when Oleg told him he and Svetlana were working with a rabbi to become more religious.

"All Sveta's idea," Oleg had said nonchalantly. "No more Flanagan's on Friday nights, I guess."

Lev's first instinct was to shout out his friend's name ("Pinkhasov!"), but he hesitated and the moment slid by. Much easier just to turn his eyes away.

Throbbing with sun, an exquisite day in Rego Park.

Lev half-expected to see the greasy landlord again, with gray-brown chest hair visible from the stretched-out collar of his T-shirt, but *she* opened the door. He had called earlier, lied that he would be in the area anyway and dear Katia was in no position to be stopping by her-self. Anna told him they were having some people over but he was welcome to join them, an invitation Lev accepted reluctantly. He would be in and out, he told himself. When he considered Anna K., his thoughts got entangled in cobwebs, surrounded by an unpleasant feeling of dread.

"Privet," Anna said, opening the door wider. "And I never managed to run out, buy a little something for Katia. What a terrible cousin I am." She wore all black, exactly as he remembered her, this time a sweater, the hint of pink underneath. Her hair appeared slightly wet, the curls around her neckline drooping from the weight of water.

"Unnecessary," he mumbled, following her up the stairs. "I can only stay a moment, my movie's at five-thirty."

"Movie?" Anna paused on the landing and turned to face him. The hallway was painted in two dreary colors—brown and beige; the floor filthy with dust balls and other detritus—leaves, crumbled branches, a child's woven glove.

"There's a Godard retrospective at the Film Forum. I'm seeing *Contempt*."

Anna, incongruous with her surroundings, was more plump than he remembered her, but again, he was arrested by those curls, wildly framing her round face. "A great movie, I hear."

"Brigitte Bardot," he said, "unhappy in her marriage." He thought about what he had just said and blushed; he hated when he blushed, his lips were so thick already, he looked grotesque. He wanted to fling the postcard at her and flee.

"Sounds interesting." Anna continuing up the stairs laboriously, as if she were older than she was, a heavy tread on each step. The apartment was on the top floor, a sixth-floor walk-up. She tapped the door open and Lev could see three men, with drinks, conversing on the futon couch.

"Lev Gavrilov," she announced, entering the room, as if graciously filling it with the unexpected. "This is David, Matt, and Jim. Two friends of David's from Columbia." Lev stared at David. This guy, what was it about him? Lev had been expecting a muscular guy, one of those beefy, assertive Americans in a jean shirt and khakis, the ones with firm opinions on any topic. Instead, this David was bespectacled, gangly, a twitching Adam's apple, a brown mop of hair half covering his eyes. Let's be honest, he was equine, possessed a kind of dopey strength. He even puffed on a cigarette and Katia hated smokers, always made a show of waving away their stench. This was the man of the Post-it notes he had found in Katia's drawer? They all shook hands.

"What do you do?" the guy Matt asked, and Lev immediately hated everyone.

"A pharmacist," he said.

"Can you swipe me a Zoloft?" Matt joked. The conversation stalled.

Anna receded to the tiny kitchen, mixing vodka with a thick, carroty liquid. It had been a mistake to come here, when Brigitte Bardot waited for him. Nowhere to be alone here; the room reminded him of the sets of those black-and-white German films with their low ceilings and uneven walls, with their shadows and unnatural angles.

"How's Katia feeling?" David asked quietly, slipping this in while his friends began a debate about something—the difference between fiction and nonfiction? A silly thing to talk about, in Lev's opinion.

"She's fine, thank God."

More blushing. In the kitchen, more stirring, the clinking of ice cubes. Lev could see Anna swaying to the jazz music playing on one of those new iPod speakers, her hips forming the number eight.

"I'm glad. She is . . . she was . . ." Thankfully, David was unable to finish that sentence.

Everything is fiction, Matt argued. No, Jim said, we've argued about this before, and you know there is such a thing as truth. An empirical truth? Who gets to decide? Perception? Schrödinger's cat? David was standing in the middle, chasing an olive with a toothpick.

"We mustn't delay our guest, he can only stay a minute." Anna saved him. She wound her arm around Lev, pulled him away from the triptych of men. Was it her scent, the cinnamon of her breath? Lev surrendered to a dizzy feeling. Hard to believe she was at least ten years older than he was, older than anyone in this apartment, lending her an air of fragility. "He has a movie to catch."

She motioned him into the foyer, she leaning against the wall. The Caravaggio light illuminated her right shoulder, the peak of her collarbone. He reached into his jacket pocket and handed the postcard to her, watching her face as she examined it, bringing it close, almost to her nose.

"From Katia?" she asked, and started laughing, a deep, sensuous laugh. She stared at it for a few seconds—mournful or amused? There was something profound in the way her lips pressed together, in the angle of her bent head; hers was a portrait worthy of framing. In the other room, Lev heard expressions of condolences from Matt or Jim. David was telling them about a book not completed despite all his efforts, a novel internally, maybe fatally flawed, an agent at her wits' end. Lev didn't understand. Hot in this coffin of a room, and yet he wanted her hand on him again.

"What is it?" David called.

"A portrait," Anna said. "A gift from Katia." She turned to Lev. "Please tell her thank you, I do appreciate it." Her face changed then, as if a curtain had been dropped, the actors on stage eager to reclaim their real lives. "But then, you said you have to leave. *Contempt*, right?"

"Yes," he said, remembering that he had never taken off his jacket and so could leave right now. But there was a duel inside him, between pity and desire.

2 7

THE CONDITION OF WOMEN

Serge's eyes were the color of blueberries. Every time Anna went to see him, she uncovered new traits—muscles, previously dormant, now fully exploited, a lisping laugh close in tenor to a hissing radiator, a birthmark next to the peak of his right elbow. "Remember, Seryozha, this is your mama," Stasia whispered to the boy. His wavy hair was parted on the right side these days. He walked by himself now, his hands still stretched out for balance.

"Mama," Seryozha said in wonder. They had a half hour this time, Serge off to a playdate at four. How she envied the child who would have her son's attention for an entire hour.

She looked around. Alex had cleaned house; not a trace of her remained. Not their towels, white sheets, not the Art Deco–style coffee table she had picked out, not a single clue to her past existence, a tube of lipstick even. The new furniture was completely different, antique where her tastes had leaned toward modern, the new china had a pink French country pattern. On the table stood a vase filled with white orchids, a flower Anna had particularly detested for its coiling blandness masquerading as elegance.

Was this Alex's taste asserting itself or someone else's, a woman's, offstage? As if in answer to Anna's query, draped over a chair in the bedroom was a baby-blue silk nightgown. Dior. It smelled of citrus.

Seryozha followed her inside, fingers reaching for her leg as she sat on the bed, gripping her stomach, hunched over. "Mama," he said again, enjoying how the word stretched across his lips.

Sometimes after visiting Serge, she would take the train to Queens. Her parents—heftier, more tired, it seemed—no longer came into the city to see her, so Anna had to return to Rego Park. She would pick them up in the apartment and the three of them would walk to a Chinese restaurant on Queens Boulevard they had been frequenting for twenty-five years, where the friendly owner would certainly give them a booth tucked inside the belly of the restaurant, away from the window's drafts. Anna didn't mind; the sizzling rice soup was a mouthful of adolescence.

At first they would all talk at once. There would be the anticipation of their favorite dishes, the pleasure at the reunion. Her father would carefully dissect that day's *Novoye Russkoye Slovo;* he would tell Anna, as usual, that at least the Russian news was focused on international current affairs, far superior to the local fluff that was on the evening news. Inevitably, though, after two beers, warmed by the shrimps' chili sauce, her mother would ask, "Any chance of getting back with Sasha?" Then the meal would be ruined. There would be tears. "Think of your son," her mother would wail, her father motioning for the check.

Anna would walk behind them, noting that the strip bar Shimmy's, the tired glow of its red sign, stood where she remembered it, across the street on Queens Boulevard. And passing her old ballet studio, where Madame Zoya used to pinch her side for excess fat as Anna stretched on the barre. Amazing, Anna would think, the durability of certain things. Didn't the owner of Shimmy's, or Madame Zoya, show up to work one morning longing to destroy everything they had built? Were they never tempted?

"I don't understand why you're doing this," her mother would say, eyelids inflamed, when they reached the Sixty-third Road subway station, as Anna reached out to kiss her good-bye.

Of course, David's father would not be staying at their studio. Taking the train from Chicago would allow him to splurge for the W Hotel, because how often did he get to New York to see his son? And of course he was looking forward to meeting this Anna, the girl—sorry, the *woman*—who had so entranced his David.

The sudden appearance of Myron Zuckerman made Anna nervous. Wasn't it uncharacteristic of his father? Didn't David say Myron planned everything weeks in advance? She teased out a long-buried anecdote from her memory—Myron with his appointment book, scratching in David's piano recital, his track meets, graduation.

And here he was, with hardly any warning, a sudden academic conference in midtown. Holocaust studies, and Myron was the pioneer in the Shoah's quotidian aspects. His last book researched a week in the life of an ordinary German family, with no ties to politics, to Jews, to Hitler. His argument: it is in the everyday that history is revealed.

And the way David presented his arrival, as if it were medicine camouflaged as dessert and dissolved in hot tea. He told Anna about it over a mediocre cheese plate at a cheap French restaurant on Ludlow. All the canonical cheeses were heaped on the wooden tray—Manchego, a goat, and a Brie, Triscuits and fruit, the wine too acidic to drink. And then, voilà, mere moments before coffee, David announced that Zuckerman *père* is to descend on New York in just four days!

"How long have you known about this?" Even the figs, dry.

"It'll be fine," David said, his mouth full of cheese, a new irritation invading his voice.

"How did it go?" His wife had waited to ask him until he had changed into his house clothes, a pair of soft sweatpants. Katia was pacing the house again, one hand on her belly, practicing Spanish on the computer. *La mujer está en el tren,* he heard coming out of the living room.

The couch was littered with index cards, a bowl filled with cantaloupe rinds. Katia's usual neatness had given way to a kind of charming disorder. Any minute and their lives would explode. These days, he was anxious every morning and right before he went to sleep. His compact world was unstable, all these new worries.

"It went fine." The first lie to his wife. Or just an omission? But something told him this was the best answer—the way Katia feigned indifference at his response, the way she returned to repeatedly click on the same Spanish expression. Her full body smelled of yogurt.

"How did you find Anna?"

"Changed," he said truthfully. The Spanish went away, and they heard the muffled sounds of a Russian argument through the wall: *Are you an idiot or what?* They were used to it, Russians fighting; in the end, it was always the wife who won the battle.

Lev prepared himself for Katia's questions about *him,* the guy with the cigarettes and that floppy hair, the American. But having met him, Lev found no foundation for jealousy. The guy was a coward; even Lev could see that was his biggest problem.

"Is she less peaceful—Anna?" Katia stood behind him now, her stomach pressing against the small of his back. Hands roaming about the inside of his thighs. He led her to the bedroom, peeled her gently. Less peaceful? *That* was what she wanted to know? The things women thought about.

When Anna arrived at the Cloisters, she found David and his father conferring like Benedictine monks. They sat draped in shade, Myron leaning against a column, David straddling the bench. Anna watched them from her place by the doors, the tenseness of David's back. As she spilled out into the courtyard, Anna noticed that Myron didn't smile, that behind his beard, he was preparing his face for the greeting. Should she call him Myron or Mr. Zuckerman? Just Myron was unthinkable for Russians, who could distinguish between the polite and the casual address.

"Hello," she said simply. "Wonderful to finally meet you."

Myron cleared his throat. "Yes," he said, less as a response than a confirmation of his own assumptions. "I've been interested in meeting you."

Why couldn't they get to know each other on the sunny side of the courtyard? Here she probably looked short on color given the navy dress she had chosen. She would get no help from David, she could see that already. He had been rendered mute, helpless. Myron peered at her through those round glasses.

"A beautiful day," she tried.

"In Chicago as well. In fact, to leave Chicago when it's sunny is a kind of crime."

Her age rested somewhere between David's and his father's, surely Myron had noticed. And Myron? How strange, how off-putting, to discover that he was barely older than Alex, and possibly even younger.

"But the bleakness of weather is nothing new to a Russian," Myron said.

"Anna left when she was young, Dad. She's pretty much an American now."

"Are you an American, Mrs. K.?"

"Dad, you know she's no longer Mrs. K., I mean unofficially! Why do you always have to do this?"

"Do what?"

Into the Cloisters ran three children, their parents behind them. They were told, sternly, to be aware of the rosebushes. Do-not-touch-anything.

David's voice was squeaky, the voice of a small cartoon animal, a beaver, Anna thought, or perhaps an aardvark who would be wearing a top hat. "You've just met her, I thought you could at least hold out until dinner!"

Myron turned away from Anna, his gaze resting on his son. "But, my dear David, that's exactly what I'm trying to find out. Who exactly she is."

Anna, now shivering, stepped away from the men, crossing the boundary into sun. Closing her eyes, she felt the late summer warmth beating on her face, cascading down her shoulders, her breasts, thighs. To her right, she heard a half-hushed fight between father and whiny son. To her left, the skipping of children, a game of hide-and-seek already in progress. "The rosebushes," she heard. "Be careful."

A cloister in Manhattan perpetuated the myth of serenity. She could remove herself, retrace her steps, get onto the A train. Where would it take her? She could switch to the E, back to Queens. Something soothing about the subways, not quite as exciting as trains, but still, the rocking of the voyage, the anticipation of reaching one's destination. How often had she stood on subway platforms, feeling the wind of a train not yet arrived, its lights, its rumble. How fast it traveled, sliding down the platform. She loved it when her train was running late and was forced to skip a station or two, thrilling past the waiting hordes, their mouths open, watching her train go by.

David left his father. "He promised he would tone it down. He just tests people so he can get to know them." She could sense him weakly pressing against her side. Oh, God, why did she love him again? It terrified her that for a moment she had forgotten. Instead of the fullness of her heart, she felt an excision. She thought of her mother crying, "Think of your son" or "You never gave your husband a fair chance, Anya." It occurred to her that in her own way, her mother was happy. If only because she limited the borders of her world. To step outside them meant chaos.

David was tugging on her arm, as though he were a child seeking validation. "Fine," Anna said. "It's fine. I know he means well." Myron, from the bench, was watching the entire exchange.

They had, all of them, drunk a lot of wine. Back in Myron's hotel room, a sliver of Union Square was visible from his window.

"What do you see as the role of women today?" he asked, opening a new bottle of Bordeaux. Was he flirting with her or testing her? These last few days, she could not be sure. They were drinking out of the hotel's glasses, stout and heavy, David and Myron in chairs, Anna sprawled upon the bed. They were to go out again, to the lounge downstairs perhaps, but Myron brought a decent Bordeaux, and the city preened outside their window, all silver-white, all yellow.

"There's Dad for you, all small talk," David said. Why were fathers these days so much more interesting than the sons? Anna thought, and then pushed the thought aside. Myron was having trouble yanking out the cork; half had come away with the corkscrew, the other half still choking the neck of the bottle.

"Well, it interests me, what women think of their condition. In my mind, it's hardly better than it was fifty years ago, hell, even a hundred years ago, in some ways." He worked on the other half; then, giving up, stuck his finger inside the bottle and pushed it into the wine.

"Their condition?" When could they take a train, she wondered, leave this room behind? But David was clearly warming himself beneath the glow of his father's attention; it would be a long night, she could tell. "This is the reason you're still single, Dad."

"I don't know what you mean. You know, I've come to the realization that marriage is no longer a viable option. We've talked about this. A social experiment, too flawed, unnatural. What do you think, Mrs. K.?"

Anna groaned. The first tendrils of a headache prodding the recesses of her brain. She had allowed the wine to take her over and now, her weaknesses had exposed her. Just two more days and he would be gone. Her eyelids, it seemed, were closing by themselves.

Myron accepted her silence and turned to his son. "But you, David, continue to be a romantic. An admirable trait in these cynical times. You always did wish you lived in the nineteenth century. Love, tragedy, conquest, Napoleon."

"Dad!"

"What?"

"It's Anna. She's asleep."

"Your Anna. I'm glad you called me to come out. And you've waded into some perilous waters, in case you didn't know."

"How can you say that?"

"She's got something, I know, but it may be depression. And she's Russian. You always did love those Russian women. Remember? Olga, Irina, and what was the name of that third sister?"

"Masha."

"Ah, yes, of course. The unhappy Masha."

Myron, his tie askew, rose to pour them another round. David emptied his glass and spread out on the king bed, careful not to disturb Anna's shrimplike pose. His hands were crossed behind his head. He chuckled. "Yeah, I guess I always did love those Russian women."

They came home to a message on the answering machine: "Hey, Dave, it's Lauren. I forgot to tell you to say hello to your father for me. Tell him I'll see him the next time he's in town." Time began its tiptoeing, making Anna aware of every blink, each palpitation of the heart. David's long eyelashes were beating rapidly, like butterfly wings.

"Anna, I'm sorry." He banged on the bathroom door, jiggled the handle. "She's been a dear friend, I wish I had been honest about that. But I guess this was what I was afraid of. I don't know, you've been so testy. Anna!"

"Here it is," he heard. "The condition of women."

She stepped into the shower and turned on the hot water. Head lowered, still pounding, she stood under its spray. (How long could she stand it? Approximately forty-five seconds.) Her scorching chest, the rash of the heat pockmarked her arms. It occurred to her that there was a chance, a good one even, of her not being able to have any more children. The first biological gift of youth may have, already, been taken away. David was no longer knocking at the door; instead, Anna heard the guitar of bossa nova on the other side. Unhurried, complacent, only a little bit mournful.

By the time she opened the bathroom door, he was already asleep. She took two Advils, washed them down with a tall glass of water. Myron's book, which she had been laboring through all week, lay on her bedside table, bookmark sticking out like a taunting tongue. She had meant to read it all, to impress him with intelligent questions on his scholarship. Never before had she done this kind of extensive research to win over a parent.

She picked up *The Truth of the Everyday: What One Week With an Ordinary German Family Tells Us About the Holocaust* and opened it.

Anna didn't understand, why bother researching such minutiae? The youngest daughter, Elsa, her love of writing and gardening, her penchant for desserts and battle with her weight, how she got punished by staying out after curfew. What did this have to do with the Holocaust? Anna's eyes began to droop, but she forced them open, turning the page. Where would Seryozha sleep here? Where would he play?

A pack of kids was screaming over a bleating car alarm, a woman berating her girlfriend: "I told you to stay away from him, bitch." "Dave" rolled over, one hand flung across her stomach, hearing nothing.

2 8

—————————

A PHARMACIST WHO
DOESN'T BELIEVE IN DRUGS

What did Lev expect? He
had expected to fall in love with his own child. It would be the way
it was with Vasilisa, one look, the churning of the stomach, an intake
of breath, the trickle toward certainty, toward helpless love. Instead,
his first reaction upon seeing the pink wriggling thing was fear. What
would this dependent child become? A mutt of old and new, tugged,
like Lev, by the world and Bukharian traditions? Lacking, like Lev, in
a kind of faith?

Both he and Katia had been treating Roman like a porcelain elephant. Lev was afraid to pick up the bobbing head, which appeared to
be held up by the flimsiest of cords. He interpreted every cry as life-
threatening, a sob of anguish. Never before had Lev appreciated the
sweetness of family with their polite intrusions, their expert handling
of his son, the soothing reminder they brought with them that this had
all been done before.

Rabbi Melman officiated at the bris alongside the *mohel*. The
clamp, the straps, the anesthetic were prepared, and the baby was
returned bawling on a board, carved like a piece of sacrificial lamb.
Lev was unable to watch; nothing prepared him for this sight, its sur-
gical violence. The men dragged him outside to take in the extended

summer evening. Conversation was kept light, about soccer matches mostly, a little politics—the new wave of anti-Semitism in Moscow—but nothing touching on what they saw indoors. Having smoked a cigarette, drunk a few shots of pepper-infused vodka, it was hunger that finally drove the men back into the building.

Then the guests left and Lev and Katia were alone with the baby again. Lev marveled that Katia knew what to do, her hushes sounded so natural, her expert flicking open of the diaper's Velcro, the way she tested the temperature of milk on her wrist. He awaited orders, but none came, which only made him more anxious.

At night, he was aware of the tenseness of Katia's body beside his own, anticipating each murmur, her breasts overflowing with milk. Her head barely touched the pillow, as if levitating in expectation. Those first weeks, Lev would get up with her, moonlight pale in his boxer shorts, passing her the Desitin, observing as Katia changed their son, as she rocked him back to silence. He had not realized their lovemaking would end so abruptly, that she would ward off all his caresses.

He wondered what Oleg had done as a new father, did he sleep? It was an act Lev was almost incapable of, his mind contorting. When he heard Roman bawling, he worried; when he heard no bawling, he hovered his hand above the baby's mouth to check on even breath. Sometimes, to fall asleep, Lev warmed red wine in a pot with some sugar.

"A pharmacist who doesn't believe in drugs," Katia would joke, on her way to the bathroom, sometimes the first words they exchanged in a couple of hours. Bare-kneed, a cup of warm wine between his palms, he would make room for her on the couch. Practically cracking open with love, with gratitude, when he saw an expression, a smile he recognized.

Two weeks later, they received a gift. A BabyBjörn carrier. The card was addressed to him alone. He read it, read it again, threw it away, then fished it out of the garbage can and shoved it in his briefcase. He brought the black baby saddle to his wife, who was breast-feeding as usual, in her rocking chair.

"From Anna," he said.

Katia smiled one of her new motherly smiles, materializing on a single side of her mouth, impossible for him to decode. The baby coughed and spat up milk, the sound of a weak old man. Back to the baby, the baby, the baby.

That night, he read the card again, studied the black loops of the letters. *As a mother, I think of you,* written in terrible Russian, the awkward construction of the sentence, the vowels in *think* were completely wrong. Still, he reread. *Think of you*—that *you* dangling off the edge of the line, as if on the verge of plummeting.

2 9

YOU ARE MAKING A MISTAKE

Anna had received an e-mail from her lawyer: "He is looking for primary custody. You living with lover in studio doesn't help." She remembered when e-mail was limited to the most innocuous correspondence or for long-distance connections, but now Serge's future would be decided by e-mail. Her lawyer, always writing from a different airport, hated phone calls.

They were escorting Myron back to his train to Chicago. Penn Station on a Sunday evening, what else was there to say? It was the usual madhouse, dark, overrun, undignified. Despite the station's lack of grace, its chunky shabbiness, Myron refused to fly, saying he preferred the train, its proximity to the ground, its romantic associations, the kinds of people it brought together.

A few trains, including Myron's, were delayed; bodies leaned on one another in the waiting room, feet stretched out on backpacks and suitcases. David wandered off in search of snacks. Myron squinted at Anna, put his hand on top of hers, but didn't say anything. She had planned to show off her knowledge of Myron's book, leave him with a stamp of herself, her appropriate intelligence. He was more appealing to her than she expected. David lacked his maturity, the strength of his jawline. Her mind returned to the e-mail: "Change living arrangements?"

"Why one German family?" she finally broke the silence, glad she had stayed up the night before skimming the book. "There was not a single word about the Holocaust. I was wondering, why should we care about someone like Elsa?"

"You are making a mistake, dear. My son, you see, he's impressionable, so easily seduced by conflict, if you know what I mean."

Did he really say this? All the murmuring around her made her unsure about what she had heard. And his tone, confidential and deliberate. He patted her hand, nodding as if they understood each other. She was terrified, mute, until David returned with pretzels.

"I propose to read history in precisely those moments which are least obvious, and in them find the strands, the link to those events we mistakenly foreground," Myron continued, but louder and brasher, as if lecturing in a classroom. Then maybe he never said those other words, she thought, maybe it was her own feverish mind feeding them to him. Anna tugged at her curls, staring at Myron's suitcase, which looked impressively light, even though she hadn't seen him wear a single item of clothing twice.

"It's like psychoanalysis. We are made to connect our neuroses to major events in our lives. I am fucked up because my father hit my mother or my mother was never home. Thank you, David." Myron sprung open a packet of pretzels, offered them to Anna. "But what about the moments we don't remember? The night Mom *was* home, but we had trouble falling asleep, the morning our zipper was snagged and we were late for school, a boring date with an optometrist, an e-mail breaking plans for a movie. No less important, if one studied the consequences of each of those events."

Anna took a pretzel. It was good, dotted with salt crystals but also sweet; it made her thirsty. Would the act of eating this pretzel alter her "living arrangements," bring about a closer relationship with her son? She took another, broke it apart with her teeth. What she wouldn't do for water.

Before he got on the train, Myron gave her a brief hug, and again

came that same pat, this time between her shoulder blades. " 'Bye,"
she heard herself calling out, even when his back was already turned,
even when the only piece she saw of him was a flap of coat, a patchy
blur of beard.

The next morning, she called her old publisher for her job back. Her
boss, a playwright on the side, had moved on and his replacement
was vague about openings. He told her to send in her résumé, but he
didn't sound particularly enthusiastic about receiving it. *Try Hough-
ton*, he said, *they might have something there. Try Norton.*

"I speak Russian," she said, a skill she had rarely needed in the job
but was useful, just in case that Russian publisher bid on one of their
most popular books—one of *The Spiritual Lives of Animals* series, for
example.

"We'll contact you if something opens up."

The back of her silk robe was wet with perspiration. The remains of
buttered toast stuck to a corner of her plate. Still morning, technically,
and nothing planned; it would be another hot one, the weatherwoman
had chirped. Anna promised David she would not be running the air
conditioner.

"You are making a mistake, dear," his father had said yesterday.
One of the dark days.

"It's highly unusual to have a person your age looking to start in adver-
tising. You realize, of course, that there will be a long period when
you'll be asked to perform administrative tasks?"

"Of course," she said. But it was David who gave her the ultima-
tum. Just take whatever, he had said, you're draining us.

"Are you absolutely sure you want this job? Do you even know
what strategic planning entails?"

"Not quite," she said, stroking her scuffed Coach bag between her
knees as if it were a reclining cat, a napping infant.

"Yes, that's what it seems. It's just not clear this is the career for you."

"Oh, well, thank you for your time." She rose, she shook another puckered hand, turned yet another knob, and let herself out.

In a magazine, she read that as people age, their memory tends to dip further and further back in time. Her parents, these days, reminisced about the early days of their courtship, a shared political economy course at college, a joke her father made at a party, after which, having been denounced by one of the guests, he was taken in for questioning. They recalled their first Moscow winter as a married couple, when they had a week without heat, only hot-water bottles and each other's bodies. Through the walls, they would hear neighbors generating heat by jogging in circles around the kitchen. The excitement of scouring a peddler's book cart, flipping past manuals on tractor operation and John Reed novels, to find that rare book in translation, a Flaubert!

"Remember, Boris?" her mother might begin, in Russian, always to him in Russian. "Remember? When you were a resident practically living in the hospital and you got sick? Remember how you locked yourself in the bathroom of that wretched communal apartment, soaked yourself in cold water to bring down your temperature? Remember that unpleasant babushka who loved to gossip and eavesdrop, how she pounded on the bathroom door, 'Boris Markovich, you've been in there for eighteen minutes'? Remember, Boris?"

"Remember, Natasha?" her father might say. "When Anna was born and they wouldn't even let me in the hospital? And I stood outside what I thought was your window, knee-deep in snow, screaming, 'How does she look?' A nurse finally took pity on me, shivering, stamping my feet in that hat—remember that animal on my head? She finally pushed open her window and screamed back, 'She's beautiful.' And you were."

And Anna's memory? At times, hopelessly pinched in childhood. Excavating the things that used to bring her happiness—lately she had been focusing on a favorite Astrid Lindgren book popular in Russia at the time, a friendship between a young boy and a rotund middle-aged man named Karlsson who lived in a bachelor pad on the roof

and traveled via a propeller attached to his back. No one, apart from
the boy, knew that Karlsson existed. The first place, Anna believed,
she learned about secrets. Hundreds, maybe even thousands of books
inhaled since then. Why, at this point in her life, was Anna K. thinking
about the rosy-cheeked, overalled Karlsson?

One morning she was filled with the overwhelming desire to get out of
the house, to leave the cereal bowl unwashed, to take the train uptown
and see her son (she had a son, after all, remember?), tell him about
Karlsson. She ran out of the apartment without changing her clothes.
On the subway, she wondered which parts of the book Serge would
like best. Would Serge be awed, as she was, by Karlsson's pithy bon
mots, the little boy's attempts to hide the existence of his new best
friend from his parents?

The number 6 train was crowded as it crawled uptown. Her subway car had no air-conditioning, usually a deterrent for New Yorkers,
but the train clearly had not come in a long time; no one was taking
any chances, wedging themselves in despite the heat.

She stumbled out of the station and ran the entire way to her
old high-rise, weaving around nannies with strollers, old ladies, young
women who appeared to have just had their hair blow-dried professionally. She ran inside the building and pressed the elevator button.
Her former doorman stepped around his desk, making long strides
toward her.

"Excuse me, miss, but I have to call upstairs. The K.s are out."

"Misha, it's me, Anna K."

"You see," the doorman said, the receiver pressed to his ear.
"Nobody there."

"But we had an appointment," she said, sounding, she knew, as
uncertain as she felt. Nothing had been confirmed with Stasia, Anna's
decision was so spontaneous she had not even thought to put in a
phone call. But surely the Polish nanny knew Anna preferred Tues-
days, when David spent the entire day on campus, the longest day of
the week.

"I saw little Serge walk out with the nanny myself. But if you want to wait, you might run into Mr. K., who asked for his car to be brought out front at noon," he said coldly, just the wisp of a threat underlying his words. That was the way of certain doormen—if you no longer lived in the building, your identity was erased, you had been demoted from resident to guest.

The doorman's name was Mike, but Anna called him Misha. It had taken them more than six months to win him over; at first he had been suspicious of the Russian couple, whom he knew had arrived on the Upper East Side directly from the hinterlands of Queens. For Christmas, they gave him vodka and Russian candies with the scampering bear on the wrapper. They wrote him a card: *To Misha.* Now Anna understood she had no right to his name, neither its American nor Russian versions.

She plopped on the red love seat in the lobby and considered her options. What would happen if she waited here to confront her husband? Would he invite her upstairs for a chat or would he publicly dismiss her—Anna knew he was capable of either. Of course, she fantasized about the moment, all its possible variants. Herself as proud, winning a verbal exchange, gaining concessions. In her wilder imaginings, he agreed to open a bank account in her name, buy her an apartment where she could live with David and Serge; in her more private ones, he would hold her face again, securely. He would lead her back to their bedroom.

But shame seeped into her, a recognition that she didn't look as she once did. Her shorts, inappropriate in this gilded lobby, her T-shirt with "Brooklyn" stamped across the chest, shrunk in the Laundromat on Broome, white foam flaking off the letters. She could feel Misha's eyes on her, so she gathered as much dignity as she could and told him she would return later. These days, putting on clothes in the morning was a chore, every day blazing the same exact way.

Thank God Alex K. hadn't seen her like this, he would have been horrified. This Anna never would have earned his love, this Anna was something new—sneaking around in deodorant-stained T-shirts like a teenager, lurking around her old lobby. This Anna was dangerously close to ordinary.

When she got home, David was back from campus. He was grading the last of the summer school papers, a messy stack, stained and paper-clipped. His head, bent low, barely registered her appearance in the apartment. He took a few sips from a Rolling Rock.

"Hot out there, isn't it?" he said, maybe seeing the way her T-shirt was hanging on her body, moist with sweat beneath her armpits. By his voice, she could tell he was annoyed—David hated teaching summer school at a community college, hours wasted on pages of student indifference. In the past, he had read to her particularly egregious student sentences; at some point, he had stopped, or had she lost interest?

She stood over him, gulped from his Rolling Rock. She didn't tell him how she had spent the rest of the day strolling the boardwalk of Brighton Beach with the Russian retirees.

When she was younger, how embarrassed she was by Brighton, that this was what Americans knew of the Russian community. The babushkas gossiping outside their buildings on rainbow fold-out chairs, their daughters in blue eye shadow carefully matching the blue of their handbags, their sons in gold chains and tracksuits unzipped just enough to reveal a smattering of wiry hairs. But now, of course, Anna was beginning to feel differently about Brighton, affectionate, wistful. Had she reached the age of the prodigal daughter? Because she was ready to be embraced again by the very people she had rejected.

Anna had walked to the end of one side of the boardwalk, then turned toward Coney Island and the shimmering dot of the Ferris wheel. Her fellow strollers, as if they had discerned her former scorn, paid no attention to her. By the time she left for the subway, they were gathering at the railing for their daily viewing of the sunset.

"To have any chance of shared custody of Serge, we will need to change our living arrangements," she said to David, a light hand on his head.

He put down his green pen, rubbed his eyes. His novel, Anna noticed, had been put aside; it no longer wound its way into their conversations. The manuscript was no longer rubber-banded on his desk, but hidden somewhere, out of sight. The grappling, the revisions, David's private torments, must have all come to an end. Some muse she was, Anna thought bitterly.

"I'm just repeating what my lawyer told me," she said.

"I completely agree." He looked up, taking her hand and kissing it. "I was thinking the same thing, that we need some kind of change." His eyes, streaked with red, made her want to embrace him. A few hints, here and there, that he sacrificed.

They made love for the first time in over two months, tucked away in their own pocket again. She had burned in the sun—all that exposed skin, neither hat nor lotion—but he made no mention of it, just ran his fingers lightly over her stinging patches. It would be fall very soon, there was bound to be a shift. She rose from the bed, naked, turned on the air conditioner. She was feeling reckless.

3 0

WHO ARE WE?

In one of his sillier daydreams, Lev imagined her coming into the pharmacy. She would not look as she had on her own wedding day, but the way he knew her—Anna of the hallway. He would tell her about *Contempt*—the lushness of the color, the languor of Brigitte Bardot soaking in the bathtub, the way the onscreen marriage cooled and congealed, the questions the movie asked about death—and she would understand that side of him too.

She would take his hand, bring him out from behind the counter. They would go to a hotel together, or another sterile place, scoured of the past. The heavy curtains would be drawn shut, the bed vast and soft. She would undress herself, Lev decided, because even in reveries his hands shook when it came time to touch her. Beneath her clothes, he would find cold breasts like that of marble statues, wide, enthusiastic hips. She would push him toward desperate acts drawn from experience, from guttural longing.

On their first vacation in America, his parents took Lev to the only place they could afford to visit—Long Island. The tour bus filled with elderly couples brought them to a local winery, where they wandered the facilities and surveyed the wooden barrels, the gargantuan silver vats where the grapes were pressed. He was sorry that the most interesting part, the physical act of pressing, had already been done, out of his sight. That was what he imagined would take place in that hotel room between himself and Anna—in utter darkness, the mashing of skin and pulp, the sticky sweetness of grape juice.

Usually he would stop himself there, pace himself, or one of those dour Bukhi caregivers would be waiting for him with a folded prescription slip and he would be forced to resume later. It had been the same with the actress Isabelle Huppert; he loved how she could summon a kind of revulsion, a messy fearlessness. A woman who looked as though she could gnaw her own leg off if it meant survival, but with an unfathomable vulnerability. Exciting.

When it came time to turn off the lights, to shut down the pharmacy for the night, say good night to the owner, and head home, Lev would dawdle. He would do unnecessary work, righting toppled bottles of face cream and sunscreen, checking that all the packages were correctly alphabetized. What awaited him at home? Errands, a sultry, sexless, sleepless night.

It was still warm out for early September, so he took to sitting on a bench on Austin Street, watching life unfold in front of the movie theater. Groups of Bukhi kids (he knew some of their parents, of course) were savoring the freedom of their little collective. Hovering on the street corner for hours in order to decide where to go, pantomiming kisses for passing blond American girls. One night, he saw a couple walking by, the man's arm resting on (what turned out to be) Irina's back like a fur stole. He had been wrong, obviously, believing his torments would dissolve with marriage to Vasilisa.

Some nights, he would go to his parents' house for dinner. His father, secretly pleased, would set the table himself. If he caught the extent of Lev's mood, he would remind him that at Lev's age, he had started over in a new country. So what was Lev's problem? A beautiful baby, a wife that turned out okay, what else did he want? At least in a communist country you knew to be happy with simple miracles. Here, health and happiness were never enough, you were always told to want more. But there is nothing more, Levchik, this is what commercials never dare to tell us.

"Za zdarovia!" he would remind his son, pour another glass of vodka.

Inevitably, the telephone would ring. "Yes, he's here," his father would admit, and watch him carefully. Lev would tell Katia that he'd be home in just a few minutes, he had been checking on the health of his parents. The slow gathering of the leftovers, plastic containers crammed with *plov,* with *samsi* from the store. A chocolate wafer cake, hard and crumbly. In a jar, he would find homemade plum preserves. A loud kiss from his father, but Lev was sure his father had penetrated all his thoughts about Anna and other shameful inner echoes. Lev's son was only one month old, and already he had failed him.

Who am I? Roman might ask him when he got older, when questions like that would begin to press their way into his consciousness.

How do I know? Lev would be forced to say. *I barely know what I want. Who I am.*

"We're Bukharian, that's all there is to it," Oleg said at Flanagan's. Since Oleg's increased religious observance, Fridays were no longer an option, but this was a rare exception—Ruben's wife was pregnant. Without celebrations, we would be animals, Oleg had said on the phone, while Svetlana clucked in the background. He was preparing them for the end, when Oleg could no longer drink beer, would be observing full kashrut.

The three of them sat in their old booth near the back, which they procured by threatening a group of underage kids in Forest Hills High School jerseys who were sitting there when they arrived. They played a round of darts, drank three pitchers. And now Lev, possibly deeply inebriated, posed this question: "Who are we?"

"Lev, your problem is simple," Oleg said. "You enjoy making things difficult for yourself. You've always been this way. Look, there are two different ways to pray in synagogue. You can enjoy the cantor's singing and think about dinner or you can sit there and resent every minute of the service. You know what I mean?"

It was odd to hear Oleg talking about synagogue, when not too long ago he was still groping the underside of the waitress's ass.

"I think so," Lev said.

"Just stop beating yourself already. Stop asking foolish questions. Come with us to Shabbos services once in a while, that'll get your head straight." Oleg still wore green, but now the color made his skin look sallow. He had lost weight, his edges defined, revealing dips and craters. He stretched in his seat as if confined.

"Aren't we drinking to my baby?" Ruben reminded them, slumped against the seat, gesturing with his mostly empty mug. They would have to put him in a cab later, wake up his wife to meet the car downstairs. The usual story.

A football game was on, the volume cranked up. Americans with their blind devotion to football; the three of them were proud soccer players, of course, the real "football." A cheer went up at the bar, fists in the air.

Lev picked up his own mug and looked up; Oleg was staring at him, eyes narrowed, as though he had grasped two dangling strands of rope and had, just now, managed to knot them together.

"A toast to Ruben and fatherhood," came out of Lev's lips. He sipped his beer and grimaced. The quality of beer in this place had always been poor, frothy water passing for ale; Lev didn't think he could continue drinking the stuff. Their bar, their longtime haven, Lev realized, wouldn't last much longer. They were still so young, and yet it felt otherwise, like they were shrinking, graying, disappearing. Outside the bar, Lev and Oleg watched Ruben's cab peel away. They said good-bye, slapped each other on the back. Lev was alone.

And again Anna materialized in his mind. With her image, the old discomfort returned. "Poor Anna," his wife had said. That was it, what was bothering him—in that studio apartment, Anna didn't match. Like a sleek modern couch among antiques, there had been a grotesque discrepancy. That was how he remembered her from her own wedding, out of place there too.

So who was he? An observer, nothing more. In the hallway, he had wanted so badly to reach out his hand, to settle it on Anna's collarbone, a move worthy of Jean-Louis Trintignant. But it was a ludicrous, dangerous fancy. He was a passive watcher of film. This was the role life had for him.

And somehow, with that thought, Lev could breathe again. He quickened his step, widened the distance between himself and Flanagan's. A bodega was still open at two a.m. He grabbed a bunch of roses out of a bucket; they were already decomposing, the lips of their buds shriveling. An Uzbek shopkeeper handed him change, a gold-toothed smile, an exchange between men. The guilty flowers for the wife, the man thought, hadn't he sold a million such bouquets?

Lev ran the entire way home. Katia would wake up to roses in the vase, red, resplendent, and then, just maybe, she would be at peace. No more tears. No more "You don't love me's." She would welcome him inside her again. He stepped into the apartment, which was tinted, dipped in nighttime black. The roses he placed on the table, next to a covered plate of what he assumed was his dinner, already cut into digestible pieces. In the bedroom, his wife had wrapped the entire blanket around herself, leaving half the bed bare. And all that courage, generating strength as he ran through the empty streets, dissipated. Guiltily, he didn't look in on his son, who was sensitive to the slightest of movements. For the first time, Lev had to force himself to get undressed, to climb into that bed, to stay.

A week later, he found himself looking for her at the Ryba on Avenue O. Katia was surprised he had agreed to go, since he hated those amorphous family parties where no one really knew the birthday girl—this time a twelve-year-old relative from Katia's father's side. The guest of honor tended to be ignored by the adults, who organized the party for themselves, to gossip, fling back a few shots of vodka. Maybe, Lev thought, *she* would be there.

But when he arrived, his hopes seemed ludicrous. Would she really walk into this windowless, narrow restaurant, *Anna,* walking down the worn immigrant streets of Avenue O? It seemed all right for them, somehow, they would never fit in with Americans; no, if anything, their survival had depended on their going to places like the Ryba, Café Ellara, and the like. Even Anna's parents, forking herring at one corner of the table, were at home here. But this place wasn't for her.

She was meant for loftier places, deferential American waiters in tuxedos instead of this schlumpy server who had allowed himself to be talked into gulping down a shot of vodka along with the table and was now whistling through his teeth.

And what if she did show up? What could possibly happen between them? Maybe she and Katia would make up and one day, in the not-too-distant future, he would fling open the door to find Anna K. in their hallway. His wife would be out on an errand and Lev would invite her inside. She would shake her curls out, still wet from the late afternoon drizzle. She would be wearing, well, anything (his imagination faltered), something soft, close to the skin. She would watch the procession of his hands on her body, first there, dip under there. She would smother him with her scent. Still naked, he would make her a strong cup of tea and listen to her, and then he would talk. Someone tugged on Lev's sleeve; it was his turn to make a toast from himself and Katia, and with relief, he let the scenario shimmer away, out of his mind.

In the middle of the table, a whole red snapper was privy to the drunken conversations, its center already disemboweled, its eye gazing upward, moist and languid.

"Did you hear about Anna K.?" somebody said.

"She'll lose her son and doesn't seem to care."

"An unnatural woman. To not care about her own child."

"As soon as a young man shows up, she up and leaves her husband."

"Unnatural, really. Her child, a baby—what else does a woman have?"

"That man—it won't last long."

"No, that's obvious."

"With a woman like that, the man never lasts long."

"Shh, her uncle is right across from you."

"But it's true."

"It's a regular scandal. But still, Marinachka, speak softly, have some pity. That's her uncle in the gray tie."

"You don't have to tell me twice."

"But you're right, of course, every word. It's unnatural. That's exactly what it is."

3 1

——————

MOTHER, CHILD

And so it happened that dur-
ing this particular clandestine visit with Serge, he walked in, with
his Burberry jacket, his laptop, a tie gleaming silver. Even Stasia was
flustered, dropped dishes in the sink, and ran to the door. There was
nowhere for Anna to run; reclined on the couch, her son on her lap, the
Astrid Lindgren book spread open before them. (For she had found
it—*aha!*—at the St. Petersburg Bookstore that afternoon on Brighton
Beach Avenue. Her childhood returned to her, the very same pictures;
Karlsson stuffing his face with Swedish meatballs.)

"What? Here?" Alex sputtered. How old he looked, Anna thought, the
trimmed beard, the crocodile skin. He was heavier, not just around the
middle but everywhere—heavy face, thighs, the dense fabric of his suit.

"It is my fault." Stasia ran out of the kitchen, a towel twisted in her
hand. Because, really, what was there to explain? The scene was fairly
self-explanatory—mother, child, a book about an overweight man with
a propeller on his back.

"Papa!" Seryozha said, pleased.

"So you've been doing this, then, under my nose?"

Anna took Serge off her lap, placed him beside her on the couch.
He hoisted himself down and Stasia took him by the hand.

"My fault," Stasia repeated, but Alex K. waved her away. He was still staring at Anna. Clearly, an action was required of her. Taking stock of the situation, she realized she had a limited arsenal at her disposal: her voice, her body, the appeal of motherhood. She could burst or beg, she could weep. Inside, she felt dull, sapped of strength. Fighting him felt pointless.

"Why are you here?" he said, in Russian. He was rooted to that corner by the door, bald spot reflected in the small oval mirror, keys dangling from his index finger.

"Did you think I wouldn't see my son? This has all been impossible." She had risen from the couch, but kept her distance. Whatever she used to see in his eyes was now gone.

"Why won't you admit this is all your fault?" Alex said. "So why here now?" He used the formal "-vy" address with her; she hated how Russians could do that, withdraw their intimacy. He used the same tone as the one he saved for wait staff, for his administrator.

"I was wrong, Sasha. What else can I say?"

"You never said a thing. That's the problem. You never said a word," he said, pulling open the door. And then, softly, "And now, why don't we let lawyers handle this?"

Anna picked up her bag. "But my son," she tried, even allowed herself to touch his arm meekly. It had soothed him in the past, this touch, dissipated his stress or anger. No matter how busy, he had always made time for her touch. This time, he jerked his arm away, so sharply that the keys flew out of his hand, colliding into the bare wall. She heard a dull thump followed by a metallic clang. Instinctively, Anna bent down to pick them up from where they lay, spooled, on the hardwood floor. It occurred to her that there were so many things she had not yet seen, her husband's shoes from this perspective, the gray filaments in his trousers.

"Goddamn it!" He tore the keys out of her hand, leaving a serrated red trail along her palm.

Down the hallway, she heard the shuffle of footsteps, the gentle pounding of a cane against carpet.

"Sasha, have some pity. I'm his mother. Let me say good-bye at least."

"Go, mother," he said, as if the word "mother" could be substituted with "bitch" or "lunatic" or something else that was far worse. He held the door open with his foot; she could feel his breath on her neck as she crossed the lintel.

She was wearing sweat shorts and flip-flops, her knees still burning red from her Brighton Beach excursion. "What *happened* to you?" she thought he asked, but when she checked behind her, he was already gone.

An old woman stood by the elevator watching, her hair the color of tangerines. Anna recognized her as the neighbor she used to avoid, a woman whose door would always be cracked open, in order to report on the collective drama of the building.

Anna readjusted her face and stood mute for the entire ride to the lobby. She had always hated that the elevator was paneled by mirrors; she had rarely wanted to look at herself reflected from all vantage points, especially with these bright lights hunting down each bodily imperfection. And certainly right now—swollen, red, her throbbing hand—it was the last sight she needed.

3 2

THE CHOSEN IMMIGRANT

How do immigrants retain their culture? By tethering themselves to the older generation, by procreating with a sharer of the language, by returning to the country of origin—taking its public transportation, staying with relatives, paying the lower museum entrance fees reserved for locals, buying potatoes in its marketplaces? But the country Russian immigrants left behind has been transformed; it has become a brand-new overcoat, unrecognizable from the old. The road back, severed. The road ahead, improvised, littered with myths. *Acquire,* a voice prods you on, *succeed at all costs; you must justify your journey.*

Once, Anna's tenth-grade class was driven to the MTV studios on a field trip. Restless teenagers waited in line for bleacher seats. If they were lucky, a camera would pan over them and they could wave to their parents. Anna, as usual, stood a few paces apart, a book in her hand. When the punked-out intern emerged with her clipboard, her purple lipstick, it was Anna to whom she gravitated, Anna who was to decorate the set, Anna who would dance in the background of the game show *Remote Control.* The rest of the class was envious, surprised, because to them Anna had been, for the most part, invisible.

She had played her role in the school to perfection: teacher's pet, sullen athlete, so few friends it was as if there were none.

Was Anna surprised at this distinction? Yanked out of line and catapulted onto the stage? Not a bit. She knew she was chosen because she was an immigrant. She put away her book and followed the intern ahead of the entire class.

She danced then, all curls and Cavaricci pants, as the host rattled off questions to the bewildered contestants. In the background, Anna swayed, arms pumping, as though in a trance.

"How ya doing?" Colin Quinn asked her during a commercial break.

She never saw this particular show, never found out when it aired. And what if it did? Her parents didn't have cable anyway, couldn't afford it or figure out how to subscribe. But she was left with a fatalistic certainty. Why was it the eleven-year-old Anna who, while on her first American vacation in a Borscht Belt hotel, won first prize in bingo, a plastic bag of saltwater taffy and Three Musketeers candy bars? And later that same night, wasn't it *she* who was brought up onstage by the unfunny comedian? Why did *she* leave the Soviet Union, but her best friend Olga had to stay?

There were responsibilities to being chosen: To keep herself open for when the moment arrived. To slough off the old country, refuse to dwell. But what took its place? For Anna, just waiting, for fate to spark. To be called into action. For the unbroken American life of her dreams to begin.

3 3

———————————

A FALL ROMANCE

The red-gold of fall; trees the color of caramelized carrots, soft and browned. The New York stage was decorated for love and Anna insisted on taking advantage of her props. A cumin accent to her Central Park strolls with David, the smell of hot dogs and peanuts. A new book started together, *The Awakening*, discussing it on benches, as he plucked twigs out of Anna's curls. Without speaking, they might decide on noodles for dinner. When they ignored the future, it was unbearably perfect, the pleasure almost too sharp.

Of course, there were less cinematic moments as well. David's impatience when it came time to shop. His rage at seeing old classmates' first books in the New Releases section at Barnes & Noble. His impatience with any display of rude behavior. Just that afternoon, a young woman pushed David by mistake and failed to apologize, and he chased her down Prince Street, saying "Would it kill you to say 'I'm sorry'?" Anna didn't understand where inside David all that anger thrived.

But those were blips, a badly spliced reel of film. He also knew how to erase those incidents from her short-term memory. He left Post-its around the house when he went to work. She found *Missing you already* stuck to the underside of her face wash. The yellow of *Oh Anna, My Anna* peeked out from beneath the sole of her shoe. A filled cereal bowl waited for her on the counter, sprinkled with dried cranberries. David even promised a trip to Edison; his mother, it seemed, was eager to meet her.

And how was this contentment achieved? By firmly pushing Alex, Serge, Nadia, and her parents, job applications, all out of her mind. They marred the uncomplicated crispness of a Fuji apple, the satisfying crumbling of leaves beneath the heel of a boot, of winter fabrics splayed out in the front of stores, the first sip of hot chocolate from City Bakery.

Another event she wished to forget: a forty-second birthday come and gone.

Fall days reminded her of Katia, their afternoons of museum trips, of girlish laughter, the younger girl's adoration. Anna waited until David went off to campus and picked up the phone. Several mornings, she had thought about getting on a subway to Rego Park to see Katia's baby. The intention alone made it hard to breathe. No right to see others' babies. But it was her cousin's baby, surely guilt should make an exception. She pressed the button on the phone marked "Talk," then pressed it again when she heard the dial tone.

That night, David would be having a drink with Lauren. He had told Anna that morning, and she had pretended to be grateful for the honesty. But she noted that he took extra care with his appearance, put on a sweater they'd bought at Banana Republic (on sale; these days everything they bought was on sale), a sweater Anna had praised as sexy. Innocently, he pulled it over his head and drew it down over his torso. Honesty had never been a cherished value of Anna's, but David swore it held a relationship together. He kissed her, by way of goodbye, on the forehead.

Anna thought of Katia's fleshy Bukharian husband, who had lumbered awkwardly into Anna's apartment. His shy demeanor, hands in the pockets of his pleated pants, his thick eyebrows, the careful way he listened to her, as though dipping his net into a pool to gather a single floating leaf. He was no writer, no intellectual, yet for a moment it felt as though he could grasp her, inscribe her story. Yes, if Anna were to admit it to herself, there had been a flash of intensity in his eyes. Was she still capable of extracting desire then? She had no plans for tonight. She picked up the phone again.

3 4

―――――

NOTHING APPROPRIATE
ABOUT ANNA K.

How different this shopping excursion was from her last preparations for Chagall and the Zavurovs' New Year's party. Now Anna was forced to trawl sample sales, request discounts for stains and unraveling thread, battle sausage immigrants for the last torn Badgley Mischka. Returning from the mirror to find a Russian woman slithering into Anna's jeans—"I thought they were for sale," she said, sheepishly handing them back.

David couldn't believe that she wanted to return to Chagall, to see all those people after, well . . . they didn't regret it, did they, but to flaunt it was another matter. Why not lay low for a while longer, he suggested, it would be a mistake.

"Mistake?" Anna K. said. "Did you say mistake?"

"Yes," he said, unblinking. "Mistake."

That discussion had ended badly, with David typing furiously on his computer on one side of the room, Anna sulking on the futon couch, pretending to flip through a magazine while waiting for an apology. In the past, he would . . . well, what did it matter anymore what he *used* to do? In any case, no apology came, so she would go to the party and she would find a dress.

When Anna had finally worked up the courage to dial Katia and

Lev's number, Katia had been home sick from work. She was so happy to hear from her, Katia had insisted, and it was then she extended the invitation, tentatively but affectionately, reminding her they were cousins, she had known and loved Anna since birth. Anna making all the appropriate noises, all the tender endearments, but secretly wondering about Lev. Yes, when she thought of it, he *had* swallowed her as men used to do, *had* gulped her down. Eyes darting around her chin as she spoke. And it had been too long since she felt her leveraging power; in the past, she never would have allowed a lover to imagine he was her sole consumer.

Once invited to the party, she was eager to get off the phone with her cousin. She would re-create her former success with the right dress. "Good-bye, Katyenka," she said.

She could still recall the faces of all those men—watching her as if transported to a time in their lives when the impossibility of love brought more pleasure than realized love. This time, however, Anna's hunt for the ineffable would have to begin at designer sample sales.

A Russian woman (they were everywhere these days, but predictably at sample sales) in her late twenties, blond hair embroidering a sweetheart face, pushed Anna's clothes to the side to make room for her own hangers. Quickly, she undressed beside her, small, perky breasts, gold belly-button hoop, trying on flimsy see-through tops. On Anna, a dress was sitting all wrong, tight around the hips, hem trailing. Time dripping between her fingers.

The dress she bought; she could tell he despised it. She herself had been torn about whether to purchase it, had stood in the common Loehmann's dressing room for almost an hour, twisted in indecision. It was tight, no doubt about it, the décolletage quite low. Out they popped, her breasts, with so little coverage. But the dress was black and lacy, a Vivienne Westwood, its price slashed by more than half. Just five years ago, she wouldn't have hesitated, she would have made her entrance at any party and taken her seat. She wouldn't have needed to rise; by the end of the night, business cards would be lining her evening bag.

"But isn't it sexy?" she asked David. She had spritzed on some perfume in the bathroom, taken some trouble with makeup for the first time in weeks. She had swung open the door of the bathroom, sashayed in her four-year-old red Jimmy Choos. He looked up at her in horror.

"Honey, you can't wear that. If you absolutely have to go, you just can't wear it. I mean, seriously, Anna, take a look at yourself."

He turned back to his papers, a flush of pink streaking from his cheeks down to his neck. He refused to attend the party, and the residue of that argument was still embedded in his posture. She began taking off the dress, a flutter of panic beating its wings against her chest.

"You won't wear that, will you?" he said without looking up, absentmindedly reaching out to stroke her hip. "You'll return it, right?"

If he waited for her answer, if he put away his work, if he kissed her on the lips, traced the outline of her jaw, she decided she would not wear the dress. She gave him time, slowly tying the sash of her robe, packing the dress back into its cellophane garment bag, squeezing it into the rickety, overstuffed closet. She put on the kettle for tea, counted out sugar cubes. The whine of the kettle, the water boiling. Yes, it seemed she would wear the dress.

There was a moment, right outside Chagall, when she was tempted to tell the cabbie to turn around and return to Manhattan. Pretending to fumble with the exact change, she watched people pouring into the Russian restaurant. Beneath her coat, she felt exposed and alone. Who knew where David went tonight; he said he would be spending New Year's Eve with Matt and Jim at a mellow Columbia alumni party, but she wasn't sure anymore. All his gestures lately felt deceptive, the gaps in his sentences indicating miles of unspoken territory.

She paid the driver and walked inside, carefully gauging the height of her heels; her feet had become accustomed to an old pair of sneakers. Her toes were already pulsating with the effort to walk, compressed into the pointy tips of her shoes. At the coat check, she gave away her protective shield, and as she climbed the stairs toward the restaurant, she glimpsed herself in the full-length mirror. What did she see? All that excess flesh, a few new spots, darker than she remembered them, dotting her chest. Her courage failed her. She would go home immediately, even if it meant spending the night alone. But first, a drink?

"Anna!" she heard. On the other side of those swinging doors, salsa gyrations were in full swing. A man with a ponytail led a band in matching silver vests. She moved toward the voice, Katia's, the voice of forgiveness. She was carrying a baby, dressed in a powder-blue jumpsuit, on one hip, and Anna was surprised to find Katia wearing black, a color she usually avoided; she always said it made her look old before her time. Katia hoisted Roman onto Anna's shoulder, the heat of his body suffocating her. Anna realized that she had forgotten the weight of a baby, heavier than she remembered, like a squirming bag of groceries.

"Take him away," she heard herself say, more harshly than she would have liked. Katia quickly removed her son and Anna forced herself to stay where she was, to caress the baby's head, to ask Katia about her health, the baby's lovable idiosyncrasies—did he sleep through much of the night, did his face bunch up when the pacifier was removed— but she was hot and thirsty. Eyes, she felt, were appraising her, and when she looked down, she was horrified to find that the transfer of a baby had caused a slice of nipple to protrude from behind the bodice. The dress was too tight, even her ribcage ached.

After she adjusted herself, she found that Katia had been called away to show off the baby to relatives and now she was standing by herself. On the other side of the room she saw a bar, and with some difficulty Anna made her way along the waxy dance floor. In the background the singer bleated, *Give me, give me, give me a man after midnight.*

Women materialized along the way to the bar to block Anna's path; like the wolf in "Little Red Riding Hood" (or to be more culturally precise, *"Krasnaia Shapochka"*), they had found their prey. Women, with their painted eyelids, their costume jewelry, asked her (vindictively, she was sure) about her son. Women—who once came to her birthday parties with a variety of immigrant presents: pajamas from Mandee's, an assortment of Revlon lipsticks—now practically drowned her in Chanel No. 5, in Red Door.

"And your son, Anyechka, how old is he now? What is he doing these days? My Larochka's children are already in kindergarten. What about your son?"

Anna forced herself to give the proper answers, to inquire about their families. She tried to think of ways to extricate herself. These faces from her childhood, already changing with Botox, equine due to minor plastic surgery, swam before her.

Discotheque lights were flashing maniacally across the dance floor. Children, chasing one another, weaved around the legs of adults. The way back to the door and out onto Brighton Beach Avenue was long and fraught with peril; she would have to glide past tables stuffed with relatives, snake around gossiping friends of the family. More Chanel No. 5, more Red Door. Her son, they wanted to know. What would she say about him, they wondered, when she never saw him? How would she put her own situation into words? If only her parents hadn't been away this New Year's, if only her mother were here to mitigate the onslaught, thought Anna. Natasha Roitman excelled at the masquerading of facts.

And then a blessed, "Can I get you a drink, Anna Borisovna?" and she was steered away from the tsunami of women. The pull of Lev's arm, guiding her toward the bar, and she was rescued.

"Vodka martini, strong," she managed, aware of the heat spreading itself down her neck, no doubt across her breasts. She watched Lev as he spoke in Russian to the bartender, his ill-fitting, cheaply made suit, the stockiness of his frame, skin the color of charred meat. His Russian so much more confident than her own, the authoritative voice her father used to attempt when punishing her as a child. The same voice that had drawn her to Alex, but this one was different somehow, speckled with longing.

She took the drink he handed to her and she felt she could hold herself upright again. They clinked glasses, the vibration of coming together, not unlike the electrifying sound of a kiss.

. . .

By the end of the night, even Katia would give up on being her defender. It was decided that there was nothing appropriate about Anna K.: her costume was that of a common prostitute, she had embezzled Katia's fiancé and was now coquetting with her husband. Was she even Russian anymore? Language disintegrated in her mouth, the words strung together as if in translation.

And there she was at the bar, gulping her fourth or fifth glass of wine, her hand on Lev Gavrilov's shoulder, breasts flapping all about. Those purple-stained teeth, that disjointed laugh. And no one had seen quite that shade of face, suffused as it was with alcohol.

It was a real pity how far off the path she had veered. A woman who only a few years ago had everything they might want—an Upper East Side condo, a lovely little boy, a *delovoy* husband who was probably rarely at home. Freedom she had, and money. And now look at her, they said, just look at her. As if she hadn't noticed their glares, cool cucumber that she was, as if she did not sense the turbulence in the air about her.

He watched Katia throwing clothes into duffel bags in the middle of the night. Outside they could hear the hoots of New Year's revelry— "*S Novym Godom,*" the screeching of tires, loud smacking kisses. Roman whimpered in his sleep. Katia's hair was piled on top of her head in a babushka bun, and she continued to pile colorful tops, her still-oversized maternity pants, Roman's tiny *kombinezony* inside those bags, pressing down on the clothes to get the zipper closed. She still wore the stockings from the party, glittery opaque casings stretched tight.

"I knew it," she said, as if to herself.

Lev, still in his suit, leaned against the wall of the bedroom. After the Chagall party, Katia had cried the entire cab ride home and he had ignored her, staring out the window onto Queens Boulevard. The purple lights of Shimmy's, the boarded-up storefronts, identical residential buildings, the hibernating heap of Queens Plaza. How he hated the way she cried, helplessly, soaked in self-pity, like a child manipulating adults with her tears. In the past, he had always melted, how could he not? He had taken Katia into his arms, had embraced her soft round shoulders, had kissed her face and watched it brighten beneath his kisses.

"Do you still love me?" she would ask timidly, and order would be restored.

Now, for a change, he longed to act against his best interests. He was at the precipice, peering down on certain destruction just moments away. Katia moved to the kitchen, stacking cans of formula on the table. Lev shook himself out of numbness.

At the party, all he had seen in front of him was Anna, vivacious body—ripe, feminine, fragrant. Did they really talk all night? He would have said no, that it was only a long, marvelous minute they stood there by the bar, discussing French movies, their favorite restaurants, then her son and parents. The vastness of an intelligent mind opening itself to him was what he was now holding on to, the acute pleasure of it pulsating in his stomach.

"Katyenka, please stop packing for one minute." He said the sentence in solid chunks, extracting air between each word. He placed his hand on the place where her back began and neck ended. If she would only let him touch her, if she would take his hand and place it on her breast, the way she used to. He had been patient with her, but he wanted her, for God's sake, he still yearned.

She slithered out of his grasp and raised her palm as though feeling her way around a wall in the dark. "I could scream," she said, red and swollen. He had never seen her look so wild, so tangled and splotchy.

A perverse, uncharacteristic instinct within him whispered, *Let her leave.*

A boardwalk in winter—fog-drenched, a bitter wind. Cold penetrating her; Anna was not prepared for the fierceness of an ocean gale. Some days she would warm up at Tatiana's; one of the few diners in the room, she ordered only those sentimental dishes from her childhood.

Herring in olive oil enveloped by shaved raw onion, hearty borscht with grizzled pieces of beef, smoked sturgeon, marinated green tomatoes, pastry crammed with sour cherries, all washed down with *kvas*. She tried to speak with the waitress in Russian, but so many words came up blank. Check? She had never had to say that word as a child and now found it was hidden too deeply, irretrievably in her brain.

"Check, please," she said in English.

Then she went back out to wander the boardwalk. At first she had no particular aim, but eventually a routine established itself—first to Coney Island, then back, stilled here and there by the sight of the ocean. *Claim me*, she wanted to say, *take me back*. By abandoning all this, had she made the wrong choice?

Her parents had probably heard about the New Year's party; her mother's messages had been escalating in volume. She was drained of explanations, guilty. Drops of ice clung to the fake fur of her collar.

Scurrying past her for refuge inside Tatiana's walls were a pair of her former countrywomen in stylish leather boots, giggling in the cold. They came in with shopping bags, their hair varying shades of beet. They stared at the figure in black, a woman alone, not quite Russian, they decided.

A few times, Anna ran into an older man coming in from the beach with his fishing rod, the hood of his windbreaker covering his bald head, brown pants rolled up to his ankles.

"Any fish out there?" she would ask.

If he hadn't ignored her each time, he might have told her, "None."

A Rego Park encrusted with snow had few lingerers on its roads. All Sunday journeys were strictly goal-oriented; only delivery people out on these roads, the sturdiest of *babushki*, the mentally dispossessed— homeless people, artists. Windowpanes rattling like chattering teeth. A terrible time for Anna's parents, whose marriage relied on out-of-doors excursions.

Her mother was computer programming from home; her father,

stalled between failed business ventures. The Russian Community Center he'd invested in had not worked out as planned. Due to the fickleness of the still-Soviet consumer, he said. No loyalty, he grumbled, rereading that day's paper for the third or fourth time, hit one little snag and they're out of there. Her mother said nothing, suppressing a verbal *I told you so,* emblazoned on her face. But she did tell him so, she'd known the center would turn out to be a disaster. In old age, just as in the past, the ex-Soviets fortified their territory; they knew when to embark and when to flee toward greener pastures. Their fighting had escalated: who got the bigger birthday cake, whose grandson was a lawyer, and whose was a loser.

In an attempt at cultural entertainment, Anna's father hired a famous 1960s Soviet actress to put on a one-woman show, but the audience was depressed that she had aged so severely. "Remember that movie she was in with Plisetskaya? My God, she was so beautiful. And now look at her," they said loudly, during the actress's tearful recitation of Tatiana's love letter to Onegin. The actress ran out of the center, but not before demanding her sizable fee. At the end, there had been a mutiny of sorts, Anna's father left with unpaid bills.

And the Roitmans' friends, who had come to the U.S. at exactly the same time, even later, in the mid-eighties, had by now moved up to Manhattan, scattered to the suburbs. They were buying and selling art and real estate, signing up for South African safari packages, retiring in their late fifties. But the Roitmans were squeezed into the same two-bedroom apartment, one flight down from an elevator stop, in Rego Park along with all the others trapped in immigrant purgatory. It was humiliating.

Who was to blame for this stasis? To start, Natasha believed she should have married that Grisha who had salivated for her at university. He wasn't as handsome as Boris back then, his teeth capped and pointing every which way, but look at him now, an endocrinologist in Westchester, his wife with her fur coat, a fresh set of teeth. Their mansion so new the soil was still warm, they said.

Anna's mother held an abacus inside her head with all her husband's missteps counted—the apartment they could have flipped, the stock they should have sold, then there was that house in New Jersey, by now tripled in price. Passing up on solid investments for foolish get-rich schemes—ach, that was the Russian way. Add Anna to this claus-trophobic scene.

"Should I take Russian classes?" Anna wondered aloud, a cup of tea cold between her palms.

Her mother looked up from the computer. Was her daughter in her right mind? Natasha didn't know whether to believe the sto-ries about her performance at her brother's party. According to her brother, Katia had left her husband, taken her son, and moved back in with her parents.

She had gone wrong somewhere with Anna, that was clear, but frankly, Natasha had no idea what to do. Should she take her aside, like Americans do in movies, tell her if Anna wanted to talk, she would be willing to listen? Her own mother used to stuff Natasha with food when she got depressed, feed her one cherry *pirog* after another to plug up her adolescent sorrow. But Anna was over forty now, and if Natasha was honest with herself, she would admit that her daugh-ter frightened her—and probably always had—with her moods, their uncompromising depths.

"Are you crazy?" Natasha finally said (because did she really need an argument now, the day was so oppressive and her husband's perpet-ual presence—the shuffling sound he made in his *tapki,* his inability to rustle up his own snack—was wearing on her nerves). "To hell with Russian classes. Get a job. You certainly need one now."

"A job, right." Anna fiddled with her curls. "I've been trying."

"You need one," her mother repeated with a meaningful look. "Now."

Natasha wanted to listen to her daughter, of course she did, but she was unable to pose the right question, to crack open the torso of the doll that harbored the final thimble-sized *matryoshka.* As long as it remained unacknowledged, the problem—whatever it was, if it even existed—could be considered harmless.

"Want something sweet with your tea? *Tortik,* maybe, a nice meringue cookie?" was what she said instead.

3 5

A WALKING MIRAGE

Valentine's Day in New York City is rarely pleasant even for those with enough foresight to have secured an eight o'clock reservation three months earlier. Vulnerable couples on street corners hailed cabs in the cold. In the vitrines, mannequin chests were sheathed in red, behind them desperate signs reading "Love Me!" "Love Me!" Chocolates with dripping centers were wrapped in red and gold foil. Anxious men with flowers jaywalked on every street.

The overbooked restaurants presented identical Valentine's menus with their tired filet mignon, the inevitable oysters and fondue. Jittery waiters rushed prix-fixe courses to the table as plastic hearts dangled from the ceiling. Starving couples stood squashed at the door, their reservation times come and gone so now they hovered like seagulls, monitoring bites of chocolate cake. Tiny dramas unfolded at each table, with expectation, then disappointment or boredom stretched across nearly every face. For one night, everyone had donned the stiff petticoats of romance.

It was under these limited conditions that David broke the news.

"Iowa?" Anna asked. The vanilla ice cream on top of the Tarte Tatin was melting, forming a lumpy, milky pool.

"The new start we talked about."

"Iowa?" She put down her fork.

"The best comp job I applied for, and I got it! Can you believe it? It'll be great for me, you know, to be so close to all those writers. The Writers' Workshop, you know, in Iowa. I can take a class, maybe there's still life in this novel."

"You never told me you interviewed. Was it by phone?"

"A new start, you said so yourself, with Serge." He continued, speaking quickly. "How could the three of us live in my apartment, but how can we afford anything else here?"

"We can move to Rego Park."

"Queens? Are you kidding?"

"Why not?"

"You're not serious. Better Iowa than Queens." Lifting his cup of coffee, he did not drink.

"Why not Queens?"

"Queens is where you start out, not where you end up." She thought of Serge, on the Upper East Side, half a world away from Queens. It didn't feel right not to think of him.

"But my son."

"Your son."

The waiter interjected, bending to speak to them at eye level. "I'm so sorry, but we're going to have to ask for the table." He gestured at the seagulls, eyes wide with hunger, itching to begin their own romantic dinners.

"Of course," David said, reaching for his wallet, hands trembling. The waiter, to Anna, a blurry apparition. Behind him, she saw endless expanses of cornfields. Did Heathcliff roam cornfields? She wasn't sure. But there was no doubt in her mind: in Iowa, she would disappear. Already she was fading—on the cruise, in the street, in the way shaggy clerks at Barnes & Noble threw change back at her, coiffed men in suits passed her by. She was a walking mirage, an unfocused image, the sharp edge of possibility smoothed away.

The waiter helped her into her coat, his fingers removed as soon as it was secured on her shoulders. *A woman your age, with dwindling*

money, be gone, he seemed to be telling her. A dozen couples, concil-
iatory glasses of red wine in their hands, were drooling over her table.
She could feel them pleading, insisting: *Be gone.*

"Is Iowa your way of breaking up with me?" Anna kept pressing. Hating
how she must have looked to him, how repetitive her tone must have
sounded as she asked the same things again and again, aging a little with
each question: Do you not love me anymore? Do you still love your ex-
girlfriend? Do I exhaust you? Why, why can't you handle me?

"You're ridiculous," he said, rubbing his eyes in front of the bathroom mirror. "I told you, you can come with me if you want. God! I'm so
tired of our fights. It's just a good job, Anna, I'm ready for a real job."

"And me?"

"And you." He squeezed toothpaste onto his brush and scrubbed
vigorously as if to buff the enamel. "Honey, I hate to tell you this, but
Russian women expect too much. Sorry, I meant Russian-American
women. They want it both ways—absolute, blind male devotion and
all the benefits of feminism. The two, they clash."

"Don't say any more," she said. "I despise it when you generalize."

The day before, when he was on campus, she scoured the apartment for relics of his past. It no longer felt like spying, but like sheer
survival. She bent over a shoe box, a potpourri of female mementos:
pictures of him and some woman on a mountain cliff, a button from
a blazer, perfume that smelled of dead flowers, a brand-new stuffed
green foot (a stuffed foot?), the FAO Schwarz tag still attached to
it. She wanted to burn the whole box, but she tried to rearrange the
trinkets just as she had found them. In the end, it was the foot she
removed, shoving it to the bottom of the garbage can, entombing it in
coffee grains, cucumber peelings, and empty beer bottles.

"No, I just need to leave," he insisted. *"We* should leave," he cor-
rected himself sometimes, but not always. "I would like my life to
begin."

And mine, she thought. To end.

. . . .

"It was me. I put in a good word for him, Anna," Myron said. "The head of the department is an old buddy of mine from grad school."

"Oh," she said. "Well, David's not home. I'll tell him you called."

"It's a tenure-track position. Do you know how hard they are to get? An incredible opportunity for David."

"Thank you," she said. What was she thanking him for? Had she really not taken a shower in three days? On the counter, the remains of her pizza no longer looked appetizing, triangles of dough stripped of sauce and cheese.

"How's the job search going?" She had not realized he was still on the line, his voice as clear as if it were buzzing between her ears.

"I'm actually on my way out now," she said. They said good-bye, and his voice disappeared. She wrapped a plaid shawl around her belly and legs, and pressed the "Power" button on the remote control. The weather segment came nineteen minutes into the news hour. Snow today, they said, snow tomorrow. Be careful on the roads. Slippery. Seasonably cold.

They woke up to two feet of snow on the ground, a mosaic of ice on the window. The sound of shoveling, the glee of scampering children outside their window. She loved those minutes before either of them rose, the morning pregnant with promise, unmarred. No other time in the day held such exquisite anticipation—a strong cup of coffee; as a special treat, she might allow herself a sticky bun. As they ate, they would dismember the thick, multilayered Sunday *Times*, each laying claim to his or her own section. They still had the option of returning to bed afterward because the light was a grayish white, that noncommittal early morning hue.

Under the spell of the burgeoning day, it was easy to imagine that all complexity could be untangled, Iowa and Serge logically united. In that light of morning, Anna was still young. She *was,* if you looked at it rationally, comparatively, if you disregarded the opinions of other people.

She opened her eyes and to her surprise discovered that David's eyes were already open. He was staring at the ceiling, his lips moving, his arms at his sides, as if he were formulating conclusions or unraveling problems. More than ever, she wanted to know what his ailing novel had been about. He had said he would show it to her when he was done and she understood, now, that it would never be done. Was he thinking about how it had failed or, to be more precise, how he believed she had failed it? Hadn't she signed on as the muse, hadn't that been her role all along? Or was she reading too much into it as usual? He could simply be thinking of coffee or countless other mundane things.

"Good morning, honey," she said brightly, turning to him. A simple American endearment Russians simply did not comprehend. Honey, dripping and sticky. Russians preferred to mold names, build out of them affectionate, individual shapes—Anyechka, Anyusha, An'ka.

David's eyes focused. He prepared to say something, the culmination of the staring at the ceiling, maybe? Fear invaded her. She could not stand it, not while enveloped in the safety of morning.

When her mother used to make her breaded chicken cutlets, her favorite dish, she had used a mallet to make the chicken flesh yield. Anna would find her banging away in the kitchen, the violent arc of her arm, up and down. This was what Anna K. thought about while waiting for her lover to say something—the mallet pounding the chicken into checkered patties.

"Coffee?" she said at last. "A nice strong cup?"

A kind of relief in his "Yes, thanks. That sounds great."

A kiss on his shoulder, she rose. But then, with the grinding of beans arrived a line from a Joseph Brodsky poem. She had never liked Brodsky much, all the thinking he required, all those inscrutable classical allusions she used to skim past. And on this morning, it materialized without bidding: *Life without us is, darling, unthinkable.* She said it out loud, traced the words with her tongue.

"What'd you say?" David asked from the bed. Her heart plunged again, because she was certain he'd heard but was pretending otherwise. These days, he was going to great lengths—failure of hearing being one example—to avoid confrontation. She said it again to herself; this time, she forced herself to believe: *Life without us is, darling, unthinkable.*

One thing after the other disappeared. His favorite cookbook, *How to Cook Everything*, was given away to Matt or Jim. The broken space heater thrown away. A similar fate befell Trivial Pursuit, Lands' End catalogs, ancient *Time Out New Yorks*, the gray Manhattan Portage bag with a hole in the bottom. Anna's belongings remained where they were—stuffed inside two bottom drawers and in plastic Century 21 bags beneath the bed. David made no comment. No "What about you?" No "You won't need your Louis Vuitton in Iowa." On that issue, silence.

Her mother called her to tell Anna that a woman had moved in with Alex and Serge. A Russian woman, of course, a girlfriend of his friend's wife, or some such connection. (Did Nadia set this up?) No, no concrete physical description, except she was a workout fiend, spent whole mornings at the gym. A little older than Anna, widowed, two semi-grown children. Soon Serge might be calling her "Mama," a possibility neither Anna nor her mother vocalized.

Her mother reminded Anna she could still act, get herself together, seize an offensive position. Maybe Alex has grown weary of the stringy lunatic who spends days rolling around on the Pilates mat, maybe he's already fed up with her veiny arms and elastic torso. No doubt he misses Anna, her curves, her real Russian beauty? And who knows the details of that relationship anyway? Until the divorce comes through, it's not really over. And even then, in the hands of a determined woman, anything is possible . . . Her poor mother was frightened by Anna's new languor, her indifferent voice. It was as though her grandson already belonged to the other faceless woman.

"Let your father and me come there," she said last time they spoke. "We'll get you out of that horrible place, bring you to Rego Park. At home, we'll figure out what to do. We'll make a plan, you and Seryozha can stay with us for a while."

She was tempted. It was on the streets of Rego Park where she dreamed—the landscape demanded so little of you that the small-est triumphs felt like world-changing contributions. In Rego Park—among anonymous buildings, Payless stores, individual trees burst-ing out of the ground like gifts from a neglectful spouse—you were left alone to be as successful or as mediocre as you liked. But Anna recalled what David had said—Queens, it's not where you end up. Naturally, she declined.

Did Anna K. still have choices? Those glorious choices so beloved by immigrants? She couldn't see them for the cornfields; she'd bend one stalk, but behind it thousands of others blocked her perspective. Of course, if someone asked her to point out Iowa on the map, Anna K. would have some trouble. And those recurring images of expansive cornfields, was admittedly a shortsighted view of a place she had never visited. But that's how it was with her: one thing stood in for something bigger, less graspable. A single image represented an entire tragedy. Despite herself, Anna K. was a believer in Big Events.

She would go, then, she decided one afternoon. In Iowa, she might take Russian classes at last, she would balance herself, send for Serge, maybe. Wasn't the air healthier there for a little boy? And without David, who would she be? A few minutes later, she changed her mind. She could never leave, a ridiculous idea, she would be more free here, there would be more places to deposit her remaining beauty. And why was it still snowing in early March? A dreary snow, incessant, wind whipping your face with it.

At the St. Petersburg Bookstore on Brighton Beach Avenue, a sales-clerk handed her a copy of Boris Akunin's latest mystery. "Just in," he announced, taking her for a real Russian immigrant, a *Novoye Russkoye Slovo*–reading Russian, an RTN-watching Russian. A *Metro* magazine–perusing Russian. A Russian who thought in Russian. Who preferred the density of Borodinsky bread, who bought the cheapest garlic, who flossed out poppy seeds, who closed her eyes when she heard the melancholy strains of Okudzhava. Anna flipped through the pages of the book, squint-ing past all that exhausting print, the labor of deciphering each word.

The young man noticed her expression. *"Shto s vami?"* What's wrong with you? he said unkindly, and turned away, shoving a book into the hands of another customer.

She was a tall, pale woman, with outstretched translucent fingers, who did not know where to go next. Just that morning, when David was out, she had excavated his novel from the bottom of his drawer. Like Zubovsky's book, it was thin, bound by two rubber bands. She had removed the rubber bands carefully, running her fingers over the remaining indentations. The paper used to be a bright, bleached white, but was now curling, yellowing at the edges. She scanned it quickly once, then returned to the first page to reread. It had to be done quickly; sometimes students forgot about their meetings with David and he came home unannounced. Something was wrong with this novel, a deep flaw she couldn't pinpoint.

She started again, one ear attuned to the sounds from the stairwell. She heard the tread of boots and snapped a rubber band in her hurry to put away the manuscript. The boots stopped on the third floor, and she began again on page one. Then it hit her. The heroine, Marina, was boring because she was idealized. This was David's biggest problem. The other characters were convincingly drawn, the plot moved along quickly enough, but every time Marina appeared on the page, the author would rhapsodize about her fragile beauty, the sweetness of her expressions, the flicker of her smile. Why did he not seek Anna's advice? She had worked in publishing, she'd read since the crib, practically, she probably knew a thing or two about character development.

Still, she had to admit the Romeo and Juliet story was well shaped: the disapproving, religious parents provided the protagonists with their obstacles. There were many lovely scenes, especially of one inside a diner where Marina, a recent immigrant, asks to sample all the American foods of her fantasies. She and her boyfriend slurp tapioca, feed one another cheesecake.

But now in the St. Petersburg Bookstore, Anna understood. All this time, it was not she who was the muse, but Katia. Young, simple, Bukharian Katia had been fueling David's creative imagination. It was

Katia's story he wanted all along, never her own. Somehow, Anna's story was yet again unpalatable for the writer. The narrative of her life would disappear.

The novel failed, Anna thought bitterly, because Katia was the only real choice he was capable of making and because he failed to understand her. The lack of insight was right there, splashed across every page. She had "an oval face framed by soft brown hair." She touched him "meekly, seeking his guidance." She was a "dark, Eastern beauty, sheltered by Judaism, threatened by the outside world."

My son, he's impressionable, Myron had said at Penn Station. And a terrible writer, Anna K. thought, yet she had put her fate in his hands.

Then *he* popped into her head, his expression as he handed her the Kramskoy postcard. He had watched as she connected with the woman displayed in the picture, regal in her lonely carriage. Didn't he have the gaze of a mystic, a transcriber of souls? A not-unintelligent kindness emanating from him, a sensation that he too questioned his surroundings. Two of Katia's boyfriends, and had she selected wrongly? The cruelty of that thought (poor Katia)—she couldn't believe herself capable of it. But that's what thoughts were for, weren't they, for their private alleyways, their hidden underbellies?

She ran out of St. Petersburg, into the battering snow. The heavy weight of the shearling impeded her, weighed her legs down. She had gotten only halfway up the next block when she realized that the clerk was running after her. Only when he caught up to her at the corner did Anna comprehend that she still held the Akunin book, firmly, almost painfully, in her right hand.

The following day, as she waited in the lobby for the elevator to descend, Anna realized she had never visited Katia in this apartment. The building was a typical Russian émigré tenement. Small windows peeking out of brick with a marble lobby and mirrored walls—a kind of shorthand Art Deco. As she expected, the complaints in the lobby were conducted entirely in Russian: joint aches, the exorbitant price of zucchini, *Master and Margarita* (the new Russian television adaptation).

She held a bag from Oilily, overpriced designer galoshes, froggy green, but only after she bought them did it occur to Anna that Katia's child was barely crawling, much less skipping puddles. Also inside the bag, she had brought the bestselling Akunin for Lev, as an offering.

She had left a message on Katia's machine two days ago, but no one had called her back. No doubt they were busy with the baby. Didn't she remember those first months, incubated in that tiny world, the stale air of domestic repetition?

In the elevator, Anna was pressed against the wall with an elderly couple discussing a daughter who never calls them back, who is out with girlfriends at those Bay Ridge dance clubs, slathering on makeup as if for a role in a horror movie, while her son runs around the streets like a homeless urchin when he's not disappearing for weeks at a time with those thugs from Sunnyside, whose divorce barely came through before . . . Anna expunged herself from the confines of that elevator onto the sixth floor. David was right: to return to Rego Park—impossible.

She rang the doorbell; the door was immediately flung open by Lev. Anna held in her breath, aware of the grooming efforts she had made earlier that day. A rare blow-dry, curls let loose around her shoulders, a satin blouse the color of unripe banana peel. And there was Lev, in sweatpants, a tank top, his thick hair snarled like the bristles of a much-used scrub brush. He smelled of black licorice, the roots of flower stems left standing in old water. Only now she recognized that David's body rarely exuded its own scent.

"Anna Borisovna, I thought you were Katia," Lev said, blushing in surprise. "I don't think I should let you in. It's a mess in here."

"I called," she said, handing over the gift bag with the galoshes.

"Really?" he said. Then, "Yes, I guess you did. I had forgotten." He took the bag, a hairy man holding a pink bag by its handles. He stood there, the door not entirely ajar, his foot holding it open.

Now that she had let go of the gift bag, her hands felt strangely empty.

"There's a book in there for you," she said.

"A book? Oh, look, the Akunin. Haven't read that one yet."

"I happened to be in St. Peter—"

"Thanks." Lev made no move to open the door wider, to extend a welcome into the apartment. This was a deeply un-Russian move; Anna could only assume that something was wrong.

She checked in with her own disappointment. Had she expected to be embraced, to be told, between raw, insistent kisses, that this, this was finally right? Did she expect a larger, grander rescue than the one he had performed at Chagall? Yes, she was convinced that he was the only one who could do it—if only events had bent another way, if she had made the connections earlier . . .

"I'm sorry, I shouldn't have come. You're obviously busy." She turned around and walked the few paces to the elevator, pressed the button.

Lev stood at the door, hovering, diving for words. "Thanks anyway, for your presents, your cards," he said. "I appreciate it, probably more than you know. It's just the timing was wrong. You understand? Nothing we can do about that. The timing, wrong."

They stood staring at each other, a coil stretched out, tautly, between them. His lips were slightly open, partly camouflaged by stubble struggling to become a beard, his eyes fixed upon her. Strange, this look of knowing, it could almost be mistaken for love.

The elevator had come and gone and still Anna waited for the "but," the more hopeful conclusion, for transcendent hope.

"Timing?" she said, making a move as if to return. "What do you mean by that?"

"I'm sorry, Anna Borisovna." With a weak wave of the hand, as if in self-defense, Lev shut his door, a turn of the lock, a barricade.

In the middle of the hallway she remained, the familiar, blunt despair gathering force inside her. The light waned, succumbing to clouds. She had to get back to the city; tonight she was supposed to be introduced to Lauren at last. Still, Anna was unable to move.

In all these apartments, behind the same closed door, lurked identical immigrant stories—dimming memories of war, of empty stomachs. Their inhabitants lived with ghosts of people left behind, young sisters dead of malnutrition, of cancers that could have been treated if only there had been medicine, aunts whisked away in the night, some to return from Siberia half-blind, missing a finger. These ghosts immigrated with them, shared their wonder at the resiliency of Bounty paper towels, disapproved of waste—tomatoes allowed to grow soft and brown, a schmatte gathering dust in the closet.

The people living in these apartments cooked from recipes committed to memory but then, over time, relaxed the rigor of the original text, each serving becoming more and more Americanized. Okra in *baklazhanovaia ikra*? Shrimp in Salat Olivier? Chocolate chips in rugelach? Why not?

They spoke a new language, one not entirely digested, laden with chunks of Soviet, dribbles of Yiddish, benevolent fragments of English. They put up with errant, half-American mongrel children, who flung themselves away from their parents, who called reluctantly every night. *Kak dela, Mama? Okay. Bye-bye.*

And so? What does that all mean? Isn't that what they asked for when they immigrated? Isn't this state exactly what they deserve? Where's the tragedy? one may ask. Aren't chocolate chips the ideal addition to rugelach, with its flaky, spiraling crust, its walnuts, its plum filling? That's the nature of the world—eventually chocolate chips will be inserted into any rugelach.

The elevator waited patiently for Anna K. What would she do now? The people around her were politely shutting their doors.

Lauren was not at all what Anna had expected. She was in fact brown-haired, plump, with eyes spaced close together. David sat on one side of the table, Lauren on the other. They were nursing their beers in the subterranean Murray Hill tavern.

Anna was late to the bar; she had allowed herself only twenty minutes to make it to Murray Hill from Queens, when in the best of circumstances it would take almost an hour. At first she couldn't find them. The bar was filling up with the after-work crowd, dense with sensible shoes, wool and striped button-downs.

"You drinking something, miss?" the bartender shouted, probably to her, but she ignored him, scanning the room. Her eyes adjusted to the lighting, and she glimpsed them at the farthest table from the bar, tucked into a corner, framed by faux-Tudor beams and antique lighting fixtures. A candle flickered between them, illuminating their chins and noses, their entwined hands. David was saying something and Lauren hunched over her mug, strained to hear him.

They did not see Anna as she pivoted, as she climbed the stairs and ran out to the ice-slicked streets. Groups of rowdy postcollegiate men cheerfully moving on to the next bar bumped into her, tipping her balance. Jumbled thoughts battled for prominence in her mind, a cacophony of conflicting signals. Should she go back inside? She had not seen anything incriminating, nothing irrevocable, neither here nor inside his desk drawer. A nervous impetuousness had always been her problem, that Russian soul again, she thought. And love, what about love? She could pretend she'd just arrived, stun them with her graciousness, her curiosity about Lauren's job, her hobbies, their past together.

Or maybe she should beg Alex to take her back, as her mother wanted her to do. She never told her mother how unlikely that scenario was—Alex with his moral certainties. She had never even discussed movies with her husband—for him, the bad characters were bad, the good were good, what was there to discuss? And Anna? She was bad, it was that simple for Alex K. And her son's Russian would soon transcend her own. Her son.

Should she return to Rego Park, littered with the corpses of immigrants? Yes, she decided, she could go to Queens, there was always Queens for her, a short-term measure, a place to reconsider the options.

Again, there was Lev, his scent in the tank top, the regret in his voice as he said, *The timing was wrong.* What she had suppressed: the hugeness of what she had felt at the New Year's party. It began as flirting, as it always did, but then . . . a tug she couldn't verbalize. The fluidity of understanding between them. His strong arm as he swooped her out of the circle of women, the way he listened to her, simply, with no expectations. She had been distracted by what she perceived as simplicity, a kind of boorishness she attributed to all Russian men. In Lev, she thought she could glimpse a fellow thinker, a fellow doubter—what Russian men loved French films, for example, outside of their usefulness for impressing women?

Only Lev could help her, she thought, no longer cold despite the fierce wind that pushed her farther west toward Third, toward Lexington. She decided to use a pay phone to call him—it would be the safest way, an untraceable number. If he picked up, she would tell him what she'd wanted to tell him just hours ago, she would put her life in his hands, the rest of them be damned. She fumbled for coins, how much was a public phone these days? Since cell phones, she had forgotten what it was like to shiver on street corners, the blue receiver pressed to her ear. But, of course, there was no dial tone.

She turned downtown on Third. A snow-rain mixture began to tap across her face and she increased her speed, squinting at all four corners before moving on. Another block, then another. On Thirty-sixth, the phone worked, but the coin drop was choked by a wedged quarter. On Thirty-fifth, the receiver came loose in her hand, cord dangling down to her waist. She glimpsed a phone outside a newspaper bodega, but it was hard to hear beyond the din of Thirty-fourth Street. The snow was descending more furiously now, so she dialed the number and it rang, Anna's heart sinking with every ring. Where would she begin? What if it had all been in her imagination? But no, that wasn't possible, for hadn't he said he appreciated her gift, "more than she could know"? He was a cautious man, an honorable man, that was the closest he came to saying, *I love you*. And then the ring was interrupted, and it was him.

"Hello?" But his voice was frantic and stern, forbidding. She paused, sounds balled up inside her.

"Hello!" An aggressive hello, almost hysterical. As if he were someone else, the Lev she knew having been substituted for another man. Had she been crazy to make this phone call? This wouldn't be the answer after all. One last attempt, her mouth even formed the shapes, the tongue curling to the roof of the mouth, the *L* already in place.

Nothing came out. She hung up, the cold suddenly everywhere, filling up her lungs, numbing her toes.

Without thinking about where she was going, Anna found herself on Lexington Avenue at the subway station. She descended, swiped her MetroCard. The platform was neither empty nor crowded, a few people were leaning over the edge, checking for the lights of the train. A garbled announcement came over the loudspeaker, as if the more indecipherable the more important they were. "Due to an incident in Queens, blah blah blah," the MTA speaker tried again.

Did she react too rashly? Anna wondered. A panic she didn't recognize swept over her, made her feel as though she were dying. Nausea; she felt it in the gullet, in her spine. She tried to imagine a future to look forward to, but each narrow hallway was equally dark and foreboding. She would go to Queens, she would wind up in Queens. For her parents, staying in Queens was like telling their friends: *You succeeded and we failed. You are that story and we are this story.* And it would be no different for her.

The people beside her were already impatient, asking each other what was the matter. What did the announcement have to do with the number 6 train, a line that didn't even go to Queens? The words, as though from God, were difficult to interpret. All they wanted to know was if this incident had anything to do with them. An incident in Queens, a man close to Anna said, could be anything from terrorism to a "sick passenger"—the latter he enunciated as if in quotes.

Anna forced herself to fix her attention on something, and found it drawn to the orange-painted line separating the waiting passengers and the gaping slit of the train tracks. A faded orange, the straight line chipped, scraped, grimy. Immediately after it, the final warning of the yellow line. From a distance, she heard the echo of an arriving train.

"Jesus," someone said. "It's been more than a half an hour."

Anna inched up to the yellow line, transfixed. What if she were on the front page of the *Daily News*? Briefly, she imagined David reading the paper, Lev, the spasms of their grief. The paper would select her most beautiful picture, from before she met Alex, maybe the one where she was blowing out birthday candles on her thirty-fifth birthday, with her elongated cheekbones, hair swept behind her ears. She had been caught off guard by the camera and her eyes had glistened, as if she held within herself a bunch of unopened tulips just minutes before they were to be released in water. Or better yet, the one from the New Year's party where Katia had introduced her to David. She would want it to be the picture of herself she saw in David's eyes when she shook his hand, that woman reflected in his glasses, the soft blush of her, set off by black.

A pair of lights shimmered in the tunnel. How easy it would be after all, just one step at the right time. A choice made, a decision, a leap. Could she actually do it? She slid her right foot against the rim of the platform. She could see the blinking green circle of the 6 train, ready to squirm free from confinement.

"Careful, lady," the man who had spoken to her earlier said. "You're standing awfully close there."

She edged away, her body used to obeying commands, but then she was drawn back to the same spot. The train exploded into the station, its two white headlights searing into her. No time to think, to weigh the options. She was always weighing, she was exhausted with managing her own story. Neither here nor there, an eternal purgatory. Let's just be honest, what would she be in Queens? In Iowa? What was she now? All it would take would be a split-second choice, the tensing of muscles, the pouncing, then the relinquishing of self. This time, for once, she would make the right choice.

3 6

WHAT HAPPENED TO ANNA K.

"An incident in Queens" was what NY1 had been repeating for an hour now; the rest of the stations had moved on to their sitcoms, their reality shows—a handful of practically naked women competing for a man in a bubbling Jacuzzi. Lev turned off the television. *Kak na zlo.* This would be the night he and Katia finally decided to talk. Just the two of them back in their apartment.

The newscaster didn't say where in Queens, but the shots were of the station closest to him, the Sixty-third Road subway stop. The clip showed yellow police strips blocking the entrance to the station, a congregation of police officers, an ambulance. The same useless information scrolled on the bottom of the screen: an incident in Queens. And Katia was supposed to be here with Roman at seven o'clock, they were to have a quiet dinner. Apologies, an entire string of them, were gathered in his mouth. Lev called her parents in Forest Hills and casually asked them when Katia had left.

"Why, isn't she there already? Just two subway stops?" Calling them had been a mistake; now Katia's father was worried. Lev concocted a lie about Katia having told him she planned to stop by the baby boutiques before they closed. But they were closed already, he was certain of it. And he and Katia had decided to share a cell phone to save costs. The cell phone, mute, lay on top of his bedroom dresser.

"Call us, Lev. As soon as she gets there."

The shashliks were cooling on the table, and he would have to reheat the potatoes. Pacing, he returned his own fumbling attempts at a salad—uneven chunks of tomatoes, rounds of carrots, shavings of skin still visible in places, coarsely chopped onions—back to the refrigerator. A hastily purchased bottle of wine, corkless and breathing, on the table.

His father had repeatedly insisted he get a car, but Lev had resisted. The idea of haggling with those polyester guys, having to conduct all that *Consumer Reports* research, daunted him. And they would have sniffed him out immediately. An ignorant immigrant to bamboozle. What an idiotic reason not to buy a car, though. He could have picked up Katia, and here she would now be sitting, with Roman. Here, he could convince her that marriage hadn't been easy for him, but he was coming around.

An incident, incident. What a cold word, encompassing almost anything. Americans with their skill for understatement. Incident could be an inconvenient delay, incident could be murder.

Still holding the cordless phone, Lev rode the elevator to the lobby. He peeked his head out the front door, straining to make out the shape of a woman and her baby. Why hadn't he picked them up? He could hit himself.

"Let me come to you," she had said earlier today. "So we can be alone." He had been so distracted by the first tendrils of affection in her voice, he spent the entire afternoon cleaning, arranging her return home. Why hadn't he picked them up? Oh, God, Lev thought, simply that. Oh, God.

And it was so cold out, he could sense it from just a few seconds outside the door, a harsh, pecking cold. He could not stay at home; he would run out to the station. At least he would find out the details of this incident.

Lev sprinted upstairs, not bothering with the elevator, two steps at a time. It was only when he got inside the door that he realized the vibration in his hand was the cordless phone. He pictured Katia finally expelled from the station, her tender concern that he would be worried. He would tell her how wrong he was, how selfish, how guilty.

"Hello?" he barked. On the other end of the line, nothing. A rustling sound—wind, the rumble of the subway? Could she hear him?

"Hello!" Street noise, but no human sounds. He was anxious now, desperate to know. A low moan—did he really hear that?—a sharp, female sound. And the phone went dead. Lev threw the phone down and, in the bedroom, found a wool sweater. A scene from *Contempt* flashed across his mind. The couple in bed, the wife asking the husband if he found her body attractive. Proceeding body part by body part, What about my legs? she asks. My neck? Yes, of course, he reassures her, he loves all of them. Why was Lev thinking about this scene just now, when he needed all his faculties to devise a plan? He threw the sweater over his head, pulled it down, realizing too late, and not caring, that he was wearing it inside out. His eyes burned, head throbbed, but for once he was utterly lucid.

Just then, as he swung open the door to head to the station and wait there all night if need be, he saw her coming out of the elevator. His beautiful wife, rosy from the cold, their son wriggling in the carrier strapped to her waist. The past few months twisted themselves inside him. All his doubts, all that angst he couldn't put his finger on, the vague, incessant torment, the choices made and not made, what did it mean in light of this relief? He had been an idiot.

"What?" Katia asked, obviously pleased, but trying to hide it. She had a new hairstyle—a pretty chin-length bob. "We stopped at Mila's Records for a few minutes. I thought a Shashmakom CD might help Roman get to sleep. Why, have you been worrying?"

Lev didn't know what to say, an overall feeling of gratitude. "An incident in Queens, that's all they said on the news."

"You're silly," Katia said. "I walked the entire way. It's not so far." She handed over Roman and eyed the cold shashlik on the table. She took off her coat, scarf, gloves, and hat, hung them up in the hall closet. Turning her back to him, she poured milk into a saucepan, but he knew—from the slope of her shoulders, the easy twist of her wrists—that she had returned, that all those things she'd said to him as she was packing her duffel bag were forgiven, for now. He wondered if she had not orchestrated this subway scenario on purpose, if there were secret parts of her capable of tiny plots and manipulations. Right now he didn't care.

Lev bounced Roman on his knee, trying not to squeeze him too tightly. His baby's fragility, the shock of black hair, fingers thick and stubby like his own, pulled at him. He would take him to temple, as his own father had done, the place they had had their most intimate talks. A Bukharian Jew in Rego Park, that's what Roman would be. If Lev was lucky, he would also like movies. And that's it, thank God. There would be no need for anything more.

The baby reached out for Katia, whimpering; Lev shushed him as he had heard Katia do and tried to say, "It's Papa. It's Papa."

"Should I reheat the *shashlik*?"

The phone rang and Lev thought of the phone call he'd received earlier, the breathy female voice on the street. It hadn't been Katia, of that he was certain now, but he probed no further in his mind. To wonder about it was futile, or worse, like pressing on a three-day-old bruise, releasing anew the old, dull pain.

Katia picked it up. "I'm fine," she said, smiling at Lev. "Why was everyone worried about us?" She poured the warm milk into the baby bottle and handed it to Lev. This would be the first time he would be feeding his son. He would have to learn to do all those things, just in case; he sensed his wife would be going back to work soon. He took the bottle.

The following day, perhaps because of the excitement the night before, Roman let them sleep in until nine o'clock. Lev's mother would be coming after lunch to babysit. They called her as soon as they woke up and she was so happy to hear of Katia's return that Lev felt a tightness in his throat. They could do whatever they wanted for the remainder of the day, she assured them.

"Let's go to an amusement park," Katia muttered. "I would like you to buy me a stuffed foot." Surely she meant animal, Lev thought, his wife's hair draped like a shawl across his stomach. Watching her fall back into sleep, one hand shoved inside the pillowcase, the other cradling her head, Lev allowed himself a pinch of sadness, a few minutes of reconciliation. After all, this was the life he had chosen; as Oleg said, Lev could either enjoy the cantor's song or else resent every minute of the service.

By the time his mother arrived, Lev and Katia had decided they would go to Coney Island, and when it got too cold to remain outside, they would have lunch in a kosher place in Brighton Beach. It would be an entire day alone, the perfect time to confess to his wife that, for almost fifteen years, he had called her Vasilisa the Beautiful. Why had he never had a chance to tell her before? He used to blame it on marriage, the way moments bloomed and dissolved while words, whole sentences, sentiments, and conversations remained unsaid.

"I'll go change," Katia said, squeezing his arm, and slipped into the bathroom. His mother motioned for Lev to sit next to her at the table. She made them both cups of tea, even though Lev had had his tea earlier that morning.

"I didn't want to say this in front of your wife, to ruin her first day back," she said, her chin pointing in the direction of the bathroom. "But have you heard what happened to Anna K.?"

Lev blushed. Against his will, he thought of his final image of Anna; what he hoped would be the last secret he kept from his wife. He knew why Anna had come here, oh, God, he even wanted it. Her green eyes, made emerald by the sheen of her blouse, a pleading in them, a softness. What could he have done? Five years ago, maybe, but what could he have done now? Should he have grabbed her, tasted and consumed her, the mashing of grapes, the slickness of their bodies, the immense release from suffering, and then what? Isolate himself from the people he loved so he could be with her?

No, Anna was more lost than he was and he had resisted his impulse to invite her inside, to coat her neck with kisses, to do what heroes do in books and movies—to rescue her. In life, we must rely on ourselves, we must keep ourselves firmly on the ground—Lev had thought this, closing the door. She should live alone for a while, commune with French films, but he knew it wasn't his place to advise her.

He saw that his mother was waiting for something, a reaction, a question. "No," he admitted, taking himself in hand. He remembered the leftover cookies covered in tinfoil and brought them to the table, unwrapped them. Raspberry butter cookies, Katia's favorite; he had bought them at Dima's minutes before the old man had shut down his store for the evening. How pleasant it had felt, the simple, gratifying anticipation of making Katia happy.

Lev took a cookie and sat down again. "I don't know. What happened to Anna K.?" His mother, the eternal gossip. Was Anna K. going to be remarried, then? Was she moving back home? Did the Ashkenazi leave her too?

His mother blew on her tea. "I guess you haven't heard yet."

"Why, what happened?" It was this she enjoyed, his mother, drawing out insignificant news, inserting herself at the center. No doubt it made her feel tangible, affirmed that she existed. But this time her voice was octaves lower than usual as she glanced downward into the abyss of her teacup.

They heard Roman in his crib, the first murmurings of waking, a wide-mouthed yawn. Katia padded out of the bathroom, her hair wrapped in a towel. She was wearing a bathrobe Lev had never seen before, a thick, cozy cotton, a bright, dazzling orange color. She leaned over to give Lev a kiss, flicked a crumb from his cheek. Lev, submerged in foreboding, was not quite able to return her kiss. Again, a scene from a movie infiltrated, a Russian one, strangely, because he saw so few Russian films. But it was *Ochi Chyornye* with Marcello Mastroianni, based on some Chekhov story, he thought. He remembered a woman lying on the bed sobbing, her sleek, proud back turned to Mastroianni, to the viewer. But it was the shabbiness of the wallpaper he remembered, a woman like that with her face pressed to a fading yellowish wall.

He felt the words his mother was about to speak would grab him by the shoulders and envelop him. He felt these words would form a chasm, separating his soul from Katia's.

He and his mother waited until his wife disappeared into the bed-room and closed the door.

"What, Mama? What?"

"I guess you haven't yet heard." Lev's mother lowered her voice to a whisper. Then she told him the end of Anna's story.

ACKNOWLEDGMENTS

This novel would doubtlessly appall him, but of course I owe a special debt of gratitude to Lev Tolstoy, whose *Anna Karenina* never ceases to astound and inspire.

At the University of Pittsburgh's Department of Slavic Languages and Literatures, Helena Goscilo's graduate course on *Anna Karenina* lit an early spark for this book. Thanks also to David Birnbaum, who has been a devoted supporter of all my post-Slavic endeavors.

Attending the MFA program at the Bennington College Writing Seminars allowed me to call myself a writer. For their encouragement, guidance, and wisdom, I must thank Martha Cooley, Amy Hempel, Sheila Kohler, Askold Melnyczuk, and especially Lynne Sharon Schwartz, who read and reread this novel; her confidence in the book kept me going. I'm grateful to Tom Bissell and Phillip Lopate for their friendship.

Claire McMillan offered valuable comments on multiple drafts. For their helpful feedback, I'd like to thank Dan Zigmond and particularly Laurence Klavan, whose words of writerly encouragement have sustained me for ten years now. Among other things, Rebecca Skloot gave me a fine gift: my first subscription to *Poets & Writers*. While wrestling with the structure of this book I had the good fortune of bumping into my friend Jeff Sharlet at a café. In mere minutes, Jeff helped point me to where the novel really began, and for that I owe him.

Thanks also to the editors who supported my writing during the creation of this novel: Alana Newhouse from *The Forward* published an excerpt from *What Happened to Anna K.* before it turned out to be an excerpt. Suzanne Pettypiece and Joshua Mandelbaum pulled a story of mine out of the slush pile and have since become dear friends. Watching the brilliant Hannah Tinti edit my work was like enrolling in a master class on the short story.

I'm thrilled to be collaborating with Amanda Patten once more, whose enthusiasm, positive energy and editorial acumen are so rare and inspiring. I'm grateful to Lauren Spiegel for all her hard work on behalf of Anna. Thanks to my agent Elizabeth Kaplan, who was no less excited than I was when this book found a home.

Where would I be without the unconditional friendship of Paul W. Morris? Or Natalia Vayner-Heyraud, Dana Levin, and Karolin Shoikhet Obregon?

Sonya Bekkerman: this book grew out of our coming of age on the streets of Rego Park. If no words exist to express gratitude for her luminous presence in my life, perhaps some moment within these pages is a way to begin.

My parents gave me no less than everything: bottomless love, patience for my many shortcomings, a new American life (and thereby an endless source of writing material), and my beloved sister Elizabeth.

Thanks most of all to Adam Lowenstein—husband, partner, muse. For sharing his talents with me, for nurturing skills I didn't believe I possessed, for giving all of himself in every situation, and for lovingly tweaking my immigrant grammar. Without him, this novel (along with so many other things) would exist solely in my imagination.

What Happened to Anna K.

For Discussion

1. Though *What Happened to Anna K.* is a sharply contemporary novel, there are many structural nods to its source material, such as the introduction to new characters through the impersonal perspective of the wedding videographer. How else is the narrative like that of a nineteenth-century novel? Why do you think David's perspective is never fully revealed, unlike most of the other characters in the novel?

2. Describe the various types of romantic idealism depicted in the novel. Is there a conflict between Anna's traditional romanticism, tied to heroes like Darcy and Heathcliff, and her dreams of a Woody Allen–style New York love affair? How do these imagined passions compare to Lev's longing for the romance of French films? How do these scenarios contrast with real life? In what ways are these ideals destructive?

3. Anna is seen both from her own perspective and through the eyes of others. How does her sense of herself differ from how she is perceived? Is her own vision of herself the true one, or is she at times blind to truths that others observe?

4. In what ways is beauty used as currency in Anna's world? Why do you think Anna's aging changes her outlook so dramatically? If she had not been raised with the goal of attractiveness, would her story have been different? Do you think this standard for women is universal or specific to Anna's community?

5. Why do you think Anna never voices complaints within her marriage? Can Anna fault Alex for not knowing her, when she never truly attempted to communicate? Is she later guilty of not wanting to know the real David?

6. Anna wonders, "Is there room for the comfort of routine and the wild beating of the heart to coexist in a single life?" (page 75–76) Why are these concepts at odds with one another? Do you believe that these two aspects of love can be combined in a relationship?

7. Meeting with Nadia at Bloomingdale's, Anna notices that "it seemed that no one cared she had had an affair; her biggest crime was" in shattering their shared mythology "by acting on it." (page 137) Why do you think the "mythology" of marriage and money is so closely guarded? Why is it fragile? Why do you think these values take the place of moral consideration in this world?

8. How does Anna's tragedy compare to the histories of older generations—their tales of poverty, starvation, illness, and persecution? Why

is Anna separated from the "shared narrative" (page 40) of the more insulated Bukharian Jews? How does her broadened world and its expanded options help to create her depression?

9. Discuss the use of trains in *What Happened to Anna K.* Why do you think the train is such a powerful image for Anna? How does it evolve as a symbol throughout the novel?

10. Many possible causes of Anna's unhappiness are discussed, from her passion for the world of books to her alienation from every culture as an Americanized immigrant. Ultimately, why do you think Anna is so desperate to be saved by true love? Why does she feel the need to be a big story?

11. In both Tolstoy's epigraph and the context of David's father's book, Reyn mentions the idea that "it is in the everyday that history is revealed." (page 178) How do you think this work speaks to the history of our own time?

A CONVERSATION WITH IRINA REYN

What influenced you to become a writer?

As an immigrant, writing was the last vocation I imagined for myself. In fact, I avoided it as long as I could, waiting for a calling in medicine, computer programming, or public relations. In order to allow myself to be a writer, I first had to discard or fail at every other sensible profession.

What inspired you to update *Anna Karenina*, specifically?

In graduate school, I took a seminar organized entirely around *Anna Karenina*. It was amazing how such a protracted, close reading revealed insights hidden during my previous forays into the novel. Before, Anna had struck me as a helpless, lovelorn victim of her society and time period. However, further examination revealed her to be an artful self-saboteur, overly influenced by books and suffering from romantic illusions. Vronsky fit Anna's plot perfectly, and I could identify with her impulse to dismantle a well-structured life in order to chase the narrative arc of fiction. As I read the book, I thought of people like me who arrived in this country as children, and how often we were tempted to sabotage our parents' expectations of us, to subvert the model of hard-won immigrant success. I think *What Happened to Anna K.* must have emerged from those considerations.

Was the process of updating a classic text different from your usual way of working? How closely did you choose to follow the original structure and story, and how did you decide which elements from the original to include and which to omit?

I did not set out to reimagine *Anna Karenina*. I wrote a short story called "Vasilisa the Beautiful" and a few others exploring Anna's adolescent years (but the character had a different name then). When I looked at these stories together, perhaps with the *Anna Karenina* course still fresh in my mind, it occurred to me that these stories were all concerned with the consequences of immigration. Once I decided to make the references to *Anna Karenina* overt, I worked directly from my memory of the book, drawing on the scenes that created the biggest impression on me (when Kitty is forced to witness Anna diverting Vronsky's attention at the ball, the famous train scene when Anna and Vronsky first lock eyes, Vronsky's horse race which leads to Anna's confession to her husband, Levin and Kitty ice skating, etc.). What I did not want to do was a direct, mechanical transposition of Tolstoy's novel into my own; instead, I let it whisper to me.

How much of this novel was drawn from your own experience as a Russian immigrant?
The whole novel, I would say. For better and worse, it is the experience that defines me.

You reference Russian folktales throughout *What Happened to Anna K.*, and you've written several short stories about them as well. Are these stories a particular influence on your writing?
What is most intriguing to me about fairy tales is their undercurrent of menace. The Russian imagination tends to revere superstitions that happen to be derived from these ancient folk traditions. Some of us were raised to sit before a journey, not to sing before noon, never to step over supine legs for fear that they will cease growing. I think I was always aware that each journey, each step, carried with it potential danger. In that way, fairy tales must have always indirectly inspired my fiction.

Other than Tolstoy, who are some authors who have influenced your work?
The list is long and varied: Nabokov, Chekhov, Gogol, Dostoevsky. Benjamin Constant's *Adolphe* was a revelation at a crucial time in my artistic development. Also Bernard Malamud, Philip Roth, Grace Paley, Italo Calvino, Milan Kundera. In college, I was thrilled to discover the burgeoning genre of immigrant/multicultural writing. Having little Russian-American work to turn to, I was uniquely inspired by memoirs from writers like Eva Hoffman, André Aciman, and Richard Rodriguez, along with novels by Chang-rae Lee and Salman Rushdie. These authors first made me question the concept of "home," forcing me to grapple with what it means to live a hyphenated existence.

You enter the perspectives of several characters in this novel with very unique viewpoints. Was there a character you felt a particular affinity with or enjoyed writing about the most?
I felt very close to Anna, but living with the increasing pitch of her despair was exhausting. In that way, Lev was a more pleasurable character to inhabit because a kind of optimistic hope drove his desires and struggles. In many ways, if Anna was my past, then Lev is my future. For a long time, I reveled in the dark and pessimistic aspects of my personality, but these days, I surprise

myself by striving for happiness. Writing from Lev's perspective allowed me to consider the crucial pleasures Tolstoy so strongly advocated: a daily appreciation for the joy of being alive.

What Happened to Anna K. **raises questions about imagination and the dissatisfaction that can spring from a love for the worlds of books and films. Do you think there is a danger in living too much through fiction?**

Like Anna, I was a bookworm who superimposed fictional narratives onto my own life. The result of this was a kind of paralysis, an ongoing sense of anticipation and a deep disappointment when life began to veer from the desired arc. When I neared thirty, I realized I was in danger of leading a wholly fictional (read: delusional) life and it was time to take myself in hand. But even if I'm more centered now, I still miss that heroine of Rego Park, the tragic one of my imagination, and the glamorous life she never got to lead.

As both a published author and a teacher of creative writing, what are your suggestions for first-time writers inspired by your work?

Once I decided I wanted to pursue writing seriously, I was impatient to succeed. I hated revision, deeply craved approval from my teachers and peers, and wanted to see my work in print yesterday. My skills, alas, needed to catch up with my newly unleashed desires. It took time and work and much frustration before anything I could take real pride in surfaced on the page. So my suggestion for first-time writers is the very thing I dreaded to hear: be patient and work.

What's next for you? Can you discuss any upcoming projects?

I'm working on another novel and finishing up my collection of fairy-tale stories. I recently published a travel piece about returning to Moscow after twenty-six years (in *Town & Country Travel*). But I feel there is more material there that I need to explore, perhaps in an essay or a longer work of nonfiction.

ENHANCE YOUR BOOK CLUB

1. Next read Tolstoy's classic work *Anna Karenina*, upon which this novel is based. Compare not only the stories but also the themes within their different contexts.
2. Much of *What Happened to Anna K.* is set in restaurants catering to Russian immigrants. Plan a trip to a Russian restaurant, or liven up your meeting at home with Russian delicacies and vodka. For recipes, go to www.ruscuisine.com.
3. Explore the Russian folktales described in the novel. The stories of "Vasilisa the Beautiful," "Baba Yaga," and others can be found at www.oldrussia.net.